THE PERFECT MOVE

THE
PERFECT
MOVE

Good Intentions Aren't Always What They Seem

ALISA H. KLINGER

THE PERFECT MOVE
Copyright © 2021 Alisa H. Klinger

ISBN (paperback): 978-1-7366066-0-5
ISBN (ebook): 978-1-7366066-1-2
ISBN (audiobook): 978-1-7366066-2-9

Book design and production by Domini Dragoone
Edited by Ashley Brown
Cover images: Courtesy of OHEKA CASTLE, Korionov/iStock

Published by
YellowPig Press
Longboat Key, Florida

In loving memory of my best friend Harriet Patronis.
I was blessed to have her in my life.

"We must be careful not to believe things simply because we want them to be true. No one can fool you as easily as you can fool yourself."

—RICHARD FEYNMAN

LIES, SECRETS, AND DANGER

Hope placed her hand to her mouth, fighting back her urge to throw up. It isn't every day you find yourself hiding from a killer in a mansion.

When Hope moved into Gold Coast Estates, she fantasized about visiting the mansion that towered on top of the hill. She envisioned strolling the beautifully landscaped grounds, eating delicious delicacies and sipping fine wine from the mansion's private stock. Never did she imagine herself lying beside wine bottles, hidden in a wooden bench in the mansion's wine cellar.

Hope remained still, motionless as her eyes were fixated on the photo she held in her right hand. *You think you know a person*, thought Hope, struggling to make sense of everything that just unfolded. She shook her head. *How did I not see it? I trusted you.* Quietly, she put the photo in her back pocket. *How did it get this far?*

The hairs on the back of Hope's neck raised; her body tingled when she heard footsteps approaching.

A voice called out, "There's no reason to run from me. I just want to talk." Hearing footsteps get closer, she put her hand to her chest to keep her heart from popping out.

Hope's body tightened. She prayed that she wouldn't clank any of the bottles, or worse break one, as the sound of approaching footsteps moved ever closer.

Suddenly she heard a thump on top of her. *This is it. It's all over!* she thought.

The pounding continued against the entire bench.

On top of the bench Hope's pursuer climbed over the bench cushions, rushing over to the open window. She heard the voice shouting out the open window, "You can run, Hope, but you won't get far."

"Did you find her?" asked an annoyed voice entering the wine cellar from the other side of the cellar. "I knew I should have stayed with you when you talked with her."

"Looks like she snuck out the window."

"How much does she know?" asked the angry voice taking a seat at the table.

"She knows everything."

"Then shouldn't we be going after her? We can't let her go to the police."

"She won't get far."

"How can you be so sure?"

The pursuer's upper lip rose with pride. "I spiked her drink with ketamine. It should be kicking in about now."

Hope's brow-line creased and her eyes bulged out. *I've been drugged?* Hope did her best to control her movements. The slightest bang of a bottle would reveal her location.

"This is a big mess. We better go find her. I'll start at the back end of the mansion. We can put her in with our other unwelcomed guest."

"That makes two unwelcome guests I have to contend with thanks to you."

The pair got up and separately exited the way they entered.

Hope gasped, then forced herself to settle down. She glanced over at her left hand, which was still holding the black leather necklace with three charms dangling. *They took you. I knew you would never have left without telling me.*

Hearing the door shut, Hope waited a few moments before leaving the security of the bench. She felt a bit woozy. Was the ketamine kicking in? How much time did she have before she blacked out?

Hope wasn't sure how many people would be out looking for her. She had to figure a way of getting out of the mansion undetected and before she succumbed to the drugs. Her mind was already starting to become dazed and confused. Realizing that the second pursuer's voice entered from the other side of the wine cellar, Hope deduced there must be another way out. She remembered that the mansion has hidden passageways the servants used to get around unnoticed. There must be a door that the servants used to gain access to the cellar. This pathway would be the perfect way out of the mansion. If only she knew where it was.

Hope went deeper into the wine cellar seeking any sign of a door. Passing the Pinot Noirs, she saw nothing. Moving on, she rushed up and down the Zinfandel aisles. Still no door. Finally Hope smiled as she got to the Chardonnays. At the very end of the aisle was a narrow wooden door.

Once through, she descended down a stairway. Arriving at the bottom, she adjusted her eyes to the darkness. Her vision was starting to blur. Time was running out. She proceeded through the long narrow hallway that stretched roughly twenty yards, then turning out of sight toward the left.

Hope raced as fast as she could, trying her best to keep her balance, which was becoming more difficult with each step. Hope's stomach turned; she heard something. Was there someone trailing behind her? She wasn't going to wait to find out.

Hope kept moving forward. She was certain that this pathway led to a way out. *I must be close.* A few feet away she saw a beam of light. A light at the end of the tunnel! Unfortunately, she could not go any further. A woozy Hope collapsed mid-step.

Then everything went black.

Part One

WELCOME TO
GOLD COAST ESTATES:
MEET THE NEIGHBORS

CHAPTER 1

HOPE ARRIVES

Eight months prior.

The day had finally arrived. Hope Klein could hardly contain her excitement as she loaded up the final box into the car. Most of the stuff to be moved was on the moving truck; however, there were a few items she wouldn't risk getting lost. Parents who have experienced their child realizing they lost their beloved stuffed "friend" know the anguish, tortured continuous cries and wails that go on for days. Hope wasn't going to risk anything happening to Marc's best friend Buzz. She also took her favorite coffee mug in the car with her. Hope had grown very fond of that mug. It made her look forward to getting up most mornings. Somehow the coffee just tasted better in that mug. She could relate to resorting to bursting into tears if anything happened to it!

While slamming the car trunk closed, Jay announced, "It is time to say goodbye to the city." Jay paused taking a deep sigh. He would greatly miss the Big Apple, a place he had called home for so many years. He'd enjoyed the helpful conveniences it afforded him—walking to work, strolling in the park, going to the museums, getting a slice of pizza at two in the morning or better yet getting baby formula at two in the morning! Hope's face brightened. "Goodbye, noisy city that never sleeps. Hello, quiet peaceful Long Island suburbs."

Waving their final goodbyes out of the car window toward the iconic city skyline in the distance, the trusty old white Honda Accord steered its way onto to York Avenue heading toward the 59th Street Bridge leading to the Long Island Expressway with Jay at the wheel and an overprotective Hope in the backseat beside Marc. Jay's lips rose upward from corner to corner as he looked back at Hope; he felt a sense of pride in himself for making his wife's dream of raising her family in the suburbs a reality.

Hope had only sat in the backseat one other time, when they brought Marc home from the hospital. Other than that, she had pushed him everywhere in his stroller. After all, who needs a car in New York City? There are so many city dwellers who don't even bother obtaining a driver's license. Long Island, however, would be a different story. Hope would have to figure a way to drive Marc around and not sit in the backseat. Hope would figure it out. She always came up with creative solutions.

Jay was going to miss spending time with Marc. In New York he would be home in five minutes; sometimes he was even able to sneak out and have lunch with Marc. They sang songs, watched *Toy Story* together and played peek-a-boo, currently one of Marc's favorite activities. Jay knew he was sacrificing his time with Marc to move to the suburbs, but he knew it was what Hope wanted and he wanted nothing more than to make Hope happy.

Exiting off the LIE onto 45 Manetto Hill Road, Hope experienced a jolt of excitement and a rush of anticipation. "Are we there?"

Jay let out a chuckle, then grinned. "We're not far, only a few minutes away from arriving at our new home." Hope's excitement was contagious. Jay beamed as his heartbeat quickened from Hope's enthusiasm at starting a new chapter in their lives out in the suburbs. Hope's love for Jay always grew stronger when she observed him taking pleasure in her pleasure.

Arriving! thought Hope. Her body tingled with joy and excitement as the car pulled up to a magnificent ornate gate with gold embossed letters, GCE, in the middle.

"We are the Kleins, and we're moving into 1 Margaret Court today!" Jay informed the guard at the gate.

"We've been expecting you. Welcome to Gold Coast Estates," greeted the stout guard. "Everything has arrived. All that's left is for the three of you to enjoy your new home." He went back into the gatehouse, and the gate slowly swung open.

"I feel like a child on Christmas day," Hope blurted out. "I can't wait to move into my present."

Children do get presents they want on Christmas Day; however, they often discover it wasn't at all what they expected.

CHAPTER 2

CHANGE CAN BE A GOOD THING, EXCEPT WHEN IT ISN'T!

Hope's eyes digested the rolling green carpeted hills, the rainbow of spectacular colors bursting from the proliferous Hydrangea flowers that bloom this time of year on Long Island along the gardens surrounding the majestic brick homes. The sun was radiant, the sky a beautiful powder blue. Rays of sunshine fell upon Hope's face welcoming her into her new life. As they continued to drive along the winding road, Hope couldn't help but notice in the near distance, the grand mansion that sat atop of the hill. Gold Coast Estates is an exclusive gated community located in the heart of North Shore's Gold Coast, a region made famous for its concentration of wealth and majesty when tycoons erected grand private estates there. Maltz Mansion, the mansion on the hill as many referred to it, was one of those magnificent estates. Today it remains on top of the hill as a beacon of Old-World grandeur and has been turned into an exclusive members only social club. The lure of living beside this grand estate brought wealthy buyers to Gold Coast Estates; many became members of Maltz Mansion. Hope could not believe that she and Jay were going to be residents here. Never in her wildest dreams did she expect this. When Jay told her that as part of accepting his partnership track position with Oyster Bay Medical Group they would be provided with housing at this prestigious community, Hope was beside herself with elation.

"This place is even more incredible this time of year." The last time Hope and Jay toured the development was in the winter when the now green rolling hills were blanketed in white fluffy snow and clear spiked shaped icicles hung from the houses. It was a winter wonderland.

Hope blurted out, "Boy, have our lives changed since living in a small one-bedroom apartment in the city."

Driving up to Margaret Court, Hope admired the stately McMansions, one competing with another over which was more magnificent with the exception of one home, which was more like a shed compared to the other houses.

Hope was fascinated by this little cottage-like house the first time she saw it. It was unpretentious and inviting; it reminded her of the seven dwarfs' house. She did some Google searches about the property and found out that it was the old cottage that the groundskeeper and his family resided in while taking care of all 100 acres of the Maltz estate. The person who currently lived there fought to have the house declared a historic landmark. Once a historic landmark, it had become untouchable to the builders of this community. Hence why it didn't fall in line with the rest of the community's McMansions.

Passing the cottage and driving onto the Belgium block paved circular driveway, Jay drove right up to the black wrought iron double entry doors that made the statement, You've arrived! Turning off the engine, an adrenaline-fueled Jay quickly got out of the car, ran around to open Hope's door.

"Welcome home, Mommy Klein," Jay happily announced. "Your dream home awaits."

Hope's senses were heightened as she got out of the car. She loved the colorful, vibrant perennials that lined the walkway leading to the house. A glorious fragrant smell overcame her. It reminded her of the smells she encountered at her grandparents' house.

Hope looked over at Marc who was sitting up in his car seat. "You're just as eager as Mommy to get into the house!" Hope told Marc in a happy jovial voice that made Marc smile. Hope knew that this smile would be short-lived. The high-pitched cry alerting her he's hungry would soon replace it.

Jay took out the car seat with Marc and lifted it up into the air. "To infinity and beyond!" Jay whimsically announced, then continued to engage a huge smile and a giggle from Marc when he told him, "You ARE a BOY!!!" as he placed the seat on the stoop. Making sure Marc was settled, Jay quickly ran back over to swoop up Hope into his arms.

Hope began to giggle. "What are you up to?"

"I'm carrying my wife over the threshold!" He began kissing and tickling her.

Ever the romantic, thought Hope, as she further surveyed her new home. Out of the corner of her right eye, she spied an elderly gentleman looking between the blinds of his window inside the historic house.

"We have company," she whispered, as her eyes pointed over to the window. Then thought, *he could be one of the dwarfs!*

To Hope's dismay, Jay waved in the direction of their nosy neighbor. "Don't do that," she exclaimed. "You'll make him feel funny. He's just curious about his new neighbors who happen to be making a disturbance. Let's go inside."

Hope searched her pockets for the front door keys; they were gone. "Oh, they must be in the car. I was jingling them at Marc. You know how he loves grabbing hold of them."

Jay looked all over the car...no keys. "They're not in the car. Are you sure you brought them?"

A light bulb went off. Hope smiled, and she placed her hand around a seated Marc. "Tada!" Hope jingled the keys. "Marc had them."

With that came an even greater disturbance. A high-pitched cry. As expected, Hope knew exactly what her baby was crying out for.

Click, click, click.

In the distance, a Nikon telephoto lens resting atop of a tree branch zoomed in closer.

You're much prettier in person, Hope Klein, and it looks like you've taken off the baby weight.

Click, click, click

Aren't they a happy family? I wonder if living at Gold Coast Estates will change that?

CHAPTER 3

HOPE'S FAIRYTALE LIFE

Hope fed Marc and left him in his car carrier taking a blissful nap.

Walking around her new home, she was overwhelmed by the size and emptiness of the rooms, she giggled at how lost their Ikea furniture looked. She had her work cut out for her. She gladly accepted this challenge to make this house into a home. *Nothing a few area rugs, pictures and throw pillows won't do to turn this space around,* she thought.

There was one room, however, that left Hope speechless—Marc's room. It was perfect, just as she had imagined her baby's room would look. The room was painted a soft baby blue with black lettering embossed "Twinkle, twinkle, little star" in flowing cursive on one wall; there was a moon and stars painted on the ceiling. The crib bedding matched this twinkling theme with sparkling silver stars scattered across white cotton sheets. In the corner of the room, the piece de resistance—a brand-new comfy glider. Sitting in the glider was Jay.

"How did you know?" uttered Hope. "You never cease to amaze me." Motioning over toward the glider, Hope leaned into Jay to give him a kiss. Before she realized it, Jay pulled her in toward him and she was seated on his lap.

"You told me on our third date that you wanted children and the nursery would be designed after your favorite nursery rhyme, 'Twinkle, Twinkle, Little Star.' I always felt bad that Marc didn't have his own room back in New York."

"You are something else, Dr. Klein!" Gently touching the side of his face, she moved it closer to hers until their lips met. The moment was spoiled when Jay's cell phone went off. "To be continued," declared Hope as Jay picked up the phone and stepped out of the room.

And so it began...Jay's demanding schedule as starting partner. Hope expected as much, but would have liked it to start a day later. She would have liked to have spent their first night in their new home together.

"When was his last dose of Coumadin?" Jay asked, speaking into the phone. "Good, then let's proceed with the angiogram. I'm on my way." Placing the phone back into the front pocket of his pants, Jay went to find Hope.

"It is great to have a place to change Marc instead of on a pad on our bed!" she commented as Jay entered the room.

"That was a quick nap!"

"Yes, I guess Marc doesn't want to miss anything." She smiled and asked, "Is it one of the players?"

"No. It's a hospital call."

"When do you get to meet the New York Titan players?"

"Although the practice is the main medical provider for the Titans, in my role it is unlikely that I would come into contact with any of the players. My responsibilities are confined to the clinic and the hospital." Jay raised an eyebrow. "My best odds of treating a player would be if they end up in the hospital!"

"We wouldn't want that to happen. It would hurt our chances this year."

Hope carried Marc as she strolled with Jay to his car. "I can't believe you have to go into the hospital on our first day moved into the house. It probably wasn't a good idea to agree to be on call today."

"I really had no choice, the doctor I'm covering left this morning for his father's funeral in Florida. Besides, we might as well get used to it since I'll be on call a great deal. That's part of the reason the practice took on another doctor."

"What time should I plan to have dinner ready by?"

"I'm not sure what time I'll be home until I start the case and can assess the situation. I'll keep you posted."

"Okay, I'll wait until I hear from you." Hope was used to having a wrench thrown into her plans. Being in an elementary fifth grade classroom for over five years, she'd had her well prepared, thought-out lesson plans interrupted by the unscheduled fire drill, the special assembly, a student disruption and many other surprises that arise every day in an evolving classroom.

Jay looked around the cul-de-sac and motioned his head over to the house across the street. "You're likely to meet a player before me. Maybe you'll catch Matthew Russo coming out of his house."

"Believe me, I'll be on the lookout!"

Watching Jay pull out of the driveway, Hope enjoyed the hot sun's rays on her face. The weather could not have been more spectacular. The sky cast a deep vibrant radiating blue with an intense golden glow beaming from behind one very long wispy cloud, while the warm Long Island Sound breeze gently blew across the trees cooling Hope from the sun's rays. The birds were chirping. Summer on Long Island!

Hope felt like Snow White living in her own fairytale... But fairytales aren't real.

CHAPTER 4

SWEET AND
BITTERSWEET MEMORIES

Waving goodbye to Jay as he drove out of the cul-de-sac, Hope noticed a woman in black capri pants and a sleeveless pink silk blouse, sporting black and white Hush Puppies loafers walking along the sidewalk. She was carrying something. When the woman stepped into closer viewing range, Hope saw that it was an adorable grayish black miniature schnauzer.

The woman shifted the dog to her left side and waved in Hope's direction with her free hand. Unfortunately, this balancing act didn't end well. The woman tripped over her own feet falling to the ground.

Hope rushed over. "Are you alright?"

"I am fine, the only thing injured is my pride."

"Don't be silly, we've all had our share of tripping in public. People have said one too many times to me, nice trip, see you next fall!"

Wiping the dirt off her clothes, the woman bent down to settle her dog's cries. "It's okay, Mini, Mommy is okay." She scooped the tiny dog back up in her arms as it wiggled and barked at Hope and Marc.

Hope extended her hand toward the dog, "Is your dog friendly?"

"She's super friendly, that's why she is barking. It's her way of saying 'pay attention to me!' I'm Morgan Kingsley, Dr. Kingsley's wife. You must be Hope. Welcome to Gold Coast Estates. I'm sure you and your adorable son will love it here." Morgan's eyes gazed upon Marc, his jovial smile and glittery eyes were magnetic. "Aren't you an angel. Such pretty blue eyes."

Hope recognized the name.

That's the doctor in the practice that left so he could dedicate his time to finding a cure for Huntington's disease...

"Thanks, it's nice to meet you. This is Marc. Do you have any children?"

...But why was he so interested in finding a cure? Oh, that's right. Someone in his family had the disease...but who...

Morgan's wide smile transformed downward. "Only if you include Mini here."

His wife! It was his wife...Her, Morgan!

With a slight hesitation Morgan continued, "It wasn't in the cards for us."

Hope's face turned ashen. *Why don't I ever think before I speak?*

Morgan noticed Hope's distressed look and felt the need to clarify. "As you may have heard, I have Huntington's disease. It's a disease you wouldn't wish on your enemy nevertheless your own child. With fifty-fifty odds, Elliot and I made the choice not to take the risk."

"That's like Sophie's Choice," Hope blurted out, then wished she could take back. Her face flushed. "Now I'm the one embarrassed. What I meant to say was that must have been a difficult decision no one should have to make." Hope had no filter; if it popped into her mind, it immediately popped out of her mouth.

"No, now you are being silly. I shouldn't have been so forthright. It's just that I am a big believer in awareness. Huntington's disease needs a spotlight put onto it; it's not known by much of the public."

"That's true, I have to admit that I never heard of the disease until Jay told me about your husband leaving the practice to pursue his research full time on a cure for Huntington's." Hope recalled Googling Huntington's disease at the time, learning that onset of the symptoms was most commonly gradual starting at around the age of 35 but could show up earlier or later.

"Elliot has made great strides. Every day he gets closer to figuring out a cure. Every year we hold a huge fundraising gala for Morgan's Song Foundation. All proceeds go to research. This year North Shore Hospital is sponsoring the event. They will be honoring Elliot for his research at Maltz Mansion. Morgan adjusted her head, pointing in the direction of the mansion in the distance, atop of the hill. We would be thrilled for you and Dr. Klein to come as our guests this year."

"It would be our pleasure!" Hope accepted happily. "I've been hoping to have a reason to go to the mansion on the hill. Its sheer presence on the hill is so enticing. I've fantasized about the magnificent parties they must have thrown back in the days of the overindulgent 1920s."

Marc was beginning to squirm in his mother's arm. Tears began to flow, wails followed. Marc was ready for Mom to take him home. "I'm sorry. He's a bit cranky because he didn't take his full nap today."

Morgan rubbed her hand against Marc's face and began singing; "You are my sunshine, my only sunshine." Magically, Marc settled down, closing his eyes and resting his head on Hope's shoulder.

Morgan fondly stated, "My dad sang that song to me when I was little." She hesitated again reflectively deep in thought, then she added, "Now I sing it to him."

It's a song that brought Morgan both sweet and bitter-sweet memories. Memories that one day she would more than likely *forget*.

CHAPTER 5

PLEASE DON'T TAKE MY SUNSHINE AWAY

Hearing a familiar song, Nathan was drawn to the opened kitchen window. Looking closer he saw Morgan with the new neighbor singing, "You are my sunshine, my only sunshine."

The all too familiar melody played over and over in Nathan's mind as he went back to sit in his favorite comfy armchair, one that Archie Bunker would be jealous of! Nathan's mind went back to a time in his life he tried hard to forget.

Hidden in an ever so tiny space between two walls stood a terrified young boy, no older than ten. His body shook, sweat dripped from all parts of his body and he lost his control of bodily functions as he felt wetness between his legs. He barely made it into this man-made hiding spot before the men entered. In an attempt to calm himself, he mentally sang, *You are my sunshine, my only sunshine. You make me happy when skies are gray...*

A monstrous voice called out, "Check every square inch of this place!"

The frightened child heard the thrashing of furniture, the knocking down of books as heavy footsteps of soldiers stormed the room.

Shaking, the boy peered through the ever so slight sliver of a crack watching them destroy the shrouded place which he has called home for the past two and a half years.

It wasn't supposed to be this way, he thought.

He was supposed to be playing with his friends and helping his parents at the candy shoppe back in his hometown of Berlin. However, the candy shoppe wasn't a safe place for him or his family.

This became apparent the day SS soldiers stormed his parents' shoppe with one mission and one mission only—to shatter the store, its contents, and the Jews' spirit.

Standing beside the counter, with his hand placed inside the see-through glass jar of colorful candies, a playful young boy nearly choked on the mouthful of jelly beans he was joyfully consuming. Quickly, almost instinctively, he removed his hand from the jar just moments before an SS soldier swung his wooden baton, knocking down all of the plentiful, glass candy-filled jars.

It was a terrifying storm, raining down bitter shards of glass onto the floor like tiny daggers fragmenting this young child's world, family, and life as he knew it.

All that was once sweet turned sour that night of *broken glass*.

The terrified boy watched as his father was brutally escorted out of the shoppe by two soldiers. His mom rushed to his father's side and was pushed away by one of the soldiers.

"He is being arrested," a soldier who appeared to be in charge declared.

"For what?"

"Being a dirty Jew."

The broken-hearted mother watched her loving husband be dragged off, worrying if he would ever return. For now, she knew what she had to do. These past few months, she and her husband have been planning for the entire family to leave Berlin and go to Amsterdam. This plan was now out the *broken* window. It would be just the children who would go, escape this darkened place. She would wait and follow once her husband was released.

The thing about plans is no matter how well intentioned they are, they can be changed and sometimes not the way intended.

You are my sunshine, my only sunshine. You make me happy when skies are gray…

And gray they were.

"In here!" yelled the uniformed man, as he pressed his fingers against the ever so slight sliver of a crack in the wall…

———

Jumping up, drenched in mounds of his own sweat, Nathan stood up from his armchair.

CHAPTER 6

A CALM BEFORE THE STORM

Hope carefully placed a sleeping Marc in his crib in his very own room.

I think I bought myself at least an hour, she smiled. *Where do I begin?*

There was no stopping Hope when she put her mind to getting things done and she was determined to make as many rooms feel more like home as she could. Before long, Hope had the area rug spread out in the living room, beautifully framed family photos placed along the fireplace mantle, and warm puffy throw pillows thrown onto the couch and love-seat. She transformed the family room into Marc's playroom, with a foam floor alphabet and number mat covered with an activity jumper, a pack-n-play, swing, rattles, teether, and bouncy balls. Carefully, Hope placed Marc's favorite toy, a stuffed Buzz Lightyear complete with expandable wings and plastic helmet onto the tabletop of the swing seat.

Hope plopped down onto the big comfy couch hoping to get a little rest. She had her eyes closed for about five minutes before the doorbell rang.

Approaching the door, she asked, "Who is it?"

"FedEx, I have a delivery for Mrs. Klein."

Opening the door Hope excitedly signed for the package. She knew exactly what was inside. "The solution to my car seat problem," Hope proudly announced to the FedEx guy. "A mirror that enables both mom and baby to see each other! It plays five musical melodies that I control by a remote from the front seat."

"That sounds great! I wish they had that when my kids were young!"

"Now we can go to the grocery store together without me trying to sit in the backseat and drive!" she joked.

"I don't think you should go any time soon. A storm is brewing."

Hope glanced up at the sky. It was still postcard perfect, with beautiful aquamarine blue shades and a glistening golden ball of orange casting a golden glow around the few fluffy clouds. Everything appeared to be quiet. The birds stopped chirping. The air seemed still. Hope felt a sense of calm. "Are you sure about that?" she questioned.

"Yes, I've lived on Long Island long enough to know when a storm is brewing. Have you ever heard the expression calm before the storm?"

"Sure."

He spread his hands wide open in a presentational manner. "That's exactly what is happening. It would be best to stay indoors."

The wailing sound transmitting from the baby monitor clasped to Hope's pants pocket broke whatever calm Hope had sensed.

"Now that will turn into a thunderous storm if I don't go!" she joked as she waved goodbye to the delivery man.

Calm before the storm, thought Hope. *We will see about that.*

A calm before the storm indeed.

CHAPTER 7

NO ONE LIKES TO BE
KEPT IN THE DARK

Walking over to the crib, Hope asked, "What do you think, Marc, are you ready to go for a drive? I have a special toy that will magically let you see *me* in the car. We can be explorers, like Dora! We can discover the groceries at the grocery store like chicken, onions, bananas, apples. Mommy's getting hungry."

Hope went back to the kitchen to gather her shopping list and car keys. She couldn't believe how spacious and bright it was, with plenty of natural light coming from the two skylights, picture window in front of the sink, and huge French sliding doors. Just as that thought popped into her mind, the room darkened. Looking out the picture window, the sky had darkened to a deep gravel gray, with charcoal puffy clouds. The beautiful day had disappeared just like that.

KABOOM!

Sheets of water began falling out of ominous black heavy clouds threatening to let out another crashing kaboom. Torrential rain ceaselessly fell, and rapid winds swayed the trees from side to side. There appeared to be no end in sight.

"Well, what do you know, the FedEx guy was right!" she told Marc. "Looks like we will have to do our exploring at home."

KABOOM!

Hope could see that Marc was looking to her to make sense of the noise he was hearing. Hope needed to reassure him that these loud thunderous sounds were nothing to be afraid of.

Hope began to sing, "Rain, rain go away. Come again another day...Mommy wants to go out today! Rain, rain go away."

As the rain continued to create a pitter patter melody on the roof, another melody played on Hope's cell phone. Hearing the song "Endless Love," Hope knew it was Jay. She had selected their wedding song as his designated ringtone.

"Hi, honey, how's your case going?"

"Not well, there have been some complications. I have to stay here at the clinic, I'm sorry it's going to be a late night."

Trying to keep her disappointment at bay, she responded, "I am confident with you there, the case will work out. It's raining really hard here. It's some storm, buckets and buckets of water have come down. I haven't seen a summer storm like this in years." Hope's heart skipped a beat as the lights in the house started to flicker. "Jay, the lights are flickering!" Her voice quivered, her body grew stiff. "Do you think we might lose electricity?!"

"I heard on the news that many trees were down so that could be a possibility."

"You know how I feel about being kept in the dark. Do we even have candles or a flashlight?" she asked with a tinge of panic in her voice.

"Calm down…there is a box in the garage labeled batteries. There should be a flashlight in there."

"Okay, hopefully I won't need to go find that box."

No sooner were those words spoken that darkness filled the room.

No one likes to be kept in the dark.

CHAPTER 8

A BEACON OF HOPE

To Hope's surprise and relief, the darkened sky transformed into a magnificent yellow, fiery reddish orange postcard. Its vibrance was so strong it lit up the room.

Hope prayed the electricity would go back on before the sky darkened again.

Looking at the time on her cellphone, Hope knew that it would be getting dark soon; so, into the garage Hope went. Out she came holding a big silver flashlight casting a bright path of light ahead of her.

In an effort to keep herself distracted; Hope decided to empty a box of books. She placed Marc into his pack and play that she positioned next to the bookshelf. She began taking the books out, admiring each book as she decided where to place it on the bookshelf. Hope loved books. She took enjoyment in organizing them according to subject—*How to Raise the Perfect Child* and *What to Expect When You're Expecting* were grouped together in the child rearing section. *Board of Education Fifth Grade Social Studies Syllabus, Teaching Hands-On Science* and *Best Literary Tales* made up the teaching section. Then there were the books on the Holocaust—*Survivors Share*

Their Stories, *Diary of Anne Frank* and *The End of World War II* were among them. Darkness was making it difficult to see the titles.

The darkness continued to make her anxious, her heart quickened, she inhaled rapidly, her stomach grumbled. Remembering that she hadn't eaten anything since breakfast in the city, which was only a quick cereal bar and cup of coffee, she decided to seek out something to eat. Heading toward the kitchen searching her memory of what food she had packed, she stopped to look out the front window. She couldn't believe her eyes. One home stood aglow among the total darkness. A beacon beckoning to Hope.

How is that possible? Why aren't all the houses on the court lit up? Then it came to her, *a private generator.*

For the next few minutes Hope debated all the reasons she should go introduce her herself and Marc to their new neighbor. *It would be rude not to go over, it's nice to get to know your neighbors, it's the responsible thing to do to check on him considering his age.*

Twenty minutes later, Hope pushed a soundly sleeping Marc in his stroller in the direction of the illuminating seven dwarfs' house. Sticking out from the bottom basket of the stroller was a fresh box of biscuits that she grabbed on the way out. *Can't go over there empty-handed.*

Walking up to the house, Hope admired the well-manicured front yard. Fresh mulch filled in beautifully flowered annual beds grouped along the walkway. The gentle breeze sounded the butterfly wind chimes. This house truly had an inviting aura to it.

Hopefully the owner will be as inviting.

CHAPTER 9

THE DWARF'S COTTAGE

Nathan knew that adding just a pinch more salt into his steaming hot boiling pot of soup with dancing matzo balls on the stove was just what he needed to make it delicious. He understood that he should keep the salt to a minimum, but that was not the way he wanted to live. "I have survived a great many challenges in my life," he'd tell his doctors. "It won't be salt that will take me down."

Nathan was looking forward to having a nice warm bowl of his homemade matzo ball soup, especially after the storm that just passed. Storms brought back difficult memories of his past, with the sounds of the moaning winds and heart stopping shots of thunder. A few sips of soup would calm him down. It never failed.

He poured the first ladle into a Tupperware container, filling it to the brim to ensure that he had at least one serving of soup saved for Matthew. When Nathan got started eating the soup, he didn't know how to stop. *Better safe than sorry,* he thought. Nathan knew the soup would be good for Matthew, who could use the "Jewish penicillin" to heal his body from a brutal week of being tackled and slammed to the ground.

That reminded Nathan he needed to make more of his special turmeric rub. It worked like magic on Matthew's aching joints. Being a pro football athlete comes with a price was Matthew's pledge.

Nathan rarely made friends; for the most part he would rather go it alone. He selected this house all those years ago because there were no other houses close by. Years later the property was re-zoned, and Nathan was forced to have neighbors. Famed football star Matthew Russo bought the property next door. He had a house built, actually a McMansion. During the time it was being built, Matthew would come to see how it was progressing. He'd always wave, but Nathan ignored him. This continued when he moved in. Another year passed until Nathan caved and took pity on him. Nathan couldn't stand to watch Matthew wince in pain every time he walked up his driveway knowing he had the perfect rub to help lessen the pain. They'd been close ever since, adopting each other as family.

Nathan licked his lips in anticipation as he sat at the kitchen table overlooking the steaming bowl of soup when the doorbell rang. *Who could that be? Matthew isn't expected back until tomorrow.*

Peeking through the peephole, he squinted to see a pretty young woman standing beside a stroller come into view. Actually, she was smiling in his direction at the peephole. It only took a minute for him to place her, *the new neighbor I heard giggling this afternoon.*

Nathan opened the door. "You're the new neighbor. Welcome to Gold Coast Estates, what can I do for you?" he asked in his thick mixed German Israeli accent.

Hope blurted out in one swift succession, not stopping to take a breath, "Sorry to bother you. Our lights are out, and we noticed yours weren't. We were hoping we could stay here until they go back on. We just moved in from the city. I'm in an unfamiliar house. I'm overwhelmed with the lights on, with them off I'm a wreck. Oh, and by the way I'm Hope Klein, this is Marc."

Nathan's jaw dropped; never had he heard a person speak so fast and so much. His protective nature kicked in. "Oh vey. The lights are out? I hadn't noticed. Please, please come in. My home is your home, Hope Klein."

Hope smiled pushing the stroller through the door. "They have been out for a few hours now. I was okay while it was daylight." Sniffing the air, she said, "Something smells good."

"Darkness is no place for a pretty young mommy and her sweet little son." Extending his hand out while taking a long look at the mother and her child, he was reminded of his wife and son at that time in his life. "I'm Nathan Friedman. Of course, you can stay here. I cooked matzo ball soup. I was just about to have some. Will you join me?"

"I'd like that. If it tastes as good as it smells, I'm sure I'm gonna love it!" She continued, "The smell reminds me of my husband's grandma's matzo ball soup. She made the best matzo ball soup I ever tasted." Looking around she said, "You have a lovely home. How long have you lived here? Do you like it here? Are the people friendly?" Hope disconnected the baby seat from the rest of the stroller.

"I like it here," Nathan smiled. "Most of the neighbors keep to themselves." He motioned toward the kitchen. "Come, let's go into the kitchen."

Hope surveyed the house.

The house was small and neat. The furniture pieces were antique relics including a navy blue velvety couch, a worn brown leather armchair, and a wooden end table where two picture frames stood. One held a black and white photo of what looked like a young Nathan with a young woman holding a toddler standing in front of an olive tree. The other held a photo of Nathan and what looked like New York Titan Matthew Russo holding each other standing on Nathan's front porch. "Is that NY Titan Matthew Russo? He's one of my favorite players."

"Yes, it is," Nathan let out a chuckle, "He's my favorite neighbor!"

Hope smiles at the confirmation that Matthew Russo really was one of her neighbors.

The dining room contained a round wooden table that sat four. The table served a dual purpose, one end for dining, while the other housed the latest Apple computer with monitor. He may not have updated his 19th century interior design style but it was certain he embraced 21st century technology.

As Hope gathered up everything she needed from under the stroller seat, she noticed a small black Samsonite carry-on by the front door. "Are you coming or going?" she asked as she entered the kitchen.

Confused at first, Nathan realized she was referring to his *just in case bag*. "Staying!" he responded. "It's always good to be prepared. Whether it be a generator or an emergency to go bag," he added as he placed Hope's bowl of soup onto the table.

What happened to you to make you so hyper vigilant? Hope wondered.

Hope positioned a sleeping Marc in his car seat on the floor next to her seat. She was thrilled to have a warm meal.

"I think Jay's grandma has some competition, Nathan!" she replied after a few spoonfuls. "This soup is very tasty. I would say it may even be better than grandma's. Now let's see about the matzo ball."

"Thanks, it's an old family recipe."

Cutting off a piece of matzo ball, she hesitated. "I think it's good but not as hard as I like it. Grandma beats you on the matzo balls, but that's only because she makes them like rocks."

Nathan laughed. "My mom made them like rocks, too!" Nathan rolled up his sleeves and dug in. He liked Hope. She was genuine.

Hope happily gulped up the soup and matzo balls; they may not have been as hard as she liked, but they were still delicious. As they ate, Hope noticed black tattooed numbers and letters on Nathan's left outer forearm. She knew what they represented.

Nathan was a Holocaust survivor. Now she understood his emergency to go bag.

CHAPTER 10

NIGHT OF BROKEN GLASS

"I see you spotted my tattoo," he said, rubbing his fingers across the numbers.

"Well, you know those diligent Germans in Auschwitz and their meticulous records."

Hope's statement blew Nathan away. He slowly remarked as he tried to understand what he was hearing from such a young girl, "You know of these tattoos? Most people were under the misconception that all Jews were tattooed."

"Before becoming a stay-at-home mom, I taught the fifth grade. Every year I taught a unit on the Holocaust. I've done a great deal of research with the United States Holocaust Memorial Museum in Washington, D.C. and Yad Vashem in Israel. What I've learned is that the heart of the Holocaust is about the people. So, I've focused on real individual stories to bring historical concepts to life. I've found it's been the most powerful way to teach students about such a challenging topic. Hearing stories firsthand from survivors has really made a difference in my students' awareness and understanding of the Holocaust. In fact, it made an enormous impact on me."

Nathan was impressed. There was something about Hope that made him feel extremely at ease. She reminded him so much of his wife, Chava. For a moment he let his defenses down.

"My story begins back in Berlin. Every day after school I would go to my family's candy shoppe. I'd play with my baby sister Sadie, eat sweets and help clean the store. My papa would encourage laughter at the store. He performed magic tricks with the candy. My mother told us silly stories and sang songs in between customers."

Hope looked over at Nathan's kitchen counter and smiled. There stood a bunch of candy filled glass canisters. *A tribute to his parents' candy store,* she thought.

"The shoppe was a safe place for me, away from the bullying at school I received for being Jewish. I had a very happy sweet childhood." Nathan choked up. "Until it wasn't. *Der mentsh trakht ingot lakht.*"

"*Der mentsh trakht ingot lakht?*" Hope repeated in her best Yiddish accent.

"Man plans, God laughs." Nathan paused. "It was November 9, 1938, 8:57 to be precise that my sweet childhood was taken from me."

"Kristallnacht," Hope softly uttered. "The night of broken glass."

Once again Hope surprised Nathan. "Yes, and what a night that was." Nathan closed his eyes, lowered his head, "Everything changed that night. My parents were preparing to leave Berlin, they were making arrangements for us to be smuggled to Amsterdam."

"But now that couldn't happen."

"No, it happened, just not the way my parents planned. My mom told me that I was to take my sister and leave with the smugglers. She and papa would follow. I didn't even have the time to think what I should take." Nathan's face sunk. "I have no photos of my family."

Hope thought back to the Samsonite bag by the front door. It made even more sense now. She imagined Nathan's most treasured things were in there.

Nathan swallowed deeply. "If only my sister came with me, perhaps things would have ended differently."

"Why didn't she go?"

"She wouldn't leave my mom. She threw a huge tantrum. You'll find out when Marc goes through his terrible twos, there's no reasoning with them at that age. I had to leave without her." Nathan gulped. "It would be the last time I'd see her."

Hope wiped her eyes, "It wasn't long after that the Nazis began putting the Jews in ghettos," Hope sighed. "And then from there into the camps."

"That's how most of the Jews got to the camp; however, my story was different." Nathan wiped his moistened eyes, "But that's a story for another day."

Hope knew how difficult it was for survivors to relive their story. She waited patiently for Nathan to regain his composure when Marc's cries interrupted. Hope went into the diaper bag and pulled out a bottle. She went over to the kitchen sink and ran the hot water tap. Waiting for the water to get hot, Hope looked out the window and smiled, "The lights are back on!"

Looking over at Nathan, Hope knew it was time for her and Marc to go back home.

CHAPTER 11

MY PRINCE CHARMING

Hope was fast asleep when she was awoken by the sound of the front door opening. The digital alarm clock on the nightstand read 2:00 a.m. Hope's first thought was the poor guy. Her next thought was please don't wake the baby!

The door to the bedroom opened. Jay appeared, holding a bottle of Moscato and two glasses. He walked over to the bed. "I know it isn't exactly as you planned our first night but…"

Before Jay could finish his thought, Hope wrapped herself around him and began nibbling at his ear. She whispered, "My Prince Charming."

Jay gently pushed Hope back onto the bed, he pulled off her nightgown while kissing her shoulders, her chest…working his way down.

CHAPTER 12

BEDTIME CHIT CHAT

Jay got out of the shower and got under the covers. "How did it go with the lights being out?"

"You're not going to believe what I did." Hope fluffed her pillow and sat up against it, "I went to our neighbor's house. The one who was spying on us this afternoon."

"What? Why would you feel comfortable staying in the dark with a stranger?" Jay shook his head, "Hope, you can't let your fears get the better of you. Personally, I think being in the dark with a stranger is more frightening."

"That's just it. We weren't in the dark. He has a generator."

"Clever old man."

"His name is Nathan Freidman. He is a holocaust survivor."

"That says it all."

"You know it. I have a great deal of admiration and respect for survivors." Hope sighed, "Nathan seems like a lonely old man."

Jay rolled his eyes, "Oh no, Hope. Do not take Nathan on as one of your special projects. I am sure if he wanted friends, he'd have them. You only spent a few hours with him. I am sure he is a happy, content old man."

"I'm sure he is. I'm not looking to make him my next project! All I'm saying is that, perhaps he'd enjoy a little company." Hope took a deep breath and changed the topic, "You had a long day. How did your case go?"

"Very well." Jay yawned. "It's getting late, I need to get some sleep. Goodnight, Gracie!"

Hope pursed her lips. "Goodnight, Gracie." She never cared for what Jay thought was a funny way of letting her know he was done talking.

CHAPTER 13

THE OLD STATUE OF LIBERTY PLAY

One week later.

Hope and Marc had been enjoying the fresh air on their run throughout the community. Gold Coast Estates has a great clear path for running. It ran along the beautiful lush grounds, passed the glorious McMansions, and wrapped around part of the golf course. She was glad Jay had suggested she get a runner stroller. It moved so smoothly on all types of terrain. The wheels and steering were incredible. She especially loved the way it handled around the crowds in the city. Here in the suburbs that wasn't a concern. Hope passed only a handful of dog walkers, joggers and runners. There was a runner on her radar—famed running back Matthew Russo. A huge Titans fan, Hope couldn't believe her good fortune to be living not only in the same community but on the same block. Every day Hope looked over at Matthew's house in hopes of catching him as he left his house. No such luck. Hope questioned if she should ring his doorbell and introduce herself. She *was* his new neighbor; he must be curious who moved into the house across the street. Yet, isn't it the neighbor who already lives on the block that welcomes the new neighbor? Hope didn't want Matthew to think she was an annoying fan harassing him at his home. Hope decided she would just wait until it happened naturally.

Setting out onto the path, Hope turned on her iPod. She created a special playlist for the run that pumped up her energy and made sure Marc was part of the experience. She sang songs and at times bobbed the stroller up and down to the beat. Marc always enjoyed going on the run. One of Hope's and Marc's favorite songs to get pumped was Kris Kross' "Jump." Hope blasted up the volume as she bobbed Marc up and down singing, "Jump, jump, Marky will make you Jump!" Turning a tight corner, a distracted Hope continued singing and bobbing with Marc until she felt something hit the front of the stroller. She'd collided with something. Quickly she checked Marc, who was giggling and pointing at a man hopping up and down rubbing his knee making funny faces.

"Are you okay? I didn't see you, there's a blind spot turning that corner." Suddenly, Hope did a double take. "Oh my god, it's you!"

The shirtless man stood up and laughed. "I didn't see *you* coming!" He wiped off any residual dirt.

"You can say you were blindsided!"

"Oh, I get it!" Matthew roared with laughter. "We have a comedian here!"

"I'm so excited to meet you. I just moved into the house across the street from you. I never expected that our first meeting would be me tackling you. I'm a huge fan. I've watched football with my dad since I was ten. You are so fast, so athletic and so amazing!"

Matthew couldn't believe the speed in which Hope spoke. "Oh man, girl, you talk fast! So, you're the new neighbor? I'm guessing you moved here from the city."

Hope blushed. "Yes. I'm Hope Klein, and this is Marc."

Matthew bent down. "Hey there, little man!"

Hope couldn't take her eyes off Matthew's shirtless chest. *He's an Adonis,* she thought. *It's as if someone chiseled his chest out of clay.* Looking closer Hope noticed something actually was chiseled on Matthew's body—on his lower back was a tattoo of a football play. Hope knew the exact play. "Is that the Statue of Liberty play on your back?"

"You really are a true fan! I'm not one for tattoos but it served its purpose."

Getting a closer look, Hope noticed that three of the circles making up the play were scar markings. "That's clever!"

Matthew turned his attention back to Marc, speaking in a playful voice. "That's the play that gets me to many touchdowns. You know what happens when I make a touchdown, little man?" Matthew went into his best touchdown dance for Marc. Moving his left foot back, then his right foot, then his left again, then his right, in Running Man fashion, then shuffling from side to side a few times building up to a spectacular back flip.

Hope lifted her iPod, blasted the Kris Kross "Jump" song and did her best running man. She smiled. *I'm doing the running man with Matthew Russo. What's better than that?*

Hope was feeling so energized she challenged Matthew to a race back to the cul-de-sac.

Matthew took off, Hope and Marc not far behind.

As Hope entered the cul-de-sac, she saw Matthew was already at the end of his driveway. He called out, "I win! You're faster than I expected. You're Speedy Gonzalez."

"Ha-ha, very funny!" As Hope pulled the stroller over to the bottom of Matthew's driveway, she noticed Nathan standing at Matthew's front door holding a round Tupperware container. "Aren't you the lucky one. Nathan's delicious matzo ball soup is sure to make you feel good."

Matthew gave Hope a quizzical look of wonderment. "You and Nathan know each other?"

"Sort of, if you consider spending a lovely evening in his kitchen."

"You were in Nathan's house?!"

"You seem surprised."

"That's cause it took me a year to get that invite."

"I sort of invited myself the night we had the blackout. His house was a beacon of light in a sea of darkness." Hope curled her forehead. "A year?"

"That makes sense. He would never turn a mother and child away." Rocking his head back and forth, he said, "Nathan is a bit of a loner. He doesn't seek out relationships with the neighbors."

From her first meeting with him, Hope sensed he preferred keeping to himself. "So how did you finally get the invite?"

"He took pity on me. For months when he saw me outside, I'd wave or call out hello, but he never initiated anything other than a polite wave. So, I'd wobble off in pain. My joints give me lots of pain. Well, one day I wave and he calls me over. Tells me he has something that can help my painful joints. It's a home remedy. Amazingly it worked. We've been friends ever since."

"That's nice. You two are close?"

"He's my grand daddy! Well, I gotta get going; Nathan's waiting."

Hope waved to Nathan. "Hi, Nathan. Beautiful day today, isn't it?"

Nathan waved. "It certainly is. How's the baby?"

"He's doing great, thanks." Hope pushed the stroller toward her house. "Enjoy your soup!"

Click, click, click!

What do we have here? Zooming the 40X telephoto lens in on Matthew Russo, there was some sort of commotion. Matthew appeared to be rubbing his left knee.

Click, click, click!

The Nikon camera moved slightly over to see Hope and Marc Klein. *What is she doing with Matthew? Are they laughing?*

Click, click, click!

Now they're dancing?! Placing the camera down, the photographer went into a backpack, took out a 3x5 yellow legal pad and wrote: *Hope and Matthew?* This could be trouble.

CHAPTER 14

KEEP SUNDAY OPEN

Looking up from her computer, Hope checked the time. She didn't realize how much time she'd spent online. She got lost on Yad Vashem's website. It was so thorough and impressive. Hope searched the site until she found the tab that read: The Central Database of Shoah Victims' Names. She clicked the tab. The introduction to the page read: "Yad Vashem, together with its partners, has collected and recorded the names and biographical details of millions of victims of systematic anti-Jewish persecution during the Holocaust (Shoah) period. Close to four million eight hundred thousand of the six million Jews murdered by the Nazis and their accomplices are commemorated here. This database includes information regarding victims of the Shoah: those who were murdered and some whose fate has yet to be determined. The names of more than one million victims remain unknow—and time is running out. It is our collective moral imperative to persist in our efforts to recover their names and restore their identities." A chill ran up her spine. She felt now more than ever the necessity to get Nathan to document his family's story. Moving the cursor over to the tab entitled: Download Page of Testimony Forms. It took her to a page of links to forms written in different languages. Hope chose English. Two printable forms appeared; Hope selected the PRINT button. Shortly she heard the printer initiate the printing.

At the same time Hope heard the "Endless Love" ringtone coming from the phone on the table beside her. She smiled; she'd been waiting to hear from Jay. She was dying to tell him that she met Matthew Russo.

"Hi, Honey." Not waiting for a reply, she added, "You'll never guess who I ran into today."

"From the excitement in your voice I'd say Matthew Russo."

"You got that right. I literally ran into him. We were out running and there's this blind spot turn as you are coming up Addie Drive where he collided into the front of the stroller."

"Collided? Is Marc okay?"

"Yes, he was laughing. He thought Matthew was so funny."

"Sounds like you had a good day. My day has gone smoothly. It looks like I should be able to get home early today. Say 6:30. And I have a surprise for you."

Murphy's Law came to Hope's mind after she hung up with Jay. For the past week Hope's had dinner ready and waiting for Jay, but every night the dinner waited and waited. So, wouldn't you know it on the day Hope let herself get caught up on the computer, Jay calls to let her know that he should be home by 6:30. Not only that, he has a surprise for her.

Hope is not one for surprises. She picked out her engagement ring, found out the baby's gender in her fourth month and selected most of her birthday presents. So when Jay said he had a surprise for her, she begged him to tell her over the phone. Jay wasn't going to give in. "What's the fun in that," he retorted. Compromising Hope asked him to at least give her a clue. Jay obliged: "Keep Sunday open."

Now this clue and the surprise were consuming her. *Keep Sunday open. Maybe he's taking us to Maltz Mansion,* Hope thought. *It would be nice to walk the grounds and tour the inside.* Hope shook her head. *What am I thinking, we're not members. Maybe that's the surprise? Jay got a member to invite us.*

Hope refocused her attention on dinner. Searching her brain and the contents in the refrigerator for a simple quick recipe, Hope's pointer finger raised when it came to her. She'd make Pasta Aglio e Olio. Quickly she grabbed the garlic, lemons and parsley out of the refrigerator. Got the olive oil, red pepper flakes and the spaghetti from the cupboard. She was set. She'd prep everything so all she'd have to do is toss the spaghetti into the sauce. This aromatic flavorful dish was one of Jay's favorites.

Keep Sunday open. Maybe he is going to take us to the beach. It is the dog days of summer and we haven't gone to a Long Island beach in years.

Hope refocused. *You need to feed and bathe Marc before Jay gets home. This way he will have some time to be with Marc before he goes to sleep. This whole week Jay's gotten home well after Marc's fallen asleep for the night.*

By the time Jay walked through the door, Hope and Marc were lying together on the couch watching *Toy Story.* A ritual followed by Marc going to sleep.

Jay quietly lay beside Marc, kissed his cheek and whispered, "You got a friend in me." By the end of the movie, Marc was fast asleep.

Hope carried Marc into his room while Jay got changed.

Back in the kitchen, Hope put the final touches on dinner.

Jay dug into the spaghetti. "This is delicious. Your best yet."

"Thank you. I slaved all day in the kitchen, but it was worth it if it makes you happy."

"You do a lot to make me happy, that is why I am so happy to do something to make you happy."

Hope wiggled in her chair, leaning in closer to Jay with excitement.

"We are going to the Titans game on Sunday. You will be able to see Matthew Russo in action."

"That's amazing!" A huge smile filled Hope's face. "It will be fun to see him make moves eluding any player's attempt to take him down."

Jay laughed, "From what you told me, you and Marc nearly took him down!"

"Yep." Hope moved onto Jay's lap nibbling his ear. "Now I'm looking to take you down."

CHAPTER 15

ARE YOU READY FOR
SOME FOOTBALL!

Arriving at the stadium, Jay looked down at the instructions he was given. "It says we should go to section C, and there will be a person there that will guide us to our seats." Entering section C, Jay told the gentleman at the door his name.

"Follow me, Dr. Klein." Jay and Hope followed him down a set of stairs.

"Looks like we are going to have pretty good seats!" Jay told Hope as they walked down. To both their surprise, the guide continued down to the next set of stairs that led to an entrance onto the field. "OMG, we are going on the field!" exclaimed Hope. The man guided them over to the bleachers right on the 20-yard line on the Titans' sideline. As they approached, a man wearing a navy blue polo and khakis waved them over.

"Dr. Klein, I heard you were coming to today's game. It's a pleasure to meet you. I'm Dr. John Baker, head doctor for the team. I've heard many good things. Your reputation precedes you. The med student who saved a young man's life his first week in the ER."

"That was a long time ago." Jay blushed. "This is amazing! It's exhilarating to be on the field. It's a whole different ball game, pardon the pun!"

"It never gets dull!" Turning his attention toward Hope, he asked, "Are you a Titans fan?"

"You betcha! I'm Jay's wife, Hope." She looked around onto the sea of blue stands filling up with the many loyal Titans fans adorning blue and white jerseys, blue and white faces, some with blue and white painted chests. Fans held signs stating, "Jump, Jump, Matthew Russo Make Us Jump" and "Go Mr. Liberty." The excitement filled the air; it was contagious. "There's nothing like being at an actual game. But being on the field is over the top. We're so close we can get tackled by a player!"

Just as she said those words, a player came running straight toward her in an attempt to catch the ball flying in her direction. The player jumped up into the air no more than two feet from Hope's feet. Landing back onto the ground with the ball in hand the player turned to Hope. "How did you like that catch, Speedy Gonzalez?"

Hope smiled and started doing the running man. "It makes me want to jump, jump."

Matthew laughed his infectious laugh. "I'm impressed! Who do you know to get this kind of access?"

"I'm married to the newest member of Oyster Bay Medical Group."

"Are you telling me that my new neighbor is also my new doctor?"

"That's exactly what she's telling you," Jay interjected. "I'm the said husband and doctor!"

"That's incredible! I had no idea." Matthew extended his hand out to Jay. "Great to meet you, Doc."

"The pleasure is truly mine. You are amazing. You have

such energy, you're so fast. When the defense leaves a hole, you run through it."

Matthew let out a roaring laugh. "I do my best!" Staring intently at Jay, he asked, "Have we ever met before? There's something about your face that strikes me that we've met."

"I would remember meeting Mr. Liberty!" Jay's cheeks reddened. "I guess I have one of those faces. People mistake me all the time for someone they know."

"Really? I guess that's it." Hearing the coaches whistle, Matthew let out another infectious laugh, "I gotta go. Gotta game to play!"

"Good luck!"

"So, this is how the players see the fans!" Jay looked around at the crowd. "Look, Dr. Conrad is here. Is that Joey De Angelo with him? We should go say hi."

"Who's Joey De Angelo?"

"Come on! You don't know who Joey De Angelo is?" Jay took a second look over in Harry's direction, and there was now a swarm of reporters surrounding Joey De Angelo.

"He must be someone famous," Hope tsked. "Why don't you go? You know my feelings about Dr. Harry Conrad."

"Yes, you think he's strange." Jay made finger quotes. "And has a God complex. You know he was only kidding when he suggested designing our babies. He thought that would impress you to know what science can achieve."

"His science crosses the line. I wouldn't put it past him to cross ethical lines in his research. All in the name of science."

"That's your opinion. He's done a lot for me, for us. He did play a big role in getting me this job."

"You got this job because you are an excellent doctor. Besides he thinks because he has done so much for you that you are indebted to him."

"It was on his recommendation I got the job. Besides, he doesn't ask for a lot. I only go into his lab once a month to bring a fresh perspective. New eyes. It's the least I can do." Jay began to walk off without Hope.

"Harry, great to see you."

"You, too. How do you like the practice?" Spreading his arms out, he added, "The perks aren't too shabby."

"So far, so good. I never imagined watching an NFL game from the sidelines!"

Hope caught up to Jay. She put on her most pleasant smile.

"Well, hello Hope. You're looking good. Motherhood works for you. How is the newest addition to the Klein family?" asked Dr. Conrad. "Jay has shown me photos. He has spectacular blue eyes. What people wouldn't give to use your DNA to make a baby."

Hope took a deep breath. *He can't help himself,* she thought. "Marc is doing great. We left him with my parents…he's a bit too young to be at a football game."

Jay couldn't contain his curiosity. "Dr. Conrad, is that Joey De Angelo over there?"

"Yes, we came together. I'll introduce you." Harry waved for Joey to join them. "You're going to love Joey. He's so much fun!"

Joey began to walk over, passing the cheerleaders rehearsing. Several called out well wishes to him. Joey ran over and kissed each one of the girls.

Hope rolled her eyes and thought, *Looks like a real fun guy!*

"Sorry about that, Harry. Can't stop the people's attraction to me! That's what happens when you win a few bucks on football picks." Joey smiled over at Jay and Hope.

Most women and even some men would say Joey was a handsome man with his dark olive skin tone, piercing brown eyes, styled dark jet-black hair. It was obvious by what Hope had already observed that his looks and physique drew many opportunities his way. Hope sensed he thought he was God's gift to the world. Which is why it made sense he'd be friends with Harry Conrad who thought he was God.

Jay shook his head and whispered to Hope, "It's more than a few bucks."

"How much are we talking about?"

"Let's just say it got him on Forbes' wealthiest persons list."

Hope couldn't tell if they were all pulling her leg. She would go online tonight and check out Mr. De Angelo for herself.

"Joey, I'd like to introduce you to Dr. Jay Klein and his wife Hope."

Joey reached his hand out to Jay. "Oh, you must be the new doctor?"

"Yes I am. How did you know that?"

"It is part of my job to know. You can't win as many bets as I have without knowing all the goings on in the football world."

Jay was very impressed, Hope not so much. She challenged him, "So who should I bet on in today's game to win big?"

"I can't reveal that! I've placed a bet on today's game. If it gets out which team I've bet on, there'd be a run at the bookmakers."

"That's a cop-out."

Jay defended Joey. "Not really, Hope. There are many people who would bet the same way as him, it wouldn't be fair to the bookmakers."

"I tell you what," Joey ripped a portion of his ticket and began writing on the back. "I'm writing down my bet." Joey handed it over to Jay. "When the game is over, you can check it and see I won."

Hope sighed. *This guy's too much. He can't just give the paper to me, he had to give it to Jay.*

CHAPTER 16

WINNING AND LOSING
AT THE SAME TIME

By halftime Hope's throat was sore from all the screaming and cheering…"Go Russo!"—as he drove 34 yards, 41 yards and then another 21 yards. "Jump, Jump. Matthew Russo makes you jump!"—when he made a touchdown. And she was up on her feet screaming when he got to the one-yard line implementing the great Statue of Liberty play. He'd been a thorn in the Colonists' side. He has eluded defensive linemen Shaun Smith every step of the way. Russo had outrun and outsmarted Smith the whole first half.

Hope was looking forward to seeing what Matthew did in the second half; however, that wouldn't be much. His first play would also be his last.

The Titans lined up on their 20-yard line. A whistle blew—an encroachment penalty called on Colonists' Shaun Smith. The Titans moved to the 25-yard line. On the next play, Matthew faked left, then went right driving for 28 yards until finally being tackled by Smith. Smith tackled him hard. Russo didn't like that. A fight erupted. It got rough, and crowds of players on both sides rushed over. Players were pulling at

Russo and Smith to separate them. Russo had a strong hold of Smith's shirt. Not willing to let go of the shirt as he was being pulled away, Russo ripped the back of the shirt along the middle. At this point the referees ejected both players from the game. Before walking off, Russo turned back and rushed over to Smith, tapping him on the back. They shared words, then shook hands. Matthew watched Smith as he walked off.

The remainder of the game the Titans did not do well. They did not put any more points on the board. While the Colonists did put some points on the board, not enough for the win.

All in all, it was an incredible game to watch from the sidelines. Especially the fight! Hope would love the opportunity to run into Matthew later in the week and find out what really happened out there. She especially wondered what was said when Matthew went back over to Smith that led to the two shaking hands.

Walking back to the car, Jay handed Hope the ripped ticket Joey gave him. Hope smiled. "Let's see who Mr. Gambler Extraordinaire picked." She read aloud, "I bet on the Colonists. Aha, he lost."

"Not necessarily." Jay shook his head. "The Colonists might have lost the game, but that doesn't mean Joey lost his bet."

"What is that supposed to mean?"

Opening the car door for Hope, he explained, "People who gamble for money place bets with a bookmaker who sets a spread to be used when betting. Depending on the spread, a team can lose the actual game but win the bet. When we get home, we can check what the spread was."

Jay's phone rang. "Hello, Dr. Klein here." Jay nodded. "Sure, that should be fine. Oh, by the way, what was the spread for today's game?"

Jay hung up. "He won the bet. The spread was plus five, Colonists. With the extra five points for the Colonists in a game ending twenty-four/twenty, the person betting on the Colonists would win the bet. Adjusting for the spread, the score would be twenty-four/twenty-five."

"Was that Joey DeAngelo on the phone?"

"Yes, he got my number from Harry."

"What did he want?"

"He asked if he could stop by the clinic tomorrow. He wants some medical advice."

CHAPTER 17

GAMBLER EXTRAORDINAIRE

Hope couldn't get back to sleep as she normally would after Marc's 4:30 a.m. diaper change and bottle. Staring at the digital clock on her nightstand, it glared 5:42 a.m. Deciding that falling back to sleep wasn't in the cards for her, Hope decided to go in the kitchen and use this time to be productive.

Sipping a steaming hot cup of black coffee, her favorite drink, Hope turned on her computer. Today's search: Joey De Angelo.

Hope typed "Joey De Angelo" into the search bar and clicked ENTER. Several postings popped up. "The Biggest NFL Bets Ever Made," "The 5 Million Dollar Bet," "De Angelo Mixes Math and Social Science Data to Score Big" and a Wikipedia page on him. Selecting the Wikipedia page, Hope discovered Joey was a Wall Street guy who got taken down by the Enron scandal. He cut his losses and applied his mathematical talents in the gambling world gaining notoriety for his gambling escapades. Joey was quoted as saying he had devised a winning formula, part collecting statistical skills driven data and part combining it with information he acquired about the players' personal lives. He joked that he's what you get if you combine John Nash's mathematical ability and Jimmy the Greek's importance of learning all you can about a player's personal life. Jimmy was known to read local newspapers to learn information that would help him determine how a player might play on game day. Jimmy's favorite tale of winning was when he learned a player found out his wife was cheating on him 24 hours before a game. Jimmy won big.

Joey took this theory to the next level. He comprised a team of observers spread out across different states and neighborhoods to keep their eyes out for any pertinent personal information that could be used to hedge his bets.

Moving further down the page, Hope's eyebrows raised. "Joey DeAngelo is rumored to be worth on the plus side of 270 million dollars."

Continuing to read through the page, something caught her eye. "Mr. De Angelo has a heart as big as his wallet. Through the years, he has made many generous donations to The Morgan's Song Foundation, a non-profit organization that is researching a cure for Huntington's disease."

Hearing the front door open and shortly close, alerted Hope that Jay was getting the morning paper. She got up, refreshed her mug and proceeded to fill a fresh mug for Jay.

"Well, what a pleasant surprise. Look who's up early." Jay placed the Long Island Newsday onto the table and lifted up the mug. "Thanks."

"I couldn't get back to bed. It's that Joey De Angelo's fault."

"Come again?" Jay sat at the table and started looking over the news.

"You weren't kidding about him. I never believed anyone could do so well gambling." Bending over and tapping the back page of the newspaper, she said, "The man does his research, no wonder he knew to bet on the Colonists."

Jay gave Hope a quizzical look and turned to the back of the newspaper. The headline read: "Smith and Russo Fight Over A Girl." Underneath was a huge photo of Shaun with his torn shirt draping off his body walking away from Matthew. Jay read, "A source has confirmed that yesterday's scrimmage had nothing to do with football but a love triangle. You think Joey knew about this?"

"From what I read he has spies all over the place looking for just that kind of information. It was public knowledge that Smith has a violent temper. Joey put two and two together and gambled on the Colonists."

CHAPTER 18

THE INVITATION

Hope was on her third cup of coffee when the doorbell rang. She wasn't expecting anyone. To her surprise, when she opened the door, she found two strangers standing side by side. They were wearing what appeared to be 1920s attire. The young girl in a flashy sequined black and gold flapper dress with black leather Mary Jane strap heels, strands of white pearls hanging from her neck and a matching black sequined headband with a feather on the side. The man dressed in a white fitted suit, black tie and vest with black herringbone leather shoes. The young man stepped up and recited:

> *We are here today to pay you a jazzin' call*
> *To invite Dr. and Mrs. Klein to the North Shore*
>   *Hospital Ball.*
> *This year you'll be swinging carefree in Gatsby fashion,*
> *At the grand majestic Maltz Mansion.*

The young girl with the pearls around her neck walked toward Hope handing her a gold engraved invitation.

"You guys are fantastic!" Hope announced. "Thank you."

Opening the invitation, it read: "North Shore Hospital cordially invites you to our annual gala, The Roaring Twenties Ball. This year we are pleased to announce we will be honoring Dr. Elliot Kingsley for his exhaustive commitment and continued financial contributions toward Huntington's disease research. Please join us for a swinging good time on September 12 at 7:30 p.m. at Maltz Mansion. Dress as a character from *The Great Gatsby*—1920s attire."

Hope's adrenaline was pumping. She hadn't attended a party that sounded as grand as this in years, if ever, she realized. In Hope's desire to share her excitement, she picked up her cell phone and speed dialed Jay.

Moments later the "Endless Love" ringtone rang out in the house. Following the ringtone into her bedroom, Hope heard Jay's cell phone bellowing and vibrating on the nightstand. Hope pursed her lips. "He forgot his phone." She couldn't wait to call and tell him. The shoe is usually on the other foot. On any given day, Hope was known to leave her phone somewhere.

Hope dialed the number to the clinic. The person who answered was very friendly. They connected her to the head nurse, who would be able to patch Hope through to Jay.

"Hello, this is Nurse Harriet. How may I help you?"

"Hi, this is Hope Klein…"

Before Hope could continue, "Hi, it is so nice to get to speak with you. Your husband is such a dedicated doctor. It's been so nice having him join our team."

"Thank you. It's nice to hear. I'm sorry to bother you. Normally I wouldn't bother Jay at work. But I let my excitement get the best of me. It's not every day you get invited to a Great Gatsby ball by two actors adorned in 1920s attire standing at your front door."

Harriet smiled and said, "That's Morgan for you. She puts in a lot of effort into making the annual fundraiser into an extravaganza. Last year she had royal court jesters present a scrolled invitation to The Medieval Ball. They tooted horns and everything."

"Will you be going to the ball?"

"Most certainly, I go every year. It's a lot of fun. I look forward to meeting in person. I can transfer you over to Dr. Klein now."

"Thank you, Nurse Harriet."

"Hi, Hope, what's up?"

"First I have to say what a sweet nurse. She really thinks highly of you."

"Harriet is terrific. She has been spending a lot of time helping me get to know the patients. I don't know what I'd do without her. She knows most of the patients and their medical history by heart."

"She sounds like a great nurse. I'm glad I got to speak with her. That reminds me of one of the reasons for my call—are you missing something?"

"What?! Oh, I did leave my phone at home but I wouldn't say it's missing." Jay knew all too well the point Hope was attempting to make.

"Yeah, yeah. You left it at home on purpose! Whatever, that's not why I called. We got our invitation to the Kingsley's ball. Two actors dressed in 1920s attire presented it to me. It was very exciting."

"I'm glad you're excited. Can we talk about this later? I'm with someone right now."

"Is it Joey De Angelo?" Hope recalled that Joey DeAngelo was dropping by the clinic today. "Ask him if he knew about the love triangle!"

Jay laughed; he put the receiver back onto the base and put the phone on speaker. "My wife wants to know if you knew about the Russo Smith love triangle before yesterday's fight?"

Joey's eyes twinkled, "What do you think?"

"I think Joey the Greek's spies are on top of that sort of private intel," Hope joked.

Joey let out a hardy laugh and replied in a cocky tone, "It appears you have done some spying yourself."

Hope objected to Joey's insinuation that she was like him. "I do research on a person based on information that is publicly available. You, however, hire..." Hope paused for a moment searching her mind for the precise word..."Stalkers, that lay in waiting until they find a person's private secrets."

"You just compared me to Jimmy the Greek who used personal information he learned about the players from their local newspapers to figure out what their mindset would be on game day and decide what bet to place. I just do what he did on a much bigger scale. I guess you can call me the box-score for the personal triumphs and failures a player has or is facing in his life."

"What's a boxscore?"

"It provides you with a statistical look at how well a team and its individual players performed for any given game, season or career. In football it will give you the statistics for passing, running, receiving, yards from scrimmage, return, kicking, punting, and defensive."

"Whatever happened to just getting the score?"

"It gives you that, too. The boxscore is a bettor's handbook in understanding the players and the team. Knowing all that statistical stuff will help determine how well a team might perform with the players set to play in the game being bet on. But that will only get you so far. If a player's mind is not in the game, it doesn't matter what his passing statistical score is. That's where my personal boxscore comes in. I collect personal data on players that will help me determine what frame of mind they might be in for a particular game. An expectant wife goes into labor, a son gets into a car accident or there's a death of someone close, all play a part in a player's performance."

"Joey De Angelo, you've taken gambling to a whole new level." Jay wiggled in his chair. "Hope, I know you love a good debate; however, I need to get back to work."

Before Jay hit the disconnect button, Joey added, "Everyone loves learning other people's dirty little secrets. I bet you have indulged in reading stories in gossip magazines, even if it's while waiting in the grocery line."

Hope shook her head. *Leave it to Joey to be able to belittle her and all women in one single sentence.* Walking over to the coffee pot, she heard voices coming from outside. Loud, angry voices!

Hope opened the front door and looked around. She spotted a bit of a commotion at Matthew's house. There was a man sticking a newspaper into Matthew's face. Hope's eyes got a closer look at the paper. It was today's *Newsday.* Matthew took the paper from the man and stared at it. Words were exchanged, but Hope couldn't make them out. Shortly after, Matthew put his hand in his pocket, took his wallet out and gave the man money.

Hope found this all very curious. *What did this man say and show Matthew that made him decide to give him money?* Hope walked back into the kitchen and picked up the newspaper, staring at the back photo picturing Smith storming off and Matthew glancing over at him. Looking at Matthew's expression, she thought, *I've seen that face before. Matthew, you discovered something.*

Click, click, click.

Well, isn't this curious? The photographer's camera lens zoomed in closer. *What are you up to Hope Klein? Spying on your neighbors! Oh Hope, don't you know nothing good happens to those who don't mind their own business?*

CHAPTER 19

ONLY YOU WOULD GET EXCITED OVER AN 85-YEAR-OLD MASSEUSE

"Hey, man, what the fuck were you thinkin' yesterday?" shouted a man in his late 20s in ragged clothes that looked slept in, shoving the newspaper in Matthew's face. "You cost me a lot of money."

"Who told you to bet?" Matthew took the paper. "Bryce, you of all people should know I don't back down from a fight."

"I know, but was it worth getting fined and kicked out of the game for that asshole?" Bryce waved his arms in the air. "You know he likes to get a player's goat. Remember at MASS Football Camp he enraged everyone by claiming he was going to set the record for the forty-yard dash and then didn't even come in first in his group."

"Oh yeah, I think he did that to motivate himself to get faster."

"It was pathetic how little endurance he had back then. I guess there's something to be said about mind over matter."

"Mind over matter? I don't think there is any will that could have helped him overcome what he lacked." Matthew flipped over to the back of the newspaper and stared at the photo showing Shaun Smith's exposed back where his shirt was torn. "If that were true, you would have willed your situation with your shoulder away."

Bryce rubbed his hand over his shoulder and raised his brow. "I see your point."

Matthew put his hand in his pocket and pulled out his wallet. "Here, I feel bad I had anything to do with losing your bet." Looking past Bryce, Matthew smiled. "My masseuse has arrived."

Bryce looked over. "Only you would get excited over an eighty-five-year-old masseuse."

Nathan walked up the pathway to Matthew's garage carrying a brown burlap bag overflowing with maroon splotched spotted rags.

"Don't knock it until you try it. Nathan has a magical rub that makes all my aches and joint pains disappear."

"Hello, boys." Nathan extended his hand out to Bryce. "How have you been, Bryce?"

Folding the money and putting it into his pocket, he answered, "Better now. I have to get going. Good to see you, Nathan. You do your thing for Matthew, and maybe one day you can rub some of your magic on my shoulder?"

CHAPTER 20

WHO DOESN'T LIKE BILLY JOEL?

Nathan followed Matthew into the house and entered the window filled sunroom that looked out onto the backyard. Standing along the back of the room was a massage table. Matthew turned on the radio. Nathan began to unpack his bag, and he chimed in with the music finishing the lyric, "It's still rock and roll to me."

Matthew let out his roaring laugh, "You never cease to amaze me. You know this song?"

"A Mr. Billy Joel was all you heard on the radio when I arrived here from Israel. 'Just the Way You Are' is still one of my favorites."

"My favorite is 'Keeping the Faith.' I always wanted to make it with a red-haired girl in a Chevrolet. Come to think of it, I did!" boasted Matthew.

Nathan ignored Matthew when he spoke this way. "I see you gave Bryce money again."

"If I can help him out, why not?"

"That is your guilt talking. The car accident was not your fault."

"We both were in the car on our way back home from practice. I remember we were going over plays when all of a sudden, the driver in a blue Honda minivan lost control of the car. Next thing we knew, we were both in traction, confined to a bed for months. Bryce a broken shoulder, me a broken knee." Matthew took a deep breath, sighed, then continued, "I came out better, stronger, a superior athlete—with multiple college offers that led to NFL prospects. Bryce came out weaker, permanently injured. All athletic college offers were pulled and never offered back. The accident had injured Bryce's shoulder beyond repair. I expect Bryce would have been an NFL quarterback if it weren't for the accident. Now I'm the closest he gets to football. That and when he helps out at the summer camp."

Expectations are the root of all heartache, thought Nathan.

"You can never rely on expectations in life. You were fortunate, and perhaps one day your friend will come to terms with losing his ability to play ball and embrace that he still has a life worth living."

Nathan dipped his latex gloved hand into a glass Bali mason jar containing a buttery, dark honey russet looking substance. It only takes one time to learn that the cayenne soaks into your open fingers burning your eyes upon contact.

"There's the stuff!" exclaimed an exuberant Matthew as he jumped onto the massage table. "Oh, how I love your homemade magic muscle rub."

A giggling Nathan continued to rub in the ointment, careful not to get any on his open skin or clothing. Nathan learned the hard way how permanent the stain is.

"That feels sooooo good! I love that hot sensation. It penetrates directly the area where the pain is and makes it feel sooooo much better."

"That's the capsaicin—it's a key element within the cayenne that blocks the substance that causes pain." Lowering his concealed hand down Matthew's knee, Nathan massaged his calves.

Matthew rolled onto his back. "Too bad I didn't know you when you got this scar. I would have applied my special vitamin E lotion and you would have no more scar."

"Then I wouldn't have the cool tattoo." Matthew lifted his head up focusing his attention out the window. He bolted up. "I think someone is out there." Sliding off the table, Matthew opened the French door leading outside, surveying the yard. "They're gone." Turning to Nathan he asked, "Have you noticed anyone hanging around my house? I get the feeling I'm being watched."

Nathan shook his head, "Not that I'm aware of, but I will be on the lookout." Continuing to apply his muscle rub, Nathan's face brightened. He greatly appreciated their friendship. It gave him a purpose, a reason to make his special muscle rub once again.

CHAPTER 21

EXPECTATIONS ARE THE ROOT OF ALL HEARTACHE

On his way back home, Nathan recalled the last time he made his rub...

There wasn't a spot to be had on the kitchen table blanketed with open silver metallic tins and their clear covers. Steam was coming out of the huge double burner sitting on top of the stove. Nathan had been cooking cayenne and olive oil for the last eight hours. Stirring the condensed liquid substance, Nathan determined that it was the perfect time to add the beeswax. Nathan was being more careful than usual in making this batch of rub. This was a special batch... it would be traveling to Munich, Germany...to the Summer Olympic Games.

A young olive-skinned, sun-kissed sabra woman with deeply intense cognac-colored eyes walked over to Nathan tapping his shoulder. "You've worked so hard to get Ari to this point. Won't it be something to hear our Israeli National Anthem in that place!"

Nathan met Chava shortly after he arrived in Israel. Both worked on the kibbutz. Nathan was an orphaned lost soul, wandering in search of something...what, he didn't know...something to fill the void he was left with. Chava's heart sensed an immediate bond to Nathan. She recognized that he must have gone through a great deal of trauma and patiently gave support and love until he felt comfortable opening up to her.

Chava knew how much it meant to her beloved husband to hear the Jewish state's "Hatikvah" in the place where he was persecuted and tormented, where his entire family was murdered, where he once called home—Munich.

Ari would make that happen. Nathan had coached Ari his whole life to get to this point. Ari was a natural athlete; wrestling came easy to him. In addition to training, Nathan took on the physical therapy component. He even created a special muscle rub to help with his son's aches and pains.

As Nathan poured the rust-colored liquid into the tins, he dreamt of the day his son would stand tall on the podium in the center position to receive the gold Olympic medal in wrestling while the Israeli National Anthem echoed through the stadium, out onto the streets of Munich and out to the entire world. Nathan's face appeared both satisfied and solemn.

Unfortunately, Nathan's dream would not come to fruition...Nathan *would* hear the Israeli National Anthem, but not in Germany.

That was the last time he would make his special rub... until Matthew.

Expectations are the root of all heartache.

"We will end today's service with the singing of our homeland's National Anthem. Based on a poem written in 1886 entitled 'Tikvah Tanuh,' it means Our Hope. It's a deeply heartfelt prayer that suggests as long as the heart within a Jewish soul yearns, hope is never lost." The rabbi glanced down onto a couple whose hope had been ripped right from them with his most sincere and concerned eyes. "Let us all rise...*Kol od balevav penimah nefesh Yehudi homiyah Ulefa-atej mizrach kadimah 'ayin Letsion, tsofiah...*"

Nathan wrapped his arm around his wife, aiding her in standing up; his eyes welled up as he gazed upon her. He had felt starvation, brutality, humiliation, desperation and loss; however, nothing prepared him for looking over at his grief stricken, broken and lost wife. Nothing prepared him to hear the "Hatikvah" in Israel instead of Munich. Nothing prepared him to be dressed in black attending his only son's funeral.

A pang of pain rushed throughout his body that he didn't know he could ever feel—and he had felt pain. He knew he would have to be strong for the both of them if they were going to make it past this darkness into the light. The rabbi was right—as long as a Jewish soul yearns, hope is never lost. For his whole long life, as long as he could remember, he had been battling external forces that tried to extinguish this hope. He would never let that happen; they would never win.

The rabbi approached the couple. "I was very fond of Ari. He was a strong, dedicated athlete who was determined to represent our country and show the world our strength."

Nathan faintly uttered, "We were just watching *Fiddler on the Roof* with him and the other wrestlers. How could this be? We were supposed to be hearing Israel's National Anthem in Munich as Ari stood tall in the middle of the winners' podium. You would think the Olympic Village would be safe from danger?"

Chava fell to her knees, and Nathan went down with her. Nathan's head gently touched Chava. They shared a moment of silence, then together they rose.

"Who would have ever thought our son would be killed in Germany of all places," accused Chava. "What a blunder. It is outrageous how easy it was for the terrorists to get into the village, into the camp where the athletes were. They had floor plans showing exactly who and where every athlete was housed, for God's sake."

"Okay, Chava, I think the rabbi has heard enough." Nathan's attempt to stop Chava from her rant went by the wayside.

"Then there's the German news, who televised for the terrorists the police's plan to attack the terrorists. Every step of the way Germany opened the door for the terrorists to have their way. All while the Olympics continued on as usual." Chava could not get past this injustice.

For Nathan, he would replay over and over again the lights going out that fateful night at the airport that led to his son being shot. The darkness consumed him. If not for Chava, his heart would be left in complete darkness.

CHAPTER 22

HOPE'S NEW HERO

Turning the corner Hope pushed the stroller up the hill in less than 20 seconds. Arriving at the top she gasped at the breathtaking view, a sprawling landscape of mature oak trees, sweeping green lawn and the towering Maltz mansion turrets and all. *It's something out of a storybook,* she thought. Hope's favorite spot, the perfect midpoint to take a break and give Marc a snack. She enjoyed this serene time with him. On most days the two were left alone; today, however, Hope had company. Hope heard laughing and barking. Chasing the birds, Mini pulled her owner off the path. Morgan giggled as Elliot followed.

Seeing Hope and Marc, Morgan walked over to the stroller and bent down. "Hello, Marc! Aren't you a cutie?" Mini jumped up next to Morgan onto the stroller. Marc cooed and his face brightened. "You like Mini. I think she likes you, too." Turning to Hope, "I think we have a dog lover!"

"Yes, he loves dogs. My parents' dog naps with him when we visit. It's adorable." Hope continued on, not stopping to take a breath, "Oh, we got your invitation! I answer my door to find a man and a woman donning 1920s attire. Now that's a way to get an invitation!" Looking over at the tall, handsome man with jet black hair, she said, "You must be Dr. Kingsley. It's great to meet you. I'm Hope Klein and this is Marc."

Elliot had a twinkle in his eye. "I have never heard someone speak as quickly as you do! That's a real talent; not many people can think on their feet so quickly."

A huge smile came across Hope's face. "Thank you. Most people don't see it that way."

"Most people are idiots. Never taking the time to see beyond what's in front of them."

Hope smiled and bent down to pet Mini.

"Will you and Jay be able to come?" Morgan chimed in. "It's going to be so much fun! Everyone dresses up, and you feel as if you've stepped back in time and into F. Scott Fitzgerald's *Great Gatsby*!"

"I already RSVP'd yes! And know the exact dress I will wear. It belonged to my Aunt Cheryl. She was a Ziegfeld girl."

"That sounds perfect!" Elliot agreed "You will make a great Ziegfeld girl. Did you know they were known to attend parties at the mansion on the hill in the 1920s?"

Hope's phone began playing the familiar "Fur Leis" melody ringtone. "It's my mom." Hope stood up. "I need to pick up. My father wasn't feeling well earlier."

Morgan nodded and waved her hand, "Of course, go right ahead."

"What!" shouted Hope into her phone. "You're at the hospital?"

All eyes were on her.

She continued, "No, Jay isn't with me. Why?"

Hope listened, then questioned, "Leukemia? A bone marrow biopsy?"

Elliot tapped Hope's shoulder. "May I speak with your mom?"

Hope's brow creased as she handed him the phone.

"Hello, Mrs..." Elliot made eye contact with Hope.

"Sarokoff."

"Mrs. Sarokoff, this is Dr. Kingsley. I assume they ran a blood test...what did the doctor tell you they found? Yes, that is a high number of red blood cells. Can I ask you a few questions about your husband's condition? Has your husband lost a lot of weight recently? Ah ha. Has he experienced any numbness in his hands...feet...legs...arms? Sure, ask him. Okay, I see. Ask him if he has experienced any shortness of breath...any dizziness? Ah ha. Lastly, has he had any noticeable bruising? Okay, based on your husband's responses I think there is a possibility he has Polycythemia Vera. It's a rare blood disease that they don't screen for at the hospital. I will direct the admitting doctor to do his bone marrow biopsy and have them check for Polycythemia Vera at the same time."

"Is there a cure for this poly...blood disease?" Hope interrupted.

"It's actually a blood cancer that begins in the marrow of your bones. This is where new blood cells grow. Polycythemia Vera occurs when your marrow makes too many red blood cells. Your blood thickens, which can lead to a clot, a stroke or a heart attack."

Hope stood still, frozen in Elliot's words. "Here I was worried about my dad having leukemia."

"I left out the most important part," Elliot smiled. "You misunderstand. With proper treatment, most people can live a long life. This disease worsens extremely slowly, usually over many, many years."

Hope let out a deep breath, like a deflated balloon. "Thank God. So, there's a light at the end of the tunnel. How do you treat this disease?"

"First, we need to see if he even has Polycythemia Vera," Elliot pointed out, then seeing the desperation in Hopes eyes, added, "Treatment is simply removing blood from your vein. It's a lot like donating blood. This lowers your number of blood cells, and your blood will be thinner, so no worries of clotting, stroke or heart attack."

"It's that simple...donate blood?"

"For most people it's the only treatment they need for many years."

"That's it? What happens after many years?"

"There's that quick mind," suggested Elliot. "We don't even know if he has Polycythemia. I'll direct the lab to send the biopsy and blood work to Morgan's Song's labs. It will be much quicker. We should get the results in a day or two as opposed to two weeks the hospital would take to get back to us."

Hope breathed a sigh of relief. How did she get so lucky to have Elliot in her corner?

As soon as Hope got back to the house, she called Jay.

"My dad is in the hospital!" Hope paused, concentrating on the background noise. "Where are you? It sounds like plates clicking."

"I'm at the diner. Joey's treating me to lunch."

Silence.

"Isn't that nice of him. I think he's obsessed with you."

"You're funny, Hope." Jay let out a laugh. "What's going on with your dad? Which hospital is he in? I'll call over."

"There's no need. Dr. Kingsley took care of everything."

"How'd that happen?"

"We were on our run and bumped into the Kingsleys walking Mini when my mom called. Dr. Kingsley heard how upset I was and took the phone. He spoke to my mom and determined that my dad likely has poly...polyth...vera."

"Polycythemia Vera?"

"Yes, that's it. When I first spoke to my mom, the doctors

were telling her my dad could have leukemia because his red blood count is so high. They wanted to do a bone marrow biopsy to confirm. Dr. Kingsley suggested they test for Polycythemia Vera as well. He even instructed them to send samples to Morgan's Song's labs so we can get the results faster. If it is poly…thy…vera, you know what I mean, Dr. Kingsley says it is easily treatable by donating the extra red blood cells. They haven't ruled out leukemia, but Dr. Kingsley felt pretty certain it is more likely poly…"

"Polycythemia Vera. That is true, but…" Jay paused. "You know that Polycythemia Vera turns into leukemia?"

"What? Do you mean my dad will get leukemia?" Hope reflected, "So that's why Dr. Kingsley said let's not get ahead of ourselves."

"He was right, we shouldn't get ahead of ourselves; however, many patients with Polycythemia Vera do not get diagnosed with leukemia for many, many years after they were diagnosed with Polycythemia Vera."

"I guess it's better than being diagnosed with leukemia from the onset. However, it must be scary knowing that one day you have it."

"Hope, can we continue to discuss this when I get home? I'm sorry I have to go."

"Sure, tell Joey I say hi." Hope rolled her eyes. She sat at her desk and switched on her computer. She'd learn all there was about Polycythemia Vera.

Walking back to the table, Jay apologized to Joey and Dr. Conrad for being away so long. "Let's get back to what we were discussing." Jay looked over at Joey.

"Dr. Conrad and I think it will work." Joey leaned in closer to Jay and asked, "What do you think?"

"I think he is the right choice."

CHAPTER 23

THE DAY OF THE BALL

Lifting up her aunt's stunning 1920s vintage dress from its box, Hope stared at the finely detailed embroidered flowers of teal and ruby red crystal beads sewn onto the cream-colored lace of the car wash paneled flapper dress. The embellishment of all the crystals made the dress spectacular in both weight and style. The weight allowed for the dress to have a gorgeous swing while you danced, but it also was the culprit in the destruction of so many dresses. Having a dress such as this was rare. Hope knew this and took great pride and joy in wearing it to the ball.

Realizing that a lot had changed since the last time she wore the dress, Hope grabbed it, crossed her fingers and entered the bathroom wondering why she waited until now, the day of the ball, to put the dress on. This was so unlike the proactive, organized person she's known to be. To Hope's delight the dress slipped right on, be it a little bit snug in some areas. She especially appreciated the way she filled out the top portion! A perk from having Marc.

Checking herself in the full-length mirror inside her closet, Hope smiled. *Not bad...buying that baby runner stroller really paid off.* Hearing the front door opening, Hope felt a sense of relief overcome her. *Jay is home in time to change and be on time for the party. Just maybe tonight will work out as well as I hope,* she thought.

Hope's relief quickly changed to disappointment when she heard a female voice coming from downstairs. "Hope, honey, we're here! Where is my joy of joys?"

Rushing out of the closet, through the bedroom door, taking the stairs two steps at a time, she shushed, "He's napping." Upon reaching the downstairs landing, she added, "If you don't want a cranky baby on your hands tonight, let's keep it down." Hope leaned in and kissed her dad's cheek. "Hi, Dad, you look great. How are you feeling?"

"Fantastic! Ever since I started donating blood, my itchiness has gone away, I'm not dizzy or tired. I'm so grateful to Dr. Kingsley. Those doctors at the hospital never would have checked for Polycythemia. It would have gone untreated and I'd still be feeling awful."

"He's our hero. It's such a rare disease, many doctors miss it. It was good that you were able to test for it at the same time you did the biopsy for leukemia. I wouldn't want you to have to go through that twice."

"Actually, it wasn't as bad as you think once the doctor inserted the needle in the right spot. It took three tries, but the whole procedure only took twenty minutes, and I only have slight pinhole scars from it."

"The wonder of science!" Hope leaned in to kiss her mom looking over at the wall clock. "You're early."

"We were lucky; we didn't hit any traffic. Now I have time to help you apply your makeup."

Hope's mother had a gift for all things beauty—fashion, makeup, the latest trends. Her mother dreamed of passing on all her beauty knowledge to Hope who wanted no part of it. Hope was more of a tomboy than a cover girl.

Staring at her daughter, she suggested that Hope would look more 1920s if she had her hair scooped up around the beautiful glass beaded headband that matched the dress. Hope agreed and off the two went, quietly up the stairs into the master bath.

"So how are things going with you and Jay?"

"They could be better. Work has really consumed him. I mean, he has always been consumed with work, but he made time to make me feel like he was consumed with me, too."

"Give him some time, Hope. He probably wants to make a good impression. Once things settle down, he will be back to the old Jay attached to your hip!"

"I hope you are right. Maybe I can distract a little of his attention tonight. Remind him of what he is missing."

"The way you look tonight, I expect you will."

Expectations are the root of all heartache.

CHAPTER 24

IS THAT TONIGHT?

Sitting around the kitchen table staring at the clock, Hope picked up her cell phone and dialed Jay for the fifth time.

As the melody for Lionel Richie's and Diana Ross' love ballad "Endless Love" filled the room, Hope disconnected. She knew where Jay was. Hope instituted her old birthing breathing exercises. *Don't blow up, you want tonight to be wonderful.*

"I'm home! What's for dinner, I'm starving." announced Jay as he slammed the front door shut and proceeded to walk toward the kitchen. Jay's surprised reaction to seeing his father-in-law seated next to his wife at the kitchen table indicated to all that he had no idea there was a gala tonight.

"Cliff! What are you doing here? Is everything okay?" Jay demonstrated genuine concern.

Clifford's upper left eyebrow rose. "We came to babysit."

Hope stood up and added, "Tonight is the gala event at Maltz Mansion for the Kingsley's foundation. Wasn't everyone in the clinic talking about it?" Hope hesitated and put her emotions in check. *You want tonight to be a success, limit your negativity.* "Dad and mom came to watch Marc so we can go."

"I was busy working. It totally slipped my mind."

"I bet if this was with Joey you wouldn't have forgotten."

"You know Joey is going tonight?"

Hope raised two fingers to her forehead. "That figures, now that you say it. He is a huge financial donor to the charity."

Looking down at his clothes he asked, "Can I wear what I have on to this party?"

"I think it's a bit too casual," Hope stared at the huge maroon colored smudge on the side of Jay's beige khakis. "Is that blood?"

Jay wiped at the stain. "No, it's just dirt. I'll go up and change."

"Put on your wedding tuxedo, it's in the back of your side of the closet."

Twenty minutes later, Jay strolled down the stairs wearing a blue business suit. Hope did not have to utter a word. Her face communicated it all.

"I guess I put on a few pounds since our wedding," he stated sheepishly. "Are you ready to go?"

"In a minute, I can't find my keys. I wanted to leave them for my parents in case they wanted to go out. Marc's car seat is in there."

"I bet you gave the keys to Marc to play with?" Jay shook his head. "You know he crawls now; they can be anywhere."

"Not anywhere, just somewhere in the house."

Hope's mom directed the two with her arms toward the front door. "You two kids go. Dad and I will find the keys."

The evening was not off to the start Hope was expecting…

CHAPTER 25

WELCOME TO MALTZ MANSION

In less than ten minutes, Jay's beloved ole reliable car with all the windows rolled down turned onto Black Oak Drive. Hundreds of fully green-leafed red cedars lined both sides of the long narrow drive leading to Maltz's stone archway entrance. The scent of cedar filled the car and reminded Hope of her college days and the cedar chest she kept her sweaters in. The early fall breeze felt good; Hope could taste the salt from the Long Island Sound on her lips as they drove through the stone archway that led up to the fabled estate.

As the car wobbled onto the cobblestone courtyard, Hope couldn't keep her eyes off the majestic palatial manor that towered, perched in all its regal glory in front of her. A 120,000 square foot brick French chateau with slated roof, towering spiked turrets with peaks and slopes that rivaled Disney's Cinderella's Castle. It defined the word opulent.

Parked along both sides of the huge wooden front doors leading into the mansion were two flawless vintage cars from the time period: a chestnut brown Studebaker President Eight Roadster and a cherry red Chrysler 75 Roadster.

Staring out of the car window, Hope felt transported to the Jazz Era of the 1920s. Women strolled in glittery sequined flapper dresses with equally glittery sequined headbands with feathers sticking out. Alongside many of the women were men decked out in formal black tuxedo suits. Some with tails and a top hat! Others had their hair greased, slicked back at the sides, poofed at the top.

Hope imagined she was at one of the famed parties, one with such guests as the likes of F. Scott Fitzgerald and Charlie Chaplin.

"I wonder how many famous people we will meet tonight!" she said, itching in her seat.

Jay smiled.

A young man sporting tall argyle socks over his four plus pants, wearing a sweater vest with custom dress shirt underneath and a white newsboy cap approached the driver's door preparing to valet the car when Jay stopped him from opening the door.

Jay questioned, "I'm Dr. Klein and I'm on call tonight. Is there any place I can park the car for quick access?"

"Sure thing, doc." Motioning both his hands in the left direction, he instructed Jay to pull up alongside a shiny silver Aston Martin. "You can hold on to the keys."

Pulling alongside the one-of-a-kind convertible, Jay's mind appeared to be reawakened, his mouth watering, eyes gawking out the side window. "I never thought I'd see an actual James Bond car in person! Look at those gorgeous rims, the curvaceous hood, the sexy mesh bumper." Jay ogled like a lovestruck high schooler.

That's the exact reaction Hope was seeking from Jay when she decided to wear her aunt's nearly see-through mesh Follies dress. *To think, you can focus on something other than your patients…just not me. What do I have to do to get your attention?* she wondered.

Jay popped out of the car and glided over to inspect his object of desire, unaware that the driver and passenger were still inside. "She is stunning. Look at those smokey tail light lenses and diamond black wheels," Jay spoke out loud to himself; Hope was still in the car.

Pushing open the driver's door, Joey De Angelo called out, "She's a real beauty! Isn't she?"

A wide smile came across Jay's face. "Very fetching, indeed." The two shook hands.

Leaning in to see if the inside was as impressive as the exterior, Jay added, "Wow, the red stitching up against the black leather really makes those seats pop."

"The quilted black obsidian leather doesn't hurt either," Joey boasted as he walked around the car over to the passenger's side. Opening the car door, Joey held his hand out to aid the woman with slender shapely legs out. Wearing a short blond bob hairdo and a sparkly red sequin fringe dress that draped just above the knees, the woman portrayed the quintessential flapper girl—with a red boa and long cigarette holder in hand to complete the look.

Witnessing the female's appearance reminded Jay of his own lady. He hightailed it over toward his car, only to be stopped in his tracks. After several minutes waiting in the car, Hope knew that her dutiful husband had forgotten about her.

"So sorry, honey. This spectacular car must have enchanted me. I seem to have gotten lost in its allure."

"That's some car Joey De Angelo has." Hope turned her attention to the woman with Joey. "Who's the beautiful blonde he has with him?"

"You mean Harriet?"

"Is that the same Harriet I spoke to over the phone? The head nurse at the clinic? I didn't realize she knew Joey. She's very attractive."

"She's normally a brunette!" Jay walked over to Harriet. "You look terrific. This is my wife, Hope."

Giggling and bopping her hand in her wig, she commented, "I've always heard blondes have more fun." She smiled warmly at Hope. "I'm so happy to finally meet you. I love working with your husband. He is such a dedicated doctor."

Joey, in his dapper shiny crimson sports coat with wide navy and white stripes, suspenders, black and white laced Oxford shoes finished off with a black skimmer hat, came up to Harriet and twirled her around, "Doesn't she make the perfect accessory?"

What does Harriet see in this guy? thought Hope. "How long have you two been together?"

"Oh, we are old friends," Harriet blushed. "We both support Morgan and Elliot in hopes of finding a cure. It is because of Morgan I became a nurse. She literally filled out the forms for me many years ago." Harriet moved over toward Hope and said, "I hope I'm not being too forward, but I have to say, you look amazing in that dress, it is truly spectacular."

Hope lifted her shoulders back and stood a little taller. "Why, thank you so much. It's my great aunt's. She was a Ziegfeld Follie back in the twenties." Hope moved her finger across the antique rose mesh fabricated dress touching the shimmering glass beads attached to cover just the right provocative areas.

Harriet smiled, then motioned closer to Jay. "Can you do me a favor and get to the clinic a half an hour earlier tomorrow? There's this patient I'm concerned about, and the only way I can get her to come in is when no other patients are around. I know it's crazy but if that's what it takes to get her to be treated it's worth it."

Jay's cheeks raised; his lips spread upwards. "Sure thing, Harriet. The patients at the clinic should only know how lucky they are with you in their corner."

Harriet folded her arm around Hope's, and the two began to stroll up the red carpet toward the two huge front doors of the mansion. "The party has already begun...we better get going."

"No party really starts until I get there!" Joey boasted as he tapped Jay's shoulder and the two started off toward the mansion.

This guy is a real jackass, thought Hope. *What could Harriet possibly see in him?*

Walking through the towering two story front doors, the couples found their host and hostess awaiting them atop of a grand staircase that rivaled that of the famous exterior staircase in Chateau de Fontainebleau in France. A horseshoe shaped wrought iron banister intricately spun into a flowing design that winded its spiral way around wide gray stone marble steps connecting at a joining second story landing leading into the main foyer of the mansion.

Making his ascent, Joey broke away from the group taking two steps at a time. "Look at you two, Daisy and Jay! Or are you supposed to be Tom Buchanan? Ha, ha-ha."

"I'm Jay Gatsby, of course. Welcome to my party." Elliot attempted to be *in* character. "Daisy here was so kind as to give up her time to help me organize this glorious affair. Thank you for coming, Mr. Carraway!"

"That's me, your trusted and faithful friend."

Passing Joey, Harriet embraced Elliot. "You make a great Jay Gatsby! So suave and confident."

Elliot gave Harriet a warm hug. "You look terrific, blond hair and all. You're as beautiful today as you were at our prom."

"Thank you," she said, twirling her boa, in her best Mae West voice. "Why don't you come up and see me sometime?" Harriet's bright red lips popped out longing to be kissed.

"So, you three all grew up together?" Hope deduced.

"We were three peas in a pod back in high school." Harriet looked at Elliot. "Later Morgan joined and we became the Fantastic Four!"

Elliot nodded, then *in* character declared, "The glasses are overflowing. The bootlegger did a great job. There's plenty of liquid happiness to go around." The boisterous sounds of the sax roared the "Take Five" catchy blues melody as Elliot tapped his feet to the beat.

Swinging his torso from side to side, Joey shimmied over to Morgan. "You did an amazing job and look impeccable." Her figure loving silhouette long black gown complemented Elliot's custom tailor fitted tuxedo. "You have brought an air of elegance and grace to this event, so why the Mona Lisa smile?"

Morgan's cheek bones raised. "I can't hide anything from you. You know me so well. It's my dad. I got a call from the nursing home—he had a very bad day. My heart breaks that he is all alone. Maybe I should have kept him at home with me."

"You know you couldn't maintain taking care of him once his symptoms reached the late stage. He lost all motor control. He was extremely irritable and easily agitated." He touched the side of Morgan's face, gently rubbing the lightened red line scar covered up by makeup. "He hurt you."

"That wasn't his fault, it's this terrible disease." Pulling his hand away from her scar, she explained, "He was swallowing his tongue, causing him to forcefully swing his body and arms inadvertently hitting me. I wanted to go right now to the nursing home to see him, but I don't want to ruin Elliot's big night. I plan on going first thing tomorrow morning."

"Does Elliot know?"

"Yes, he tried to make me feel better in his own scientific, clinical way. Telling me how my father's cognitive abilities are seriously waning, it wouldn't matter if I went today or tomorrow morning." She took a few deep breaths. "I understand that on some cognitive level, but my emotions run high."

Joey hugged Morgan. "How could it not." He thought to himself, *Not only are you concerned for your dad's well-being, you are getting a firsthand play by play of what will ultimately happen to you.* "You should have someone go with you."

"I don't want to pull Elliot away from the lab. He is working so hard to find a cure."

"Then I will go with you, of course."

Morgan was living the story for which the ending had already been written, but it's the details that were most frightening. The last few years, she witnessed the heartbreaking depletion of motor and cognitive functions she knew she would be experiencing in her future. Morgan was in college when they discovered her father had Huntington's disease. At the time, they told her she could get tested by providing doctors with a blood sample. After much thought she decided she didn't want to know. However, when Elliot entered her life and there was talk of starting a family, Morgan changed her mind and got tested. Testing positive, Morgan made it clear to Elliot that this was where the heredity line for this monstrous disease would end.

So far, her early symptoms had been kept at bay. A few missteps, trips, falls and hand tremors. Every day felt as if there were a ticking time bomb inside set to explode without any warning. When it does explode, there is no turning back. Morgan knew that all too well.

Recognizing the two stragglers coming up the stairs slightly behind Joey and Harriet, Morgan motioned toward them. "Hope! I'm so glad you made it," she said, extending both arms around Hope.

Hope felt like she was being wrapped in the sun's rays. Their embrace was reminiscent of the ones she shared with her mother whenever she'd come home from college. In fact, her mom still embraced her that way—as if she hasn't seen her in forever. You would think that this kind of embrace from a near stranger would feel strange, but it felt genuine and welcomed.

"How is our little bundle of joy?"

"He is doing great. He is with my parents tonight!" Hope glanced around. "It's amazing how well they restored the mansion."

"You know Morgan had a hand in that. She recreated the interiors to reflect the time period in which Maltz thrived, a huge undertaking. Years in the making." Elliot reviewed Hope. "Your dress fits this place perfectly."

Hope's face reddened. "It should, it's my Aunt Cheryl's dress from back in her Ziegfeld Follie days."

"I believe it. Actually, I recall looking at photos of Ziegfeld girls all lined up on the grand staircase you just walked up. The mansion had all the photos organized and bound into a photo album they keep in the library as part of the restoration. It helped Morgan to make authentic choices in design based on the old photos."

"I can't believe that in all likelihood I might be standing on the same staircase that my great aunt once climbed." She tilted her head in Jay's direction. "It's that six degrees of separation thing." Hope's voice trailed off as she became aware of

Jay's absence. Searching the area, she discovered Jay's location a few feet away, nestling his cell phone against his ear. Turning back to Elliot, she said, "I would love to look at those pictures and see if I can spot my aunt."

"Sure, it would be my pleasure. I can take you over to the library."

Looking at her watch, Morgan suggested, "I'd appreciate it if you did that later. Right now, as we speak, the egg hunt I planned is happening in the formal gardens, and I would really love for Hope and Harriet to enjoy their chance at finding an egg."

Elliot interjected, "Morgan wanted to recreate the excitement of the lavish Gold Coast parties. She did some research and found out that one owner held an annual egg hunt where he hid eggs with a $1,000 bill in them. She liked the idea of having an egg hunt during the cocktail hour. It added pizzazz to what would normally be a ho hum cocktail party outside." Elliot continued, "Morgan hid four eggs, minus the $1,000 bill of course, throughout the formal gardens. The lucky person who finds an egg will receive a complimentary overnight stay at the mansion. Typically, only members can pay to stay overnight but they made an exception for Morgan."

Harriet began walking toward a door leading to the formal gardens. "I'll meet you all there. I could really use a restful getaway here at the mansion."

Hope smiled. She was impressed that Elliot who was occupied trying to find a cure still took the time to know what his wife planned. Hope sighed thinking to herself, *Jay can't even stay off the phone long enough to pay attention to me at a party.* "Jay and I could certainly use a night alone together!"

Jay returned to the group. "Sorry about that, I'm on call tonight. I think I bought myself an hour or so."

A frown came across Hope's face.

"Maybe Jay will find one for you?" interjected Joey. "He is a radiologist—aren't they good at spotting the un-spottable?"

"I'm a mom. I find the needle in the haystack on a daily basis. You don't know how many times a day I am searching for Marc's binky."

"I sense a bet coming on." Joey proposed, "I bet Jay will find an egg before you find one."

"You're on!" Hope agreed as she took hold of Morgan's arm. "Let's head out to the formal gardens."

CHAPTER 26

LET THE EGG HUNT BEGIN

Hope looked out onto this bucolic setting—a magnificent parterre manicured with lush emerald green boxwoods pruned to create a stark border around several symmetrical patterns, which were separated and connected by gravel pathways. Inside the symmetrical shapes were reflecting pools, fountains and stone statues. At the center of this massive labyrinth was a circular fountain surrounded by a bouquet of colors. Fragrant yellow, pink, red and white roses created a welcoming pop of color among the intense greenery surrounding the rest of the garden.

The lively loud jazz musicians stopped playing as Morgan approached the center of the stage with a microphone. "Welcome to our egg hunt. I'm enjoying watching everyone's enthusiasm in searching for the coveted eggs. I have just been informed that the third egg has been discovered." Matthew Russo held up a magnificent bejeweled Fabergé-like egg. "That leaves one remaining egg. Remember, find an egg and win a luxurious night stay at Maltz Mansion. So get out there and search! Good luck!"

Morgan rejoined Elliot and Joey.

Hope wanted to go over and congratulate Matthew, but she was on a mission to find that egg and put that egocentric gambler in his place. Based upon what she saw and just heard, she moved toward the center of the garden.

Elliot leaned into Joey. "I know people speak of you in terms of being sharp, a gambler who always seems to end up on the right side of things. However, I think this wasn't such a wise bet."

"I don't think so," said Joey, watching Jay walk along the hedged perimeter of the gardens. "He is estimating that the colorful stones of the Fabergé design would stand out against the stark greenery."

"That was all good when there were four eggs to find. There is now only one, one very well hidden egg." Elliot motioned his eyes toward the center of the garden where Hope was purposefully wandering. "She is thinking that the colorful colors of the roses will shield the colorful design of the stone egg."

Matching his fingers together at their tips in a steeple formation, Joey admitted, "Clever, let's see how this plays out."

"I'm so glad you find this so entertaining. You never cease to amaze me how you can figure a way to make a simple egg hunt into an OTB event."

Morgan laughed, "Do you remember when we were freshman at NYU and Joey would organize weekly gambling pools based on freshman firsts—first freshman to get locked out of the dorm, first freshman to act like a drunken fool, first freshman to drop out?"

"He bet on me being the first freshman to be a drunken fool!" Elliot jokingly pushed Joey with his right shoulder. "And then snuck alcohol into my drinks!"

They all laughed; it very much felt like old times. A time when their biggest worry was being the drunken fool.

"I've never been so embarrassed or hungover like that again."

"It did get you to loosen up and ask me out." Morgan laughed as she reminisced, "I'll never forget watching you jump on the bar and do your best Tom Cruise's Maverick impersonation from *Top Gun* singing 'You've Lost That Lovin Feeling.'"

Just then, Jay screeched in excitement as he ran his fingers along the inside hand of a tall female stone statue feeling something inside. He grabbed hold of what felt like an oval figure and very well could be the last egg. Bringing the figure into view, Jay's excitement turned to disappointment as it became clear that he was holding an acorn. To make matters worse, Jay's cell phone went off at the exact time he heard Hope call out, "I found the last egg. It is beautiful."

A bolt of adrenaline rushed through Hope's body—there was no feeling like that of vindication. Unfortunately, Hope didn't get to hold onto that feeling for long. Looking over at Jay on his cell phone once again, she knew they would be leaving sooner rather than later.

So much for a romantic evening of dining, dancing and rekindling old feelings. Hope was about to walk over to Jay and prepare to say her goodbyes to their host and hostess, when something inside her made her reconsider. Hope decided she'd make the best of her evening without worrying about a crying baby. She'd stay and have an Uber take her home.

Lifting the egg, Hope glanced over at Joey until she made eye contact and gave him a huge smirk. Joey bowed, conceding her win, then walked over. "You win!"

Hope had the widest grin across her face. "Never underestimate a mom!"

Jay joined them. "I'm sorry, Hope. That was the hospital.

The patient we've been monitoring will need emergency angio-plasty. We need to leave now, so I can drop you back home."

"I decided to stay at the party. I'll get an Uber."

"If that's what you want to do, okay then." Jay leaned in, giving her a kiss on the cheek. As he walked away, he turned to Joey. "I wouldn't bet on New York tomorrow."

"Is that so? Your patient is a player? Which one?"

Jay smirked back at Joey. "Doctor patient confidentiality."

CHAPTER 27

AN ELEGANT AFFAIR

Hope walked hand and hand with Morgan into the intimate dining room, about 52x30 with an 18-foot ceiling, yellow stone walls with many architectural details including wide crown molding, hollowed out archways featuring marble female statues, huge framed murals and a stone fireplace. But it was the striking centerpieces that caught Hope's eye.

On all ten round tables cloaked in black linens stood the most amazing tree centerpieces—actual mini trees, filled with white orchids and hydrangeas nestled upon thick sprawling brown branches with draping white Spanish moss and hanging twinkling candles. It was as if the magnificent gardens Hope just left outside were brought inside!

Hope's lips parted as her eyes moved around the room. "I have never seen tree centerpieces. I'm blown away."

"They're Manzanita trees," Morgan declared. "They represent life. Trees are powerful symbols for growth, death and rebirth. I truly believe that Morgan's Song Foundation represents life. We seek to find answers, raise awareness, and help families."

In that moment Hope thought about Nathan. He embodied the tree of life theme. "I can't think of a better way to evoke that sentiment than what you did. This whole room feels alive."

Morgan nodded in agreement. "The florist really did a fantastic job on what was an ambitious task."

Hope rummaged her bag in search of her seating card. "I can't remember my table number."

Morgan placed her hand over Hope's arm. "Why don't you join me at my table? There's plenty of room to add an extra seat."

Standing beside their table, Hope and Morgan watched as the servers moved the place settings making room for an additional guest. Out of the corner of her left eye, Hope noticed Dr. Conrad. *It's Dr. Frankenstein, the mad scientist, playing God with his Petri dishes,* she thought, turning her body away from his view. She had no intention of ruining her evening speaking with him.

No such luck.

"Hello, Hope. Don't you look beautiful tonight. Where's Jay?"

"Thank you, Dr. Conrad." Hope sighed. "Jay got called in. An emergency angioplasty."

"Hope, you don't need to be so formal. You can call me Harry or Harold. I think we're beyond Dr. Conrad." Harold smiled. "Can I get you ladies anything at the bar?"

Both women shook their heads no. Harry walked over to the bar. Hope smiled as she watched Harry leave.

The clacking sound of a spoon tapping the edge of a crystal champagne flute rang in the air silencing the chatter as the last few guests took their seats. Joey De Angelo stood at the podium holding his champagne glass up. "Tonight, we are here to honor my best friend, Dr. Elliot Kingsley, for his groundbreaking research and determination to find a cure for the monstrous disease known as Huntington's disease. Before I invite him up, I would like to first take a moment to recognize his better half, Morgan Kingsley, who spent many volunteer hours orchestrating and creating this glorious event. Let's all give Morgan a round of applause." Joey began to clap. "I'd like for Morgan to please stand and take a bow on a job well done."

Morgan blushed, waving her hand and shaking her head at Joey.

"Thank you, Morgan," Joey continued. "If everyone will humor me for one more thank you. I would like to thank all of you here tonight. Without your continued unwavering support and generous contributions to Morgan's Song Foundation, we could not have gotten as far as we have. We have raised a greater awareness of Huntington's disease among the public, and as Dr. Kingsley will be explaining to you shortly, have made some headway in our goal of fighting this disease. So, thank you, thank you, with all my heart, thank you. Ladies and gentleman, Dr. Elliot Kingsley."

Hope was taken back by Joey's heartfelt demeanor. But that would be short-lived.

CHAPTER 28

WE ARE HEADED IN THE RIGHT DIRECTION

Shaking hands and then hugging tightly, Elliot whispered into Joey's ear, "Thank you, man, I couldn't have done any of this without you." The men released each other's hold, and Joey stepped off the stage as Elliot moved closer to the podium moving his hands slightly up and down in the air, his attempt at silencing the audience.

"Thank you all for honoring me and my work. I am very pleased to stand before you tonight with very exciting news. Earlier today I got approval to move my research drug therapy into a safety trial on humans." The room roared with applause; everyone stood up.

"It has been over twenty years since eight MIT biologists identified the Huntington gene along with its sequence. Each one of us has the Huntington gene. It is when this gene's DNA mutates creating an oversized chain translating into an abnormal Huntingtin protein that attacks brain cells...I know that's a mouthful. Let me see if I can break this down. Most of us have seen the illustration of a DNA strand. It sort of looks like a twisting ladder. Well, the rungs of this ladder are nitrogenous bases. There are four nitrogen bases and they are represented by letters: A,T,G,C. When these bases pair up, that can be considered the step of the ladder. The order these base letters follow determines the genetic code, or DNA instructions if you will. This sequence forms genes, which is the language of the cell. It tells the cell how to make the proteins." Elliot brought a glass of water to his lips, took a quick sip, then continued, "Now a normal DNA sequence or code for the Huntington gene has a repeat in it of the CAG base. If this pattern repeats thirty-five or less times, your body makes a normal protein. Thirty-six or more repeats and your body forms abnormal proteins leading an attack on the brain cells, resulting in Huntington's disease." Elliot lowered his head. "This makes me think about Ravel's instrumental movement made infamous in the Bo Derek, Dudley Moore movie *10*." Elliot motioned the band to play a bit of "Bolero." "In his composition, Ravel makes the conscious decision to repeat a melody eighteen times. In doing so he creates this masterpiece. I think to myself; how did he decide on the number of repeats? Why eighteen? Why not twenty? But in the end what really matters is that going over the set number of repeats is overkill, it ruins the piece. The same can be said about the CAG repeat in the Huntington gene. Produce more than thirty-five repeats and your brain cells are ruined. As an intriguing side note, it has been said that Ravel was possibly battling progressive aphasia when he composed 'Bolero.'"

Leaning the right side of his face in the palm of his hand, Elliot considered, "If only it was as easy as removing a few extra repeats. I'd love it if we could take an eraser and just make them go away; however, it doesn't work that way. Most treatments for Huntington's disease have addressed the symptoms as opposed to modifying the disease. I, however, have been working these past years on a drug therapy DNA molecule that can bind to the Huntington message reducing the production of Huntingtin protein in the brain. I won't go over the scientific terminology. Suffice to say, if the protein's message is blocked in the brain, no symptoms." Applause. "Today we celebrate the beginning of safety trials on humans, which brings us one step closer to getting this drug therapy to everyone who desperately needs it."

Hope clapped loudly as she stood up and joined the standing ovation. "He is incredible. It is amazing how far scientists have gotten in their understanding of mapping the DNA of the human genome," she whispered to Morgan.

"In closing, I would like to end with a Bil Keane quote: 'Yesterday is the past, tomorrow is the future, today is a gift, which is why we call it the present.' I believe today is a gift, and the future is brighter than it has ever been. With that I would like to dedicate the first dance of the evening to my beautiful wife, if she will do me the honor. Let's all celebrate."

The band began playing, and the lead singer crooned in his best Billy Joel voice, "Don't go changing to try and please me, you never let me down before..."

CHAPTER 29

MAKING MEMORIES

⌒

"Two hearts, two hearts that beat as one…" bellowed Lionel Richie from the iPad resting on a nearby bench, as two young lovers gazed intently into each other's eyes.

Slowly swaying back and forth, Jay affirmed, "I knew you would figure it out."

Hope's left upper lip slightly lifted. "Yes, it was a very clever message you left. Meet me at the place where I impressed you with my eye for great artwork. Our first date at Soho Guggenheim, of course!" Hope closed her eyes for a brief moment. "We walked around the museum, and you informed me, with great authority I might add, all about the paintings we toured. I was so impressed. I remember telling my parents who are avid art lovers what it was like going on a date with an art historian. Weeks later, we went to the MET, and I realized where your art history knowledge came from. Those small gold-plated information signs posted alongside the framed artwork!"

Jay threw his hands up into the air. "Hey, I wasn't trying to hide that from you. I thought you knew that was what I was doing!"

"They are so tiny; I didn't think anyone could read what they say without getting up close. You never cease to amaze me. Like tonight. How in God's name were you able to get a private gallery room at the Soho Guggenheim?"

"I have my ways." Jay pulled Hope in closer, singing along with Lionel Richie. "Lionel says it perfectly how I feel about you. I am so glad Bubbie introduced u*s.*"

The band leader announced, "We'd like to take this time to invite everyone on the dance floor to join Dr. Kingsley and his wife." Joey nudged Hope's arm, snapping her out of her daydream, "Can I have this dance?"

A startled Hope reoriented. "Ah sure, why not?" As they walked onto the dance floor, Harriet smiled approvingly at Joey, then at Hope. In that moment, Hope knew it was Harriet who had Joey ask her to dance.

Stepping onto the dance floor, the two slowly danced to the song. Hope was relieved that Joey didn't awkwardly stare into her eyes. He used them to gawk at the other women on the dance floor. *What did Harriet see in this jackass?* Hope thought again.

Thankfully the song came to a quick conclusion, enabling Hope to disengage from Joey's embrace. Looking in the direction of the tables, she said, "I think they are beginning to serve dinner."

On her way back Hope was approached by a couple laughing.

"Hey, Speedy Gonzalez, why are you hurrying off the dance floor? The music is too slow for you?!" Matthew Russo giggled. "Mom, this is my new neighbor Hope Klein."

"Ms. Russo, it is so nice to meet you. Your son is such an incredible athlete."

Matthew's mom smiled. "He is an even better son! I am very lucky."

"It is so encouraging to see that a son still enjoys spending time with his mother. Hopefully Marc will take me out to a fancy party when he gets older!"

"Mom and I have been through a lot together," Matthew interjected. "I wouldn't be here now if it wasn't for her."

Matthew's mother shook her head. "I provided support, but it was your determination that rescued us both."

"Couldn't get a real date, Russo?" Joey leaned up against Matthew. "What ever happened to that pretty girl that was attached to your hip?"

"Why don't you mind your own business. Keep your eye on my stats, not my personal life." Matthew looked over at Hope. "Where is Dr. Klein? I know my mom would like to meet him."

"I wouldn't put it past Joey to have eyes on you 24/7," Hope interjected, recalling what Nathan had told her about Matthew's stalker. "Jay got called to the hospital to perform emergency angioplasty on a football player."

"I don't have the players stalked, Hope," Joey stated flatly.

"Oh, which player?" Matthew inquired.

"Someone from your team. Jay wouldn't give out the name." Realizing that maybe she shouldn't have said anything, Hope changed the subject. "Oh look, the first course is being served. Great meeting you. Enjoy your dinner, I hear the food is amazing."

Hope arrived at the table to find the most colorful salad plated around the table and an overflowing basket of rolls with Maltz's famous cinnamon butter. Harriet called out to her, "It's as tasty as it is beautiful." Hope was looking forward to the meal. She read great reviews about the chef's demi-glace filet mignon and amazing creamed spinach. She was especially excited for the dessert portion of the meal, a decadent chocolate flourless torte.

Joey took his seat by Harriet and gave Hope a sinister smirk.

This guy is something else, thought Hope.

The salad did not disappoint; neither did the dinner or dessert. Hope's taste buds were awakened by the explosion of flavor each dish presented.

As the night began to wind down, Hope pulled out her phone to arrange for an Uber.

"I think I'm going to head up, I have a trying day tomorrow." Morgan turned toward Joey. "Speaking of tomorrow, I'd like to head out early, how does eight thirty sound?"

"Eight thirty should be fine. It's a good thing I decided to stay over tonight and not bother driving back to Jersey City. If you need me, I'll be in my usual room 505, my home away from home."

"Thanks for taking her tomorrow." Elliot patted Joey on the back.

Hope joined the conversation. "Thank you so much for inviting me. I had a great time. I think I'll start heading out. My Uber will be here soon."

"There is no need for an Uber. I can drive you home. Let me just walk Morgan upstairs to our suite. If you'd like I can meet you in the library and get you that photo album I told you about."

"That would be great. I'd love that. Are you sure it's no trouble?"

"Not at all, and to make your waiting time more fun, I challenge you to figure out why they refer to the library as the Escape Room. I'll leave you with this clue: things aren't always the way they seem."

For a moment Elliot reminded Hope of Jay.

CHAPTER 30

NOT TO BE UNDERESTIMATED

The creaking sound alerted Hope that someone had entered the library; however, when she turned to the entrance of the library no one was there. Startled by a tap on her shoulder, Hope turned to see Elliot standing behind her, photo album in hand.

"Where did you come from?" She twisted her head from side to side looking for a possible clue.

"You'll find out soon enough. What do we have here?" Elliot placed the album onto an end table and focused his attention on the set-up Monopoly board.

"I found this vintage Monopoly game on one of the bookshelves. I haven't played in years. I always remember getting so enthralled in the game. It was a great escape." She smiled.

Elliot gave Hope a sly smile, knowing where she was going with this. "Now that was pretty clever thinking. I never would have thought of playing Monopoly in the library as the reason for it to be referred to as the Escape Room." Elliot laughed, "With all the books in the room, you pick Monopoly!"

"You said things aren't as they seem. A book would be too obvious."

"You do have a quick mind."

Once again Elliot noted Hope's fast intellect. She liked that!

Elliot moved toward the large wooden desk over in the corner of the room, "Monopoly, however, isn't the correct answer." Elliot tapped his knuckles three times on the wooden desk. "Do you hear that?"

"Yes, it sounds like you're knocking on wood."

Walking over to the fine wood grain paneled wall, Elliot tapped three times. "Do you hear the difference?"

"Yes, but how could that be? Wood is wood."

"Precisely. This is not wood. It is made to look like wood. A process called faux bois gives plaster walls their grainy wooden look."

"Incredible, I guess things aren't always what they seem."

"Now that's an understatement." Elliot moved over to the bookshelf and placed his hand onto the spine of a book. Not just any book, F. Scott Fitzgerald's *The Great Gatsby*. "You may have wondered earlier how I entered the library without you seeing me walk through the entrance? The answer will reveal why this room is referred to as the escape room." Elliot tilted the spine of the title forward. Suddenly the wall to her left began sliding to one side, revealing a hidden passageway that led to another room.

Hope was giddy with excitement. "Does it lead to the bat cave?"

Motioning Hope toward the opening, "Let's find out!"

When Hope looked inside, she wasn't disappointed. The walls of the room were paved with orange tinted bricks that formed an archway; the floor was lined with burnt red Spanish tile. There were rows and rows of racked bottled wines. The sliding door automatically slid shut just as Hope proceeded further inside. She was surprised at how vast and deep the room went. "I should have guessed, a wine cellar! What a great place to escape to! What would a mansion be without a wine cellar? This one is truly remarkable. It really has an Old-World European feel."

Elliot pointed at the first archway filled with racks of wine bottles. "Here you have your reds—Cabernets, Merlot, Pinot Noirs, Syrahs." He pointed over to the opposite archway, deeper inside the cellar. "Over there are the Chardonnays, Sauvignon Blancs, and Pinot Grigios." Elliot moved toward the wine tasting section, a nook area with wrap around wooden benches, table and a single hung window. "And here," lifting up the top of the closest bench, "is the piece de resistance, my special stash."

"A secret compartment! This mansion is full surprises."

"You'd be surprised at all the secret places there are in this mansion." Elliot smirked. "There are many passageways and tunnels throughout the mansion. It was a means of getting around the mansion for the servants. The staff was never to be seen, unless needed. Invisible but visible if you will."

"A perception of privacy."

"True, I bet the staff could have told some interesting tales considering the family believed there really was privacy.

He took out a bottle. "Have you ever had ice wine?"

"Can't say I have!" Hope smiled as she looked out the window at the glistening full moon. *If only Jay didn't get called away, we would be gazing at it together.*

Elliot filled two wine glasses and handed one to Hope. "Let's fix that now." He lifted his glass. "Cheers to a fun evening that continues with a friendly game of Monopoly!"

"Oh," Hope blushed. "I only set that up because I thought it answered your riddle!"

"Nevertheless, I've always liked board games and Monopoly was one of my favorites." Moving back to the library's sitting area, Elliot picked up the dice, then rolled them onto the board. "Let's play a game. I'll be the Scottie dog. Which marker do you want? The iron?" he joked.

"Ha, ha, ha." Hope picked up the boot. "The boot is perfect, because I'm going to kick your butt."

It didn't take Hope long to do so!

"I can't believe you beat me by building on the least expensive properties! I didn't see that coming."

"It doesn't always work, but with just two people it is more advantageous to build on the least expensive properties. It costs less to do so, and you can afford to put more buildings on them, which gets you more rent money when someone lands on you. You have just as good a chance, if not better of someone landing on you than on the most expensive corner."

"I underestimated you, Hope Klein!"

Most people foolishly do, thought Hope.

CHAPTER 31

FUN AND GAMES

The clock struck twelve alerting Hope to the late hour. "Gee, where did the time go? I need to get home and relieve my parents so they can head back to Jersey."

"Don't you have a guest bedroom so they can sleep over?"

"My father prefers to sleep in his own bed." Gathering up her belongings, Hope noticed the photo album. "Oh, I never got the chance to look through the old photos."

"Take the album home with you. This way you can spend the time enjoying it."

"Thank you, I look forward to seeing if my aunt is in any of the photos. That would be so thrilling."

"If that thrills you, you can expect to be thrilled in the next few minutes." Escorting Hope out of the library, down the grand stairs, through the huge wooden doors exiting the mansion, Elliot walked them over to the passenger side of the yellow and black 1929 Series 75 Roadster and opened the door. "Your chariot awaits!"

"And what a chariot it is!" She moved her hand smoothly around the wide whitewall spare tire accented with red rims side mounted in front of the passenger door. "Jay and I were admiring it when we drove up earlier. I can't wait to tell him that I not only got to sit inside the car but got driven home in it."

"Why should he miss out? Give him a call. We can drive up to the clinic and let him experience it himself."

Placing the phone to her ear, Hope anxiously waited as she listened for the ringing sound to be interrupted by Jay's voice.

A groggy voice came on. "Hello?"

Hope could tell she had awoken Jay. "Sorry I woke you up. I thought you were still at the clinic."

"No, I got home about an hour ago. I sent your parents home."

"Oh, how's Marc?"

"He's sleeping. Your mom said he was a joy of joys! He fell asleep about a half hour before I got home."

"Wasn't that convenient for you?" mumbled Hope.

"Did you say something?"

"Oh, just that you won't believe what I'm doing right now."

"Getting the better of Joey De Angelo," Jay guessed.

Leave it to Jay to make this about his boy crush, thought Hope. "No, I'm driving in the yellow and black roadster that was parked outside the mansion! Elliot says you can give it a spin, if you'd like. We should be home in a few minutes."

"Oh, thank him for me, but I am so pooped. Maybe another time."

"Are you sure? We will be there…"

Jay interrupted her, "Say goodnight, Gracie!"

Knowing where Jay was going with this, Hope responded back, "Goodnight, Gracie."

CHAPTER 32

THE PLOT THICKENS

Arriving back at his house after dropping his mother off, Matthew entered the sunroom, walked over to his desk and sat down. Taking out his cellphone, he Googled the number for Huntington Hospital. He tapped the number on the screen, "I'd like to know how Andy Rees is doing?"

"Are you family?"

Matthew hung up. "I knew it!" He lifted up a pad and stared at the chart on the page. He read the names on the chart: Matthew Russo and Shaun Smith. He lifted his pencil and wrote "Andy Rees" underneath the last name.

Matthew moved over to the window. Something or someone had caught his attention. He quickly pulled the drapes shut, then rushed outside yelling out, "I know you're out there. I'm on to you!"

Click, click, click.

The photographer looked down at the time. *How did you*

get back so fast from dropping your mom off? I thought I had more time to position myself. Damn it, Matthew. Did you see me?

Click, click, click

What do we have here? Is that Dr. Kingsley laughing with Hope? Why did he drive her home?

Click, click, click

Aren't you the belle of the ball? It appears that the men in this community have certainly taken a liking to you.

CHAPTER 33

SWEET DREAMS

Entering the master bedroom, Hope carefully maneuvered the darkened room to the bathroom. She looked over at the black silk negligee hanging on the back door hook that she laid out earlier in the day in preparation for quality time with Jay. She peeked out the bathroom door, letting out just enough light for Hope to see a sleeping Jay. It looked as if he had been knocked out by a dump truck. Hope bypassed the negligee and put on her customary pjs—a plain tank top and sweatpants.

Quietly and gently, Hope entered the bed. She stared at Jay, hoping he'd feel her presence and miraculously get up and they would share an intimate moment. That wouldn't be the case, so Hope drifted off.

Feeling the heat coming off the body moving closer to her, excitement and arousal erupted throughout Hope's body. A warm hand caressed her right arm, as moist lips blew butterfly kisses all around her ear, then down her neck, tickling Hope. Repositioning herself to face her engaging lover, their lips connected. Their bodies entwined. Opening her eyes to gaze into her husband's loving eyes, Hope was startled. They weren't Jay's eyes she was gazing into.

———

A startled, now awake Hope looked over at her husband, who was still in a deep sleeping state.

Another time Elliot has stood in for Jay tonight, thought Hope as she went back to her dream.

CHAPTER 34

DIFFICULT TIMES CALL FOR DIFFICULT DECISIONS

Morgan descended down the marble staircase that led to the entrance of the mansion. Joey would be pulling up any minute. Her body sagged with dire despair, distraught with concern for her father. She didn't know how much longer he could go on living an unlivable life. If only she knew a way to help him escape the tormented, tragic existence he had been sentenced to since reaching the last stage of this horrible disease.

Hearing the revving engine hum up the drive, Morgan peered out. The sun had cast a shiny bright light onto the approaching car. *Here comes the sun*, she thought, knowing that Joey would bring in the light forcing the darkness out.

Jumping out of the car, Joey rushed over to Morgan. "Your chariot awaits." He guided Morgan into the passenger's seat. "Wait until you hear the songs I've selected for our car ride sing-along."

Morgan managed to lift up her cheeks in an effort to make her smile look effortless. "I love our sing-alongs; however, I was hoping to get a little nap in before we get to the nursing home. I didn't sleep much last night. You know this will be the first time I'll be seeing my dad, since his last episode. You know I never wanted to put him in a nursing home."

"You had no choice, Morgan. You took care of your dad as long as you could, but his symptoms got to the point where he needed to be in a full-time nursing care facility. You found an incredible institution with knowledgeable staff that are trained to care for someone with your dad's severe episodes. Imagine if you were alone with him at home and not at the nursing home when he had that last episode."

Morgan replayed the event in her mind...

Standing beside her father's bed she sensed that something was wrong. By this time, the disease had reached its final stage. Her father had become a prisoner in his own body, trapped inside a soundproof glass room, longing to be heard. He was fully aware, seeing and hearing everything that was going on around him, but unable to communicate with anyone. He was completely paralyzed, dependent on others for all his needs. Morgan watched in horror as her father's left arm involuntarily jerked, smacking his face red. His body twitching, he started gagging from his tongue forming a swallowing motion. Calling out for help, Morgan was relieved when she saw the nurse enter and rush over to her Dad and stick a wooden tongue depressor in his mouth. However, Morgan's relief was short-lived. The nurse seemed to be overpowered; she called out for more help. Four other people rushed into the room. They did something Morgan had never seen them do before; they used physical restraints to keep his arms down, in an effort to protect him from hurting himself. Morgan made eye contact with her father. There was always a glimmer, a hint of her dad that she sensed when she looked into his eyes. Morgan fell back into her chair. Her father's eyes lost whatever sparkle he had. Morgan sensed a feeling of humiliation and embarrassment projecting out of them. She felt her father's devastation; she knew that it was a lot for him to bear the burden of this disease, but it was over the top, too unbearable to see his daughter witness it. Morgan came to the decision that would be the last day she visited him.

"You know I did go back a few more times?" Morgan confessed. "Without my father seeing me."

"Why would you put yourself through that?"

"It's like when you re-watch *It's a Wonderful Life* and you get to that scene where Uncle Billie misplaces the eight-thousand-dollar deposit, and you think to yourself, maybe this time he won't. But sure enough, he does because it's a movie, and you can't change it." Morgan took a deep breath. "I thought just maybe over time my dad's condition would change; however, like *It's a Wonderful Life*, that wasn't to be." Snuggling into the soft leather passenger seat, Morgan closed her eyes.

"We have about thirty minutes until we get to your dad." Joey reached for the blanket he kept in the backseat and placed it over Morgan. "Try and get some rest. Switch that channel in your mind to a happier channel."

Morgan laughed, "You and your mind channel changing analogy." Closing her eyes, Morgan began to hum. Joey hummed along. He knew the exact channel Morgan turned on...

CHAPTER 35

I DREAMT I HELD YOU
IN MY ARMS

"It is now that special moment when we call upon the father of the bride to come onto the dance floor and dance with his lovely daughter."

Clapping erupted as Morgan's mother wheeled her father to the dance floor.

Morgan and Elliot were holding hands. Elliot released his hand and walked over to the right side of the wheelchair, placing his hand under his father-in-law's right arm, while Morgan's Mom placed her hand under the left. The band began to play a familiar melody to Morgan. She smiled as she watched her father get up from his wheelchair, stand up and take a step toward her.

"May I have this dance?" Her father smiled as Morgan grabbed hold of him in a tight embrace.

In an amazed tone Morgan whispered, "You never cease to amaze me."

"I was not going to miss the chance to dance with my beautiful daughter on her wedding day. There was never a more stunning bride. A dad could not be prouder than I am today. You truly are my Little Miss Sunshine!"

As the band played their song, Morgan and her dad joyfully sang along... "You are my sunshine, my only sunshine. You make me happy when skies are gray. You'll never know, dear, how much I love you. Please don't take my sunshine away..."

For most of the car ride, Joey continued to whistle the "You are My Sunshine" tune; he couldn't seem to get it out of his head. Staring at Morgan, his wide smiling lips turned upside down; he got himself thinking. *I don't know how much more she can take. Time is running out.* Joey gazed over at Morgan. *I promise you; I will not let you share the same fate as your father.*

Sensing Joey's intense gaze, Morgan whispered, "Shouldn't your eyes be on the road?"

Joey's left upper lip rose. "We are at a red light, sleepy-head."

"We must be close." Morgan's voice had a little pep to it. "Thanks for letting me sleep. I needed it."

"Sure thing. We should be pulling up to the nursing home any minute."

Taking out a lipstick tube and compact from her handbag, Morgan began to touch up her face. "I hope Dad does not get mad when he sees me. I can always sense in his eyes what he is feeling. His eyes truly are a guide to his soul."

Pulling into the driveway of the nursing home, Joey secured a space close to the entrance. "I am certain your dad will be very happy to see you."

Walking through the automatic front doors, Morgan stood up straight, gaining her strength in preparation for what she was about to encounter. "Let's stop by the nurse's station; I'd like to get an update before going into my dad's room."

Recognizing Morgan, the nurse exited the station, extending her arms out. "Mrs. Kingsley, it is so good to see you."

"You, too, Nurse Ileen."

"We wouldn't have called, but your dad has been so worked up lately. We can't seem to get him to calm down. We think it's his way of letting us know he is looking for you. Your father's disease never took the knowledge of you from him. We showed him your picture and he got more agitated. Usually it calms him down, therefore we concluded it's his way of asking for you." Walking alongside Morgan, Nurse Ileen hesitated. "At least that's our best guess."

Pushing the door to her father's room, Morgan said, "I'm thankful that you reached out. Either way I need to be here."

Grabbing Morgan's arm, the nurse sighed, "I need to prepare you. He has changed since you last saw him."

"I expected as much." She continued to walk through the doorway up to the bed, unprepared for what it looked like to witness another human being's agonizing descent.

Expectations are the root of all heartache.

CHAPTER 36

OPEN WHEN I HAVE
DISAPPEARED FROM MY MIND

Entering the room, Morgan's eyes welled up as they gazed upon her father helplessly lying on the bed, his gaunt and emaciated body shaking, his pencil thin bony arms strapped to the bed rails, blackened eyelids closed. "He was shriveling away when I last saw him, but this?" She took a deep swallow in an attempt to force down the tsunami about to erupt inside her. "He has become a husk of his former self." Morgan's eyes were fixated on the ribs bulging from beneath his hospital gown. She fell silent. "He has become a living corpse."

"I'm so sorry for what you must be going through. It's not only the patient that suffers." Nurse Ileen approached the other side of the bed, and she gently placed her arms around her patient lifting him into an upright position. Suddenly his eyelids opened up.

Morgan stared into them searching for her father's piercing ocean blue eyes that spoke to her. What she found were black, listless vacant eyes, devoid of any communication staring back. Unblinking, unfeeling. Difficult to look at.

Morgan gently rubbed her hand against her father's pale drawn sunken unfamiliar face. Leaning in she faintly whispered, "Hi, Dad."

His body continued to shake. His eyes remained dark as coal staring right through her.

Any hope of finding her father's condition improving was as good as Uncle Billie not losing the deposit money. It wasn't ever going to happen. In fact, his condition had worsened. At least in *It's a Wonderful Life*, everyone rallies together to fix the dire situation Uncle Billie caused. There would never be a rally Morgan could create that could fix her dad's dreadful situation.

A situation she too would be enduring. A fearful reminder of what she had to look forward to.

Morgan mournfully reflected, "I've witnessed my father's life being torn away from him, symptom by symptom. The innocent stumble, the occasional forgetful thought, an unexpected twitch, turning into harmful tumbles, frequent memory lapses, slip of your tongue moments, unwanted leg jerks while driving, jaw locking when eating..." Morgan took a moment to catch her breath. "You'd think that would be enough torture to place on someone but not for this monstrous disease. No, no siree, it won't let up until you're living a speechless and bedridden life, beholden to others for all your everyday needs. Every day waiting to take your last breath, to be set free, free from the torturous nightmare you have been forced to live, wanting to die." Morgan's body collapsed further into the chair, beaten and scared, as a foreboding premonition of her predestined future played out in her mind. *I won't do it. I cannot bear it.*

Hearing the vulnerability in Morgan's voice, Joey bent down and wrapped his arms warmly around Morgan's shoulders. "Elliot will find a way. He is getting closer every day to a breakthrough."

"I know and I hope he does, but who knows when my symptoms will worsen. Once that happens, there's no turning back, no stopping this disease from taking over. It's like beach goers watching the waves get bigger, higher, stronger. They start to realize, maybe it's time to get off the beach, but they stay just a little longer. Suddenly, a huge tsunami wave appears and it's too late." Morgan's forehead scrunched up. "If that time ever comes for me, you still have the letter I gave you?"

"You mean the one you marked on the front of the envelope, 'Open when I have disappeared from my mind?' Yes, I have it."

"Good, you are to do exactly what I request of you in that letter." Morgan's posture took on a serious repose as she grabbed his hand tightly. "Promise me, Joey."

Joey looked down at her with concerned eyes. "I promise. I will do as you ask."

CHAPTER 37

I LOVE YOU DAD

Morgan couldn't get up from the chair. She didn't want to leave. Leaving would mean giving up on her father. She couldn't do that. She wouldn't do that. Staring at the Gollum-like figure in the bed, one taken over not by a ring but a monstrous disease, Morgan knew her loving, caring dad was somewhere within, deep inside.

"The last spark of light has been drained out of him. The last means of communication we shared." There was a tremor in her voice. "I never got to say goodbye. Tell him how much I loved him."

"Your dad knows how much you loved him," Joey said flatly. "Weren't you his Little Miss Sunshine?"

Morgan laughed, wiping her eyes with the palms of her hands. Leave it to Joey to point out the obvious. Warm, happy memories sang through Morgan's mind as the melody of a familiar song played in the background.

Morgan felt the warm sun's rays beat on her from the large window to the left of her father's bed. Up until now it had been gray out. At this very moment, she had an epiphany and felt a sense of closure.

Her dad may no longer be inside the body before her, but his presence surrounded her.

Determined to leave her father's bedside in a manner fitting all her love for him, Morgan began to sing their song. Her final goodbye.

As she sang, the sun's rays felt brighter, warmer. She stood up and leaned in to give her dad a kiss on the forehead when she noticed something.

Was it her imagination?

Was she seeing something she so badly wanted to see, like a person stranded in the desert sees a mirage of water?

Was that a flicker of light she saw in her dad's eyes, a mirage?

Joey moved closer. "What is it?"

Morgan didn't speak. She cautiously motioned her head in the direction of her father's face. Hoping, praying that Joey would see it. The change in the darkness of her father's eyes.

She continued to sing, "You make me happy, when skies are gray…"

There it was again; this time more light than darkness seemed to appear in his eyes.

"Is it me, or did your dad's eyes seem to lose some of their darkness?"

Morgan's eyes began to dance. "You do see it. It's not my imagination." Leaning even closer to her father, she whispered into his ear, "You do recognize me!" She kissed him on his forehead. "I love you, Dad."

CHAPTER 38

IS SOMEONE THERE?

Whistling the theme from *Fiddler on the Roof,* Nathan stirred some salt into the simmering pot. Stuffed cabbage was one of Nathan's go-to dishes when the weather got cool. Nathan went over to the kitchen sink to wash his hands and stared out the kitchen window. Sometimes he'd catch a glimpse of Hope and Marc on their run. Currently the street was empty. At least, that's what he thought. At second glance, Nathan saw the backyard entry gate to Matthew Russo's yard swing open. *Matthew should be at the stadium by now.*

Quickly, Nathan rushed out his front door and in the direction of Matthew's yard. Feeling the gust of cold air rush right through him, Nathan quickly regretted not stopping to put on his windbreaker. Entering the yard, he walked toward the impressive all glass extension attached to the rear backside of the house. It was an all-year-round addition, complete with a built-in kitchen, bathroom, family room with 50-inch television screen, and Matthew's most prized possession—his hot tub. Nathan had viewed this area coming from the inside of the house when he massaged his magic rub on Matthew, but it was truly an impressive sight viewed from the outside.

Surveying the rest of the property, Nathan didn't notice any-thing out of order. In fact, the place was sealed up tight; all the furniture and pool were covered up in preparation for the snowy freezing cold winter.

Nathan attempted to slide open the sunroom door, but it wouldn't budge. He began to walk away, but something caught his eye. The rocking of Matthew's favorite armchair. *Was someone in there? Could it be Matthew's stalker?*

Nathan leaned into the glass pane peering inside. He shook his head. Nobody. Did he really think there would be someone lurking inside? *Nathan, you are being paranoid. Mat-thew only said he thinks there's a stalker.* Making his way out of the yard, he took one last look back. *I'll keep watching,* he thought. *If Matthew does have a stalker, I'll find out.*

That was close, thought the photographer bundled up like a ball hiding behind the armchair. The photographer's quickened heartbeat settled down. *Good thing I knew where Matthew keeps the spare key. Nathan, you are becoming a problem.*

CHAPTER 39

HOW'S MY LITTLE BUBULA?

Walking out of Matthew's backyard, Nathan listened for the clicking sound to let him know that the gate door had been secured. To Nathan's surprise, he also heard giggling. Nathan looked around to see where the laughter was coming from. His face brightened and a warm sensation ran through his body when he discovered its source.

Hope and Marc strolled over toward Nathan. "Is Matthew home? Shouldn't he be at the stadium by now?"

Nathan shook his head. "No, he isn't here. I thought I saw someone."

"You saw someone go into his yard?"

"I saw the gate swing open from my kitchen window." Nathan bent down. "How's my little bubula?" Marc giggled.

"Maybe this wind swung it open?" Hope swung her right hand up in the air.

"Maybe?" Nathan rubbed his chin. "I guess I let my imagination get the better of me. Ever since Matthew told me he thinks someone is watching him, I've given his house extra scrutiny."

"Matthew thinks someone is watching him?"

"Yes, he feels someone is stalking his every move."

"I wonder if Joey De Angelo has something to do with this?"

"Who?"

"Joey De Angelo, gambler extraordinaire; Jay's newest best friend! He sends out spies to collect personal information on players so he can use it to determine what bet to place."

"Interesting. Is that legal?"

"I guess it's like hiring a private eye." Hope placed two fingers to her lips. "Sometimes he gets the information first-hand. When Jay and I were at the Gatsby party, Jay got called in to do an emergency angioplasty on Andy Rees. Joey found out about this and deduced that Andy wouldn't be playing in the game set for the next day. This information was not public information yet, so Joey was able to use it to place a winning bet on a spread that was set based on Andy Rees playing."

Nathan raised his voice, "I think people who secretly watch other people are rotten."

Hope sensed there was more to Nathan's declaration. "I get the feeling you had a bad experience with someone watching you?"

"I think you could say that. As I have told you, I was forced to leave Berlin alone and go to Amsterdam. My mom and sister were moved into a ghetto while waiting for my papa to get out of prison. So when the Nazis came to Amsterdam, I went into hiding. I would not leave Amsterdam—Mama knew that's where I would be. That was the plan. I was able to take shelter in the cellar of the family I'd been staying with. The family pretended that I left to ensure that the neighbors wouldn't know I was still there. On most days I had to keep quiet and alert. The moment I heard any noise, I retreated to a two-and-a-half-foot by two-and-a-half-foot crawl space secretly created just for me in the rear cellar. I entered through a panel that could be removed. I always needed to be sure to align the panels. I would spend many tireless tortuous hours motionless at times in the shadow of darkness, staring at the panel, listening for that moment I could move again."

"My God, how awful. How did you ever stay still for so long?"

"I trained my mind to entertain myself, calm myself and protect myself. One is never the same after that. I rarely went outside. When I did, I had to be extremely careful. On rare occasions, someone would come down to read and talk with me, and this was my salvation."

"Thank God for that," Hope uttered. "How long did you hide?"

"I successfully hid for just over two and a half years; until a suspicious nosy neighbor contacted the SS. The SS had come many times before to search; however, this time they searched more intently due to the neighbor's tip. They discovered the crack in the wall leading them to me." Nathan's disposition altered. Hunched over, he added, "I was taken to Auschwitz." Looking down at his tattoo worn after all these years, while rubbing the unusual charms that hung from the necklace around his neck, Nathan told Hope, "It was there that I discovered the fate of my family. A neighbor from Berlin recognized me; he was in the same ghetto as my mama and Sadie. He told me that my papa was killed in prison. My mama attempted to escape from getting onto the train to Auschwitz. The SS shot her. She was carrying Sadie when she attempted to run. The neighbor recalled how even in death my mama lay over Sadie's body, one last act of protection."

Hope focused her attention onto the charm Nathan rubbed. She knew it must have special meaning for him. Unfortunately, she could also sense that he had more tragic stories to share.

"I like your necklace. Are those charms Jewish stars?"

"Yes, they are three dimensional Jewish stars!" Nathan lifted up the charms away from his neck and began to stroke the charm with the red stone in its middle, "This one was my wife Chava's." Moving his finger over to the charm with the green stone in its middle, "And this one was my son's."

"They are very unique. Where did you get them?"

"Back in Israel, at a shop at the top of Masada. Ari discovered them." Nathan smiled, "Chava fell in love with the charm and said we should each have one. She said it would be a great reminder of the glorious day we had at Masada. So, we did. From that day on we never took it off." Nathan sighed, "Well, not until...." Nathan's voice trailed off, as he lovingly put his entire hand over all three charms.

Hope sensed Nathan's heartbreak, "You have all three linked together. A reminder of that happy day you shared with them."

"Yes, a day I think back to everyday. They are forever close to my heart."

Marc began to wiggle and whine, seeking attention.

"What's wrong, bubula?" Nathan bent down, grabbed hold of Marc's hand and swung it playfully.

"He's letting me know it's lunchtime."

"I just made stuffed cabbage. I'd love for you both to join me."

Hope took a moment to consider Nathan's offer. "I can't see why not. Jay won't be home for hours."

As she entered the house Hope took a deep breath, taking in the wonderful smells coming from the kitchen. In such a short amount of time she had come to feel so at home here. She'd always gravitated to the older generation.

"Come, come!" Nathan motioned them into the kitchen. "I can't wait to see Marc's reaction to my stuffed cabbage."

Hope bit her lower lip. "This could get messy. Marc is an extremely picky eater."

After positioning the stroller seat into the right position, Hope placed a Buzz Lightyear themed bib on Marc.

Nathan rushed over with a bowl in hand. "My little Ari loved my stuffed cabbage when he was Marc's age." Sitting on the chair next to Marc, he took his spoon and scooped out mushed meat. Nathan got a spoonful into Marc's mouth. Marc began eating the stuffed cabbage.

Hope breathed a sigh of relief, as her left eyebrow raised. "How did you do that?"

"I didn't do anything special; my food is just that good!" Standing up, he motioned over to the stove. "You continue to feed our little guy, and I'll fix you a bowl."

Hope continued to feed Marc, who happily opened his mouth with every spoonful. "You must give me this recipe."

CHAPTER 40

A ROMANTIC NIGHT AT
MALTZ MANSION

Two weeks later.

Hope sat down in the wingback chair just outside the Great Concessions Restaurant and pulled out her cell phone. "Hi, Mom! How is Marc? I'm glad. Yes, we have been having such a wonderful time. Thanks again for watching Marc for us. We really needed this quality time together."

Looking up, Hope waved to Jay pointing up one finger and whispered, "I'll be just a minute." Nodding her head, she returned her attention back to the call. "Yes, we just finished dinner. It was delicious! I am addicted to their cinnamon butter. We spent the day on a guided tour of the grounds. We got massages in the room and then I took a long hot bath in the huge clawfoot tub. The suite itself is huge; there's gorgeously painted murals on the walls, a seating area with two large couches and a four-poster king size bed. It doesn't feel like we're staying in a hotel room. It feels like we are houseguests, or should I say mansion guests? Let's talk tomorrow, Jay is waiting for me."

Hope placed her arm through Jay's right arm and nestled in. "It is so nice to have you to myself."

Jay smiled. "Yes, I haven't realized how occupied I've been lately. I've missed us."

Hope rested her head onto Jay's shoulder. "I've missed you, too. I wish we could always avoid our outside pressures."

Just as she uttered the words, the outside entered their world.

"Hey guys, I see you cashed in on that golden egg prize I helped you win," announced Joey De Angelo.

Jay lit up, disengaged his arm with Hope and extended his hand out. "How do you figure that?"

"By placing a bet on who would find the egg, I motivated you both to be even more determined to find one."

"That's some creative thinking," Hope interjected. *Can this guy's ego get any bigger?* she thought.

Joey laughed. "It's my out of the box thinking that has made me a successful gambler. Speaking of gambling..." Joey turned his attention toward Jay. "We are about to start our weekly poker game. We play in the mansion's own private man cave, downstairs hidden away from the public. One of our regulars is running late. I'd love it if you would join us until he gets here." Turning now toward Hope, he said, "I promise it will be less than an hour. How many people can say they played poker in a secret room of a mansion?"

Hope shut her eyes, took a deep breath, then looked over at Jay. The look he returned back clearly stated—Can I go? Please?

"To make your decision easier, I'll treat you to an after-dinner drink or dessert. They offer homemade delicious desserts at the Green Light Bar. By the time you finish, Jay will be returned to you."

"You don't need to buy me off. If Jay wants to go, he can go. I'm not his keeper."

"How about this?" Jay suggested. "I will go down for just a half an hour if you think you would be okay hanging out in the Green Light Bar?"

Hope really wanted Jay to turn Joey down and say *I'm not here to play games with you, I'm here to spend time with my wife.* However, she at least got Jay to limit the time of being away to just a half an hour. She could handle that. "Sure, I think a table by the fireplace with a nice glass of ice wine would be lovely." *Old Jay would never consider missing a minute of time with me.*

Jay's face brightened. "Thanks, darling." Then he leaned in and whispered in her ear, "I'll make it up to you tonight."

Hope walked into the bar, ordered herself an ice wine and found the only opened table by the fireplace. Shortly after, a man approached her table. "Is this seat taken? There are no other open tables."

Hope looked up and smiled. "Sure, no one is using that seat. I'm flying solo for the next half hour."

"Where's Jay?"

"Your best buddy Joey took him away from me."

Elliot's upper lip raised. "Poker night in the Man Cave."

"You guessed it. How come you're not down there?"

"I don't care much for poker."

"How is your research coming along?"

"We are moving forward and making strides." Elliot hesitated. "I just don't know if I will be able to cure this monstrous disease before it takes over Morgan beyond curing."

Hope's heart ached with pain for this poor man's situation. What a lucky girl Morgan was to have such an incredible husband. If only Jay would focus on her and Marc just a fraction of the time. Hope wanted to distract Elliot from his worries. Noticing a Monopoly game stored on top of a bunch of other board games, she motioned over to it and asked, "How about a rematch?"

Time went by, and before Hope knew it an hour had passed. *Where was Jay? So much for him returning in a half hour.* Hope couldn't hide her disappointment.

"Why the frown. You're winning?!" Elliot joked.

"Jay was supposed to meet me here a half an hour ago. I guess playing poker is more attractive to him than spending time with me?"

Elliot shook his head. "I don't believe that. No man would ever find you unattractive."

Just then Jay came rushing in. "Hope, I'm so sorry. I lost track of the time."

Hope's face frowned. *You've lost more than that.*

Part Two

———— ❧ ————

TRAGEDY

STRIKES

CHAPTER 41

FOOTBALL CAN BE A DANGEROUS SPORT

Nathan plopped down onto the couch. "Today should be a great game. Both teams haven't had a loss yet."

"They haven't played each other yet. Let's see how well they defend Matthew."

"Taylor won't be able to stop Matthew." Nathan focused on the television screen. "Maybe I'll spot Jay among the players?"

"Jay isn't there yet; he had to first finish his shift at the clinic. I don't expect him to be there until the second quarter, if he's lucky."

"That's a hectic day. Doing a full shift at the clinic and then the long drive to the stadium."

Hope sighed and her eyes lowered. "That's what Jay does when he gets consumed. He burns the candle at not just both ends, but multiple ones."

"That's not good."

"You're telling me."

"He's on the fifty...the forty...the thirty...the twenty... he's going all the way!" The announcer called out over the roaring crowd.

This got Nathan and Hope's attention. They intently watched the television.

"Matthew Russo is like a bullet explosively taking off right from the trigger handoff, gliding past the Pittsburgh defense. He finds that hole and immediately takes advantage of it. He went all the way!" added the second sportscaster.

Pumping his right hand in the air, Nathan rejoiced, "That's my boy!"

"Making the kick, that's seven to zero. All in the first three minutes of the game!" stated the first sportscaster.

Pittsburgh's first attempt with their ball possession didn't go as well. The Titans got back the ball.

"All eyes are on Patton. Will he hand off the ball again to Russo? It looks that way, but Sanders and Riley are aware, they close the hole. Russo backs up, finds another opening. Jones rushes from behind, gets a piece of Russo's leg. It doesn't stop him. Russo wobbles on. He's met by Taylor, and he's down."

"Not before getting that first down!" added the second sportscaster. "Russo is like a Weeble Wobble! Remember? Weebles wobble but they don't fall down."

Nathan smiled recalling playing with those toys with Ari. "Ari spent hours with his Weebles Circus Tent set. He favored the Strongman."

"My favorite was the treehouse set. I favored the mommy."

"Titans first and ten, Patton taking the snap from the center, dropping back, and gripping the ball with two hands. Who is he throwing it to? Wait! It's a trick play. It's a fake throw, he's passing it to Russo. Taylor recognizes Patton's still got the ball, it looks like he's going for the Statue of Liberty play, Taylor rushes over to blitz him but not before Patton releases the ball. Russo's in position. The ball is high. Russo there! Jumps up and makes the catch, landing hard. Wait," the sportscaster gasped. "He's not getting up. He's grabbing his right knee, rocking back and forth writhing in pain."

Another sportscaster whispered, "There's a deathly silence in the stadium, everyone on and off the field are on their feet, you can hear a pin drop. Something is not right with Russo. Here comes the medical team. Let's look at the slow-motion replay. There's Russo jumping to make the catch. And there's his landing, it seems as though after landing he rotated his body in relation to the planted foot, placing his weight on it, then dropped to the ground."

"Our announcer, who is currently down on the sidelines said he heard a popping noise."

Hope sheepishly turned away, while Nathan moved in closer to the television. "How can you watch it? I can't stand to see Matthew in so much pain."

Nathan lowered his head. "These eyes have been forced to witness far worse."

Hope motioned over to him and rubbed her right hand across his back.

"Hope, isn't that Jay rushing toward Matthew?"

She looked closely. "It certainly is!" She shook her head. "He had to have driven well over the speed limit to get there this early."

Hope didn't like this side of Jay.

CHAPTER 42

GAME OVER

Waking up in a room he wasn't familiar with, Matthew was not quite sure where he was. He surveyed the room. The walls were painted a depressing green puke, there was a beeping sound coming from a computer-like screen with a bunch of numbers and lines blinking, something was attached to his heart. The last thing he remembered was being on the field, jumping up to make that incredible catch. Then landing and feeling a throbbing pain around his knee. Then it went black. Putting everything together Matthew realized he was in the hospital. Continuing to look around, Matthew's eyes landed on a chair. A chair currently being occupied.

"You're finally awake! You've been sleeping all night and most of this morning." Nathan stood up and lifted the pink water pitcher beside Matthew's bed, pouring some water into a cup. "Your throat is probably very dry...here."

"I think I popped my knee." Matthew swung the sheet away from his body. A black brace surrounded his right knee. "Yep, I knew it from the moment I heard that popping sound."

"A popping sound is never good."

Matthew's face turned intense with deep thought and concern. "Did we win?"

Nathan was surprised by the question. He thought he would ask when will his knee heal? Will he need surgery? With Matthew it was first things first—his team and teammates were his first concern; he would address his knee in due time.

"No, they lost ten to twenty-one."

Matthew closed his eyes. "What happened?"

"Simply put, they fell apart."

Matthew rolled his eyes. "Can you give me a little more than that?"

Just then the door to Matthew's room opened. "That was some gruesome entertainment you provided your fans yesterday," Jay announced as he approached the bed. Noticing Nathan's annoyed face, he extended his hand out. "Hi, Nathan, you know I'm just joking, trying to lighten the mood."

That's a strange way of going about it, thought Nathan.

Looking over at the monitor, Jay said, "Your vitals look good. With the exception of tearing your ACL, you are in great physical condition."

"Is that what happened? Will I be able to play again?"

"It's too early to say."

Matthew's face grew concerned. "What does that mean?"

"It means we won't know until we do the surgery and see what is going on there. Your records show that this knee has been injured before."

"Yeah, in a car accident. Please, I can't stop playing ball, football is all I know."

"I'm sorry I can't give you a better answer. Everyone recovers differently."

"When can I have the surgery?"

"In two weeks. I want the swelling to go down. That allows for an easier and better recovery." Looking over at Nathan, he said, "If you don't mind, Nathan, I need to examine my patient. Can you give us a little privacy?" His eyes motioned over to the door.

"Sure, of course. I'll go get some coffee from the cafeteria. Can I bring you back anything, Matthew?"

"I'm starving. I can really go for some of your stuffed cabbage." Looking in Jay's direction, he asked, "If I'm not having surgery today, what am I still doing in the hospital?"

"I'll have you out of here soon."

"I'll bring you back a ham and cheese sandwich; that ought to tide you over till we get you home."

Jay walked Nathan to the door and closed it behind him. "Now that we are alone, there's just one more issue I need to address with you."

CHAPTER 43

AN UNEXPECTED VISITOR

"It's been two weeks since Matthew Russo tore his ACL on the field. Disappointing many thousands of Titans fans, including some big time bettors who lost big money on that game who are now wagering on whether or not Matthew Russo will be able to come back to football and play at the same pro elite athlete level he's played at prior to his ACL surgery," declared the sports commentator. "ACL injuries are the Achilles heel for athletes, especially football players."

"Years ago, a torn ACL was considered a career ending injury," continued the second commentator. "Thankfully due to exemplary strides in medical science this is no longer the case. However, whether a football player, more specifically a running back, can come back to play at the competitive record-breaking level he once had is the question."

"And I'm sure it's a question that keeps Matthew Russo up at night," added the first commentator. "Russo is expected to have the surgery this week. We wish him all the best."

Matthew grabbed the remote and clicked off the television. "Why can't they just leave me alone. I don't need the extra pressure." Spread across his coffee table were more frivolous sports news commentaries…"Titans' Matthew Russo's Season

Ends and It Doesn't Look Good For the Titans," "Torn ACL Keeps Russo Off the Field Along With the Titans," "Will Russo Be Back Next Year?," "ACL Tear Stops Titans From Moving On." Glancing over at the stack of printouts Nathan had been bringing over the past few weeks, Matthew smiled and wobbled over to them. Sifting through them helped build Matthew's confidence that he would come back to play ball better than he had. These printouts ran the gamut from "Preparing for ACL Surgery to Ensure Maximum Motion" and "ACL Recovery Timeline and Tips" to Top Running Back Players Have Speedy Recovery from ACL Surgery.

Nathan had been extremely supportive and encouraging. Any time Matthew began to doubt his recovery, Nathan would be there with statistics: *Eight-five percent of players who return get back to playing at the same or higher level of football...* and success stories: *Adrian Peterson, after intensive hard work and dedication to get back, led the NFL with one thousand four hundred and forty-six rushing yards. That's three hundred and eight more than Number Two Marshawn Lynch. Then there's Jamaal Charles. Five weeks into his comeback season, he led in rushing yards.*

The ringing of the phone startled Matthew. "Hello?"

Speak of the devil. "Hi, Nathan. Yes, I'm fine. Just getting my mind wrapped around the challenging journey I'm about to face."

Matthew shook his head up and down as he concentrated on what Nathan was saying. "Yes, it will all be worth it, if I can play again. I just love that feeling of running on the field hearing the fans cheering your name, or the exhilarating sensation of finding a hole and rushing a hundred yards, making that uncatchable catch. I don't know life without football."

Rubbing his nose, he said, "Yes, Nathan, I love your brisket.

It's the perfect choice for my last meal, so to speak! We are still on for tomorrow night. I'm sure you will have more print-outs for me," Matthew joked.

Not only had Nathan been feeding Matthew up with emotional support, he had also been, well, feeding him! Matzo ball soup, stuffed cabbage and his mouthwatering restorative brisket.

"I've been doing what you suggested, I've been icing and elevating, exercising my hips. The swelling has really gone down." Matthew sat up and motioned his leg slowly up and down. "I think my knee is as ready as it will ever be for the surgery. And with your brisket tomorrow, my body will be fueled and ready to take whatever that doctor gives it. I intend to rest the rest of the night." Matthew admits "I know rest is as important as exercise. I'll see you tomorrow."

At precisely the same moment he put the phone down, there was a knock on the door.

"Well, isn't this a surprise, I didn't expect you to be knocking on my door," announced Matthew, staring at the uninvited guest at the door.

Click, click, click

Now isn't this a surprise! What brought you to Matthew's door?

Click, click, click

This can't be good.

CHAPTER 44

REAL RAMIFICATIONS

The moment Matthew shut the door, he rushed to find his phone. "We've got to talk," he uttered into the phone in a don't-mess-with-me kind of tone. "I just had a visitor who enlightened me about the real ramifications of our arrangement."

"Calm down," announced the sharp-toned voice on the phone.

"Things have changed. They've gone from bad to worse to...deadly."

"You're not making sense. ACL surgeries are very successful these days. You'll be back to playing ball like nothing ever happened to your knee."

"Don't act like you don't know what I'm talking about." Matthew hesitated. "I thought you cared about me."

"Isn't this about your knee?"

"This has nothing to do with my knee and you know it."

"I really don't," the voice on the other end indignantly announced.

This statement appeared to flip Matthew off. His body tensed up in outrage. "You don't expect me, of all people, to believe that. We need to meet. I need to see you in person."

"That's a twist. It's usually I who needs to see you!"

"As I stated earlier things have changed. How about tomorrow morning at eight?"

"Why don't I just come by now?"

"Not tonight. I need to get my rest. Tomorrow at eight, you can come here." Not waiting to hear any other reply, Matthew slammed the phone down.

Seconds later, Matthew's phone rang.

CHAPTER 45

WHAT COULD HAPPEN?

"You were never one to take no for an answer," Matthew scolded into the phone. "I told you not tonight. But I will tell you this, I know I'm not the only one."

"Umm...uhh," uttered the voice on the other end. "I believe you were expecting someone else."

Matthew's tone was measured, almost rude. "What can I do for you, Nathan?"

Nathan sensed he caught Matthew at a bad time. "I'll call back, it doesn't sound like you're up for speaking on the phone right now."

Matthew regained his composure, his tone more welcoming. "No, don't be silly."

"I forgot to ask if you wanted me to bring some of my matzo ball soup?" Nathan always kept an emergency stash in the freezer.

There was a moment of silence on the other end. "That sounds great, there's nothing like your matzo balls! Can you come by a little earlier than dinner time? I have something I'd like to discuss with you."

Nathan believed he heard a touch of concern, almost disappointment in Matthew's request. "Of course, I can come as early as you want."

"I'm meeting someone in the morning and then my schedule is clear. How about four o'clock?"

"That's fine." Nathan paused. "Matthew, when you answered the call you sounded upset and said things..."

Before Nathan could finish, Matthew interrupted, "Yes, I know. That's part of what I want to discuss with you tomorrow."

"Okay then, tommorow it is." As Nathan hung up the phone, he couldn't help wondering what Matthew meant when he said, *I know I'm not the only one.*

Nathan went to the kitchen, opened the freezer and took out the Tupperware containing his infamous soup.

I can't wait till tomorrow to find out what's going on, Nathan thought. *What could happen between now and then?*

CHAPTER 46

WHAT'S GOING ON?

Sirens were blasting out a cacophony of alarming wails. Bolts of intense flashing lights flickered through the window. Hope's body catapulted up from what could have been the best sleep she had since the baby arrived. Sleep is a precious commodity for any mom, and Hope was no exception. Hope glanced over at the all-too-often empty side of the bed. *On my own again*, thought Hope. *My new normal.*

"We-oo-we-oo, whoop, whoop" resonated through the room.

"We-oo-we-oo, whoop, whoop." The dire sound grew even louder, more penetrating. A warning sound that woke up whatever was still sleeping inside Hope's body. Quickly, she exited the room and cautiously went over to the dining room window that looked out onto the court.

A pandemonium of colored lights and dark sounds were coming from across the street. Blue and white police squad cars parked haphazardly along the driveway, with their dual turret lights mounted on the rooftop flashing red and blue waves of light across her face. A red and white Chevy ambulance with "Cold Spring Harbor Fire Co. Emergency Medical

Services" written across the side pulled up with its multiple orange, white and red lights blinking urgently.

With all the lights flashing, one might become distracted; however, Hope's dark brown eyes were drawn to the bright flood lights illuminating Matthew's backyard. If she didn't know better, these lights could have been mistaken for those lighting up a friendly night football game. However, the emergency vehicles huddled in the front of the house indicated otherwise. These floodlights were shedding light on something much darker than a sporting event.

Hope wanted to rush across the street to see what was going on firsthand, but she wasn't going to leave Marc unattended.

If only Jay was home, wished Hope.

Picking up her cell phone, Hope registered the hour. It was a few minutes after midnight. She wondered; *He should have been home by now.* Growing concerned she began to dial his number but stopped mid-dial.

Moving closer to the window, she sharpened her weary eyes on two plain clothed gentlemen walking out from Matthew's backyard.

It couldn't be! she thought. *No way.*

As the two men walked in closer visual range, there was no question as to their identity.

It is!

Walking in the direction of her house was Joey De Angelo and...Jay.

CHAPTER 47

SOMEONE'S DEAD!

Side by side, chatting like two school girls about the latest juicy bit of gossip, Joey and Jay walked past a legion composed of cops, EMS workers, and paparazzi all huddled around Matthew's front lawn. A young female reporter with a blonde bob cut wearing a red sheath dress with camera crew in tow rushed toward the two. Sticking her microphone in their faces, she forced Jay and Joey to talk to her.

After what seemed like an eternity, but was actually only two minutes, Hope watched as the two split up. Joey walked to his Aston Martin, and Jay proceeded on his way back home.

Hope bursted out the front door. Her patience was wearing thin. She greeted Jay with a slew of questions. "What's going on? Why are reporters here? Is Matthew alright?" She caught her breath, then added one final question. "Where's your car?"

Jay stepped back as if he was hit by a bulldozer. "Calm down, let's not get hysterical. My car died. I left it at Joey's house; he drove me home. I'll have to take your car to work tomorrow. When we got here Joey saw the lights were on in Matthew's yard. He decided he'd go wish him luck on his upcoming surgery. He went in through the opened backyard gate. That's when he discovered Matthew."

"Discovered?!" Hope couldn't help but interrupt. "Is Matthew okay?"

"Joey found him lying face down in the hot tub. I was heading home when I heard him call out to me. It was clear when I got there it was too late." Seeing Hope begin to tremble, wobbling back a few steps, Jay quickly grabbed hold of her and guided her to the couch.

Hope could hardly find her voice, but she squeaked out, "Matthew's dead?"

Jay nodded his head. "There was nothing that could be done. All it takes is being submerged under water for just a few minutes to block the air passageways closing off oxygen flow."

Hope's protective mind quickly went to Nathan. "I don't know how Nathan is going to take this. Matthew was like a son to him." Hope took a deep breath. "At least he won't find out like this, I can go over there tomorrow."

"Nathan knows; he was entering Matthew's yard as we were leaving," Jay stated as a matter of fact.

"What?! I should go over there. He will need me."

Jay looked at his watch. "I need to get some sleep; my shift starts in less than six hours. Keep an eye out for him. I'm sure they won't let him stay there long."

Hope's face reddened with disappointment, or was it anger? "Can't you spare a little more time for your wife?"

"Say goodnight, Gracie!" Jay called out to Hope as he walked to the bedroom.

Hope stood there stunned. Then she stormed into the bedroom, but Jay wasn't in there. He was in the bathroom. Hope yelled through the bathroom door, "I can't believe Matthew is dead and all you can do is go to sleep!"

"There's nothing any of us can do for him now." Jay sat on the toilet seat holding Hope's diaper bag, slipping something inside. "Now this should do the trick," he whispered to himself. He placed the bag on the floor and proceeded to brush his teeth.

Jay left the bathroom, kissed Hope on the cheek and collapsed into the king size bed. "Hope, I'm so tired. I really need to get some sleep. I've got patients who are depending on me."

Hope let out a sigh and thought, *Marc and I depend on you, too. I guess you don't see it that way anymore.* Hope went to the bathroom to splash some water on her face. Motioning over to wipe her hands on the towel, she noticed the diaper bag. *What's my bag doing in here?*

CHAPTER 48

A DAY AT THE MARKET

Nathan never really slept. Nighttime was difficult for him. He never slept more than an hour or two without getting up. This awful habit began when he hid from the Nazis. Always on the lookout not to be caught, Nathan needed to be hyper vigilant of his surroundings. Tonight, was no different. Nathan lay in bed, his eyes wide open. Nathan used this time to remember his past—the good, the bad and the ugly. He knew that memories fade away until they disappear. He would not let that happen to his beautiful Chava and their strong, athletic son, Ari. So every night he would recreate a memory of each one of them. Nathan struggled to keep the memories of happy times, although some nights his mind would go to the darker times. Tonight, would be one of those times.

Flashing lights and screeching cries of a siren enveloped Nathan's bedroom. For most people the siren sound is a comforting one. The calvary is coming. Here they come to save the day! They find hope that an ambulance, fire truck or police car has arrived.

This was not the case for Nathan. Sirens were a trigger. A trigger taking him back to a time in his life that he kept deep in the back of his mind. A time in Israel with Chava…

They were at the Mahane Yehuda market picking up the necessary ingredients for the night's Shabbat dinner. As on most Friday early afternoons, the Shuk was bustling with crowds of fellow Israelis in search of finding everything on their Shabbat dinner list. Mahane Yehuda was an open marketplace composed of narrow aisles occupied by stalls offering an abundance of fresh produce, overflowing stainless steel bowls of fragrant spices, herbs and nuts. Full of life, the Shuk was a spectacular feast for the senses—a kaleidoscope of colors, symphony of smells and loud, chaotic, hustling noise.

It was a warm summer day, not too hot. Chava enjoyed the longer days filled with light. She and Nathan would stroll the market taking in the familiar friendly vendors, bellowing out their unbeatable prices, and the aromatic smells including Chava's favorite fresh baked challah, as Nathan enjoyed the taste of the chocolate Halvah. But before strolling together Nathan always went on ahead to pick up Chava her favorite flowers—blue and white irises. He loved the way her eyes sparkled and her sun-kissed face grew a brighter red when he came back with the bouquet. It was a ritual he started when they first began attending the marketplace. Today would be no different.

Nathan ran on ahead, making a left at the end of the aisle to where his favorite flower vendor was stationed. Mordecai, the florist, smiled as Nathan approached. He went over to the table and lifted up the blue and white iris bouquet he specially prepared and presented it to Nathan.

Nodding his head in appreciation, Nathan handed Mordecai a few shekels. "This is one of your most magnificent arrangements to date." Admiring the flowers, he added, "Chava's going to flip."

Just then, he heard an all too familiar blasting sound. Screams erupted, shoppers spread out like ants fearing they would be squashed by a huge foot. Everyone moved as fast as they could to safety. Nathan, however, raced in the direction of the explosion. Knocking into swarms of frightened shoppers fleeing the market, Nathan knocked past them heading toward the danger. He was determined to get to Chava.

Sweat dripped from his brow, and his heart anxiously pounded. He saw a black smoke cloud the street he was approaching. The street he had just left Chava on.

Chaos filled the street, and disoriented people with torn, smoke-covered clothes wandered in all directions as EMS workers carried out the injured on cardboard makeshift gurneys, while others did their best to stabilize those on the ground.

Nathan's frantic eyes surveyed the area: green awnings were ripped apart, the colorful olive, vegetable and spice stands were overturned, and blackened lemons, oranges and olives blanketed the asphalt while bits and pieces of clothing hung from the telephone lines. Wounded victims were scattered around, some writhing on the ground, others wandering aimlessly. Rescue workers did their best to comfort the distraught and injured. Huddled around what was the bake shoppe were three rescue responders leaning over a body. The only part of the body that was exposed were the feet. They were flapped out, one foot bare and the other wearing a worn brown leather sandal. Nathan's eyes focused on that sandal. He recognized it immediately.

"Chava, Chava!" Nathan pushed his way through the responders. "This is my wife!"

"Sir, sir, are you okay?" asked the uniformed officer as he put his arm on Nathan's shoulder. "I'm Sergeant Bender from Cold Spring Harbor police department. Do you know where you are?"

Nathan's eyes moved from side to side. He rubbed two fingers across his forehead. "Cold Spring Harbor? Wait. What?" Gaining a bit of his composure, he slowly registered back to present day. "America? I'm in New York?" Nathan's mind was flashing back and forth; one moment he was back in Israel reliving that horrific day when a suicide bomber entered the busy Mahane Yehuda marketplace taking the lives of two tourists and five Israelis…including Chava's. Then he flashed forward; he was currently standing in a puddle of water inside Matthew Russo's sunroom looking down upon the lifeless body of Matthew Russo.

CHAPTER 49

IT'S MURDER

Air was raging out of Hope's nostrils like one of those thrashing bull cartoons. Letting out her frustration and angst, she paced back and forth from the front window to the kitchen, while twirling a strand of her hair with her finger waiting for the coffee to brew. Coffee—nature's wonder drug. It's amazing how much better the world begins to look after a cup of coffee.

Say goodnight, Gracie. Say goodnight, Gracie. That's his response to my concerns, while police sirens blast and ambulance lights flicker into the house, Hope thought as she replayed Jay's final words before vanishing into their bedroom for a few hours' sleep. *I've got patients depending on me!*

Hope motioned over to her bag and rummaged her hand through it. *I don't remember bringing my bag into the bathroom. Why would Jay be looking in my bag?*

Looking out the window, Hope continued to stare at Matthew's house waiting for Nathan to come out. She was worried about him. The poor man had so many lives taken from him in such tragic ways, yet he defied it all. He was a survivor in more ways than one. Glancing at the clock hanging on the kitchen wall, her concern grew. He'd been in there for a long time. One would have thought they would have removed him from the scene immediately. Something must have happened when Nathan discovered Matthew had drowned. Maybe he fainted, perhaps he had a heart attack. Hope's mind raced with horrific possibilities.

She would soon find out.

Appearing out from the backyard gate of Matthew's yard walked Nathan. He was not alone; a young man, surprisingly wearing plain clothes—not a uniform, was walking closely alongside. Hope couldn't tell if the man was holding Nathan up. She rushed to the front door, turned the handle and leapt out the door. She waved her arms from side to side in a frantic attempt to get their attention. Her efforts were rewarded. They were walking toward her.

As the two approached the foot of Hope's walkway, she motioned quickly to meet up with them halfway up the walk, extending her arms around Nathan. "I'm so sorry, Nathan. Are you okay?"

"I can't believe he's gone. It was only a few hours ago that I spoke with him." Nathan softly added, "My sweet boy."

"He's in shock, Mrs. Klein is it?" interjected the young man. "He's a bit shaken up."

Looking back at the young man, Hope raised an eyebrow. "How do you know my name?"

"Nathan here told me. We saw your lights were on. Nathan shouldn't be alone tonight." He turned to Hope as they entered her home. "I'm Detective Jake Callahan."

Hope forced a smile. "Nice to meet you. Thank you for bringing Nathan here." Moving everyone over toward the couch, she added, "It's Hope. Mrs. Klein is my husband's mother."

"It's the least I can do for Coach Friedman, after all he's done for me."

Nathan lowered his head, unsure what to make of Jake's comments.

"Coach Friedman?" Hope looked at Nathan.

"Yes, he was my high school wrestling coach."

"Assistant coach," Nathan corrected, continuing to keep his head down.

"Everyone on the team thought of you as their coach. You really knew how to communicate with us. Always motivating, supporting and encouraging us. We all wanted to do our best for you."

Nathan's shoulders slouched inward. "Did you feel that way after what I did to you? I would think you'd hate me."

Jake put his index finger up to his lip and gave out a snort. "Sure, I hated you when it happened. In fact, I hated you for many years after, but time clears things up. I realized that I was responsible for what happened to me. It was because of you that I'm where I am today, Detective third grade."

Nathan's shoulders opened up. *Perhaps Jake really did come to terms with what happened.* "That's comforting to know after all these years."

Hope's brow raised. *What could Nathan have done?* She was curious, but now was not the time. She'd save that mystery for another day.

She switched her attention to Nathan. "You'll stay here tonight. This is just awful. Drowning in his hot tub. Matthew had so much to live for." Hope hesitated. "And for you to see his lifeless body. Try to put it out of your mind."

Nathan shook his head; he couldn't put it out of his mind. Matthew did have a lot to live for. "There is no way Matthew would be foolish enough to accidentally drown or desperate enough to take his own life. Does a man make plans for the next morning if he was planning on killing himself that night? I know for a fact Matthew was meeting someone in the morning." Nathan closed his eyes, adding up all that had happened. "Something isn't quite kosher." Nathan paused. "You know Matthew told me he thought he was being watched. And when I last spoke to him, he seemed upset and angered with someone." Nathan brought his fingers together forming a steeple and brought them up to his lips. "I think Matthew was murdered."

"I think you're getting ahead of yourself, Nathan. The coroner reported at the scene that there's no evidence of a homicide. He believes Matthew drowned. Alcohol was present and we all know alcohol and hot tubs aren't a good combination. It doesn't take much alcohol to become fatigued and drowsy in a hot tub."

"I'm not buying it!" Nathan shouted.

Jake shook his head. "I didn't expect *you* to."

Hope could tell by the way Jake said *you* that there was a divisive history between these two. "It's late, Nathan needs to get some rest. Thanks, detective for bringing him here." Hope escorted Jake toward the front door.

Closing the door, Hope called out to Nathan, "Do you really think Matthew was murdered?"

Tucked away behind the darkness of the trees and shrubs, a shadowy figure slowly moved further away from Margaret Court, glad not to be seen by anyone, a not-so-easy task with all the police, EMS and paparazzi around. The photographer's night didn't turn out as planned.

CHAPTER 50

SUSPICIOUS MINDS

Hope's nose wrinkled and her lower lip raised as she entered the kitchen to find Jay's empty cereal bowl on the table. Not only had Jay left before Hope arose, he also left his dirty dishes for her.

He thinks I'm like the nurses that work with him, cleaning up the mess he leaves when he's done with a patient, thought Hope as she placed the dirty dish into the dishwasher.

Hope wanted to know more. There had to be more that Jay could have shared with her. Balancing two filled coffee cups and a bag of Cheerios, Hope made her way into the family room where Nathan and Marc were happily building a great big tower out of blue and red congregated cardboard boxes.

Nathan jumped up and grabbed hold of one of the coffee cups from Hope's grasp.

Hope smiled. "That's some tall tower you boys built. I'm impressed; usually Marc knocks it down at three blocks."

Nathan laughed, "He's done that twice to me already!"

Hope took a few Cheerios from the Ziplock bag and placed them onto the counter space of the bouncer, then lifted Marc in. Marc joyfully picked up each individual Cheerio and put it in his mouth. "You certainly love your Cheerios, don't you? Just like your dad."

You are as tight-lipped as him as well, she thought. Being that Marc's vocabulary consisted of a few words—mama, dada and up—this was a fair comparison.

Before sitting down, Hope grabbed the TV remote and switched the channel from PBS to ABC. She quickly glanced over at Marc who was happily eating his Cheerios, unaffected by the channel change. Hope turned up the volume and leaned closer to the screen.

"As many of you are waking up this morning with us, we have tragic news to share. ABC News has learned earlier this morning that the body of football great Matthew Russo has been found dead at his Long Island home. His death, it appears, is from an accidental drowning. Alcohol was found at the scene. Many Titans fans know Matthew Russo for his infamous Statue of Liberty play. The incredible running back gained many yards and touchdowns with that play to help the Titans to win two Super Bowls. Most recently, we all watched in horror as he tore his ACL on the field, possibly ending his hall of fame career. ABC News has confirmed with the Cold Spring Harbor police department that at eleven forty-seven last night, a call came in notifying them that there was an unconscious, unresponsive body found at Three Margaret Court. Responders arrived at the scene in approximately eight minutes. When they got there, they attempted to resuscitate to no avail. We are told that Matthew Russo's body was originally discovered in a hot tub by one of his team doctors along with Joey De Angelo. For those of you unfamiliar with the name, Mr. De Angelo is renowned in the gambling world for his huge winnings but rose to some notoriety from his huge windfall on the Titans Colonists Super Bowl upset. Our very own Lauren Kelly was on the scene last night. Here she is interviewing the witnesses."

"I'm here with Dr. Jay Klein and Joey De Angelo. Is it true that you discovered the body?"

Jay's body was frozen like a deer caught in headlights, his jaw retracted, his neck muscles stiffened. There was a crack in his voice when he provided his limited answer, "Yes, we were."

"It appears that this was likely an accidental drowning. Do you agree?"

Jay lifted his chest as he straightened up. "Of course, it was an accident. What are you suggesting?"

Moving her microphone over to Joey, she responded, "Mr. De Angelo, as a professional sports gambler, it must have crossed your mind that a football player who loses his ability to play at the level he once played is at great risk to…"

Joey interrupted, "A great athlete has passed away." Grabbing Jay's arm, Joey began to walk away from the reporter. "We have nothing further to state."

Hope turned to Nathan. "That was odd. Joey always seemed to me to be someone that loves the spotlight. I wouldn't think he'd electively pull away from the cameras."

"He was probably in shock."

Hope was deep in thought, playing back what Jay had just said in the interview. Something about the interview was off. "Jay must be in shock, too, because his story is mixed up. He made it sound like he and Joey together discovered the body, but he told me last night that it was just Joey. He said Joey saw the backyard gate was opened and the lights were on in the sunroom and went over there to wish Matthew luck on his surgery. Jay said he was walking back to our house when Joey came out from the backyard calling out for help. Why would Jay get something like that mixed up?"

Nathan stood up; a light bulb lit up in his mind. "Wait, did you say the backyard gate was opened?"

"That's what Jay told me last night. He said Joey drove him home because his car wouldn't start and when they reached the court Joey saw the lights on at Matthew's house and decided to go over and wish him luck on his surgery. He said he went through the back because the gate was wide open."

"That doesn't make sense." Nathan shook his head. "I know for a fact that Matthew had a special lock put on that back gate. He kept it locked from the outside, but you could get out from the inside." Nathan added, "He put it in after I told him I thought I saw someone in his yard."

"I remember that day, but you didn't find anyone in the yard."

"Yes, but Matthew felt that even though I did not find anyone he didn't like that there was easy access into his yard."

"What are you thinking?"

"That the only way the gate was open was because someone left it open when they exited that way out of Matthew's house."

"Wouldn't a visitor leave through the front door?"

"Precisely."

Hope's eyebrows knit together. "What are you getting at?"

"I think it's the action of someone who panicked. When I last spoke to Matthew, he mistook me for someone else. He assumed I was someone calling him back. He yelled into the phone, in an angry tone, *you're not one to take no for an answer.* Then he added, *I know I'm not the only one.* When he realized it was me his tone softened. I asked him about it and he said he'd discuss it with me over dinner tomorrow. I knew I should have pressed him. Now look what happened."

"Nathan, this is not your fault."

"I can't help thinking that whoever planned on meeting Matthew in the morning decided they couldn't, or wouldn't wait until then."

Motioning toward the door, Nathan scooped up Marc. "How about we go for a walk, and make a pit stop at Matthew's house?"

CHAPTER 51

LET'S MEET

The photographer carefully placed the camera onto the desk and picked up the phone receiver.

The moment the familiar voice was heard on the other end, the photographer declared, "We need to meet. I have something you need and you have something I want. If you are as smart as you appear to be you will meet me at the Starbucks on Jericho Turnpike at seven o'clock tonight."

Hearing the response, the photographer replied with a gentler tone, "I'm glad you see things my way. I will be seated in the back wearing a Mets baseball cap."

CHAPTER 52

WHAT WERE YOU THINKING?

"We have nothing further to state," bellowed Joey De Angelo out from the 75-inch television screen in Joey's living room.

Joey squashed down into the couch as if a ton of bricks fell onto him. "Stupid, stupid, stupid." Clapping his hands twice, he signaled the TV to turn itself off. "What was I thinking? I never should have gone over there. I can be so impatient at times."

Joey's face turned ashen; his lips frowned down as his cell phone played an all too familiar melody.

"Did you happen to watch the morning news?" barked an angry voice.

"Yes, I saw it. I was there. One could say I was in the wrong place at the wrong time."

"What the hell were you thinking?"

"I really wanted to talk to him."

The voice on the other end interrupted, "For a smart gambler, you didn't hedge your bets well."

"I disagree, I think with the information I had, I gambled right."

"Either way, your face is all over the news."

"Yes, as a witness alongside Dr. Klein, another witness."

"That's true," the voice settled down. "Regardless, do me and yourself a favor and stay clear of any further interviews."

"I think you're wrong; it would be more suspicious if I stayed out of the spotlight." Joey shook his head as he hung up the phone.

CHAPTER 53

A CLUE!

For a man of his advanced years, Nathan was moving at lightning speed. As he pushed Marc's stroller in the direction of Matthew's house, Hope needed to push herself into a faster gear to keep up.

"Do you really think that someone was with Matthew when he drowned?" Hope stuttered out as she raced behind Nathan. "I have to admit that if Matthew kept the back gate locked, why did Joey and Jay find it opened?"

Hope's heart sank as a thought came to her. *Unless it wasn't unlocked when Joey and Jay got there? Maybe there's more to Jay's story than he told me.*

Nathan pulled the stroller up Matthew's brick walkway. Running alongside were evergreen bushes and beds that in the summer bloomed with seasonal flowers. All that remained in the beds now were gnomes, more specifically Snow White and the Seven Dwarfs gnomes. Matthew got them for Nathan because he felt Nathan's house resembled Snow White's cottage, but Nathan said that he thought they would look better in Matthew's front yard.

Nathan bent down and reached for the gnome that looked like Dopey; it sported an oversized green shirt and purple hat. He lifted it up. Nathan's eyes widened. "No key."

Hope laughed, "Is that where Matthew hid his house key, under Dopey?"

Nathan gave a half smile. "Matthew thought it was the appropriate dwarf to keep the key under. He said if he was dopey enough to lock himself out..." He continued to lift each dwarf in search of the key. When he got to the gnome that looked like Doc, it was facing the opposite direction as the other dwarfs. Nathan lifted up Doc. "What do you know, here it is."

"Maybe Matthew decided to switch it up and hid it under a different dwarf."

Nathan looked up at Hope raising an eyebrow. "I doubt that, but anything is possible."

They walked to the front door, and Nathan jingled the key in the lock and twisted the handle.

Entering the house, Nathan pushed a now sleeping Marc off to the side in a quiet corner of the foyer. "Sleep well, my little angel," he said as he went to join Hope.

Meanwhile, Hope's heart quickened, and her stomach turned entering Matthew's home. She felt extremely awkward entering someone's house uninvited; that the owner of the house was dead made it ten times worse. This was her first time inside his house. Hope's eyes scanned all around. She had envisioned a messy bachelor pad with mounds of dirty clothes on the floor and furniture along with empty takeout pizza boxes and white Chinese food cartons scattered across the coffee table and end tables.

Hope followed Nathan into the sunroom. Nathan called out, "This was where Matthew spent most of his time." Her expectations were not shattered. There were worn clothes and empty takeout cartons splattered all over. There were piles of papers spread out across the coffee table along with empty soda cans. Nathan was standing over the coffee table gathering up the papers. "These are the printouts I gave Matthew to read. They're articles about football players who went back to playing football after ACL surgery. Most went on to play at or better than the level they played prior to the surgery. Matthew knew with my help we would get him back to playing ball." Nathan lifted the papers and handed them to Hope.

Hope looked through them, then pulled a single page. "This isn't one of the printouts. It's a handwritten chart of some sort." Hope took a closer look at the chart. There were columns that ran horizontally and vertically. Along the vertical column was a list of names: Matthew Russo, Shaun Smith, Andy Rees, Tim Drady, Russell Weathers and Dylan Jackson.

Nathan moved closer to the paper. "They're all football players. Andy Rees is on the Titans, Shaun Smith is on the Colonists, Russell Weathers is Philadelphia, Tim Drady is Pittsburgh, Dylan Jackson, Atlanta."

"Don't you think it is odd that Matthew has his own name on here?" Hope points out. "It seems being a football player is all they have in common. With the exception of Andy Rees and Matthew, they are all on different teams and play different positions—either running back, defensive lineman or quarterback. So why these specific players?"

Looking at the chart, Nathan pointed to the horizontal column header. "Every player corresponds with a specific week. See...week one, two, three. It goes all the way to week seventeen."

"The exact number of weeks in a football season. He was watching football games."

"More specifically, he was watching these particular play-ers during these particular eight weeks. Look, weeks nine through seventeen are blank."

"That's because they haven't happened yet. This chart is recording this season! His intention was to watch through to week seventeen." Hope realized that the chart was filled in up to week eight. "The last game he watched was the day he drowned."

"This chart proves that Matthew wasn't suicidal! It shows he was planning on being alive to watch all seventeen weeks."

"You're right!" Hope moved her fingers across the chart. "What do you think these symbols mean?" Each player had a colored football symbol in the box that met the week with the player's name. The football was colored either green or red. Hope lifted the paper closer to her eyes. "And there are only slashes across red colored footballs."

"I think this was Matthew's way of collecting information about these players."

"That makes sense, but what does it all mean? It's some sort of code."

Hope looked around the room and moved over to Mat-thew's desk. "Maybe we will find a clue on his desk?" Hope looked over the desk. There was a desktop computer stationed in the middle, a telephone and answering machine on the right side, and on the left side of the desk were a stack of white DVD boxes. Hope looked over the boxes and read the titles out loud: "New York Titans versus New York Colonists, Pittsburgh Coalminers versus Miami Manatees..." Suddenly, Hope stopped reading.

Something caught Nathan's eye. He collapsed into Mat-thew's desk chair as he grabbed the watch sitting beside the keyboard.

Hope rushed over and bent down, gently touching Nathan's shoulder. "Are you okay?" Hope could see that Nathan was holding a watch. She could see this was not a watch from here. In place of numbers were Hebrew letters. In the Hebrew language, letters represent numbers. Hope recalled her Hebrew school classes—alef, bet, gimel, dalev, hay and vav. That's how they referred to what year you were: first, second, third year.

Nathan looked up at her. "I'm alright." He lifted up his right hand. "With everything going on, I forgot that I had given Matthew this watch." Nathan took a deep breath. "It was my son's. It means a great deal to me. Nathan's voice got all choked up. "Once again it gets returned to me."

Both Nathan and Hope huddled together so deep in thought they did not hear the front door open.

Heavy footsteps approached the living room moving toward Matthew's desk.

Leaning into the huddle, a voice asked, "What are we looking at?"

The startled duo jumped up so hard, they banged the desk knocking off the phone and answering machine.

"Jake! What brings you here?" asked Nathan.

Jake was about to speak when another voice projected out. It was an automated female voice: "You have one voice message…"

CHAPTER 54

A THREATENING MESSAGE

A forceful firm voice projected out of the answering machine, "Matthew, are you there? It's Russell Weathers. Pick up!" There was a moment of silence. The voice returned with an edgy tone to it: "I could just shoot you for your stupidity. There was no reason you needed to get the police involved. Call me in the next five minutes or else." There was a slamming sound followed by a beep; then the animated voice came back on the line: "Message recorded at ten thirty p.m."

Hope looked over at Nathan, her finger pointing to the name on the chart. "Russell Weathers!"

Nathan raised an eyebrow and turned his head toward Jake. "Now that doesn't sound friendly, does it? Did you hear anything at the police department about Matthew seeking the police's help?"

Jake dumped a dirty shirt on the floor and sat on the leather couch. "No, I haven't. I'll look into that."

Nathan sat back into the desk chair. "I see you've come to your senses. You wouldn't be here otherwise."

"I have to admit that after leaving you I got to thinking. It couldn't hurt to look over the scene a little deeper. I've learned that drowning is very tough to prove as homicide even by the coroner. Which got me thinking, doesn't that make it a perfect homicide? After everything that happened to me years ago, who am I to listen blindly to authority? We both know how that turned out for me." Jake looked over at Nathan.

This was the second time Jake alluded to something happening between him and Nathan in the past. Hope's brow raised in curiosity. *It would have to wait,* she thought. *Right now, I want to hear that message again. Was it really as threatening as I imagined?* "I believe we may have stumbled across evidence that might raise some suspicion." She picked up the phone and answering machine, placed it back onto the desk and hit the replay button.

"Matthew, are you there? It's Russell Weathers. Pick up!" A moment of silence. "I could just shoot you for your stupidity. There was no reason you needed to get the police involved. Call me in the next five minutes or else." There was a slamming sound, then beep, then the animated voice: "Message recorded at ten thirty p.m."

"He called at ten thirty. Matthew was home." Hope hesitated. "Most likely in his hot tub. What did the medical examiner say was the time of death?"

Jake rifled through his notepad. "Between ten and eleven thirty p.m." Looking up, he said, "Depending on where Russell was, he might have had time to get here, find Matthew relaxing in a hot tub, argue with him…"

Hope clutched the paper with the chart on it, raising it in her hand. "Maybe this has something to do with why his name appears on this chart Matthew wrote up."

Jake got up and took the paper from Hope. "What chart?"

"A chart Matthew created that proves he wasn't suicidal. This chart shows that Matthew was planning on watching all seventeen weeks of football."

Jake looked over the chart. "It does appear that Matthew was set to watch all seventeen weeks; however, we don't know when Matthew first started this chart. Something could have changed his mind after he made it."

Nathan had been quietly reflecting on the names on the chart. "Shaun Smith and Russell Weathers are both on this chart, and both seem to have a problem with Matthew."

"So, you're thinking Matthew is the type to keep a record of players he had issues with?" Jake rubbed his chin. "And was collecting data on how to beat them on the field?"

Hope interjected, "Why would he waste time gathering up that kind of knowledge when he wouldn't be playing for the rest of the season or next year? I think there's something else going on with this chart."

"Right now, I think I need to have a talk with Russell Weathers. Let's not get ahead of ourselves, Matthew's drowning could still end up being a tragic accident."

CHAPTER 55

WHY WON'T YOU BELIEVE ME?

Nathan's body shivered as he stood in front of Matthew's driveway waiting for Hope and Marc. The cold Long Island wind felt colder with each passing minute. Nathan wrapped his arms around himself in an attempt to warm up. *The cold weather starts earlier every year,* he thought. *Thankfully the snow hasn't hit yet.*

"Looks like you could use a thick jacket like Mini here has on!" Morgan suggested as she, Elliot and Mini approached. "What are you doing standing out here in such a lightweight jacket?" Mini galloped as much ahead of her owners as her leash would allow letting out her doggie greeting, "Woof, woof, woof!"

Elliot unwrapped his scarf as he walked closer to Nathan. He threw the scarf around him. "It's made of cashmere wool; it will warm you right up."

"You don't need to give me your scarf." Nathan pulled the scarf off. "I'm just here waiting for Hope to come. She should be here any minute. She needed to change Marc's diaper." Mini's two tiny paws scratched at Nathan's legs begging to be picked up. Nathan lifted up the pup and was greeted with kisses.

Elliot's right eyebrow raised. "Hope is inside Matthew's house?"

Nathan sensed Elliot's dismay at Hope being in a dead man's house. He also noticed Morgan's left hand had been wrapped with a beige Ace bandage. "What happened to you, my dear?"

Morgan blushed. "This morning I tripped over this little girl." She patted Mini with her good hand and looked over at Elliot. "Stop looking at me with those wounded puppy dog eyes. This fall was strictly carelessness, not my symptoms worsening. I was putting the dishes in the dishwasher; the TV was on. I keep it on for background noise. All of a sudden, I heard breaking news…Matthew Russo found dead; I couldn't believe my ears. I rushed over to get closer to the TV, and Mini here got caught under my feet. She loves to sleep right next to wherever I may be. Don't you? You're mommy's little baby." Morgan patted Mini again. "I know you two were close. I'm so sorry for your loss. Such a tragic waste of a fruitful life."

Elliot shook his head. "To throw one's life away is certainly tragic."

Mini began licking the corner of Nathan's moistened eyes, as Nathan stood up straight. "Matthew did not take his own life."

"He may not have killed himself purposely, but from what I read, his death was brought upon him through his recklessness. Alcohol and hot tubs are a dangerous combination. Especially when you are by yourself."

"Matthew was not reckless; in fact, Hope and I believe that this was not an accident at all." Nathan motioned his head over in the direction of Matthew's side door. "You can ask Hope yourselves."

Hope came out of the house, placed the key back under Doc and pushed Marc's stroller up to where everyone was standing. Mini was barking and wiggling from Nathan's hands, trying to get to Marc. Nathan gently put the pup down, which wasn't easy since she was wiggling all around. Giggling, Marc patted her as Mini jumped up on top of him and gave him kisses.

"I really think Mini thinks Marc is another puppy!" laughed Morgan.

"I'm glad the two get along."

"I'm surprised to hear that you went inside Matthew's house," said Elliot, perplexed. "I didn't realize you two were close."

"Regrettably our relationship was just beginning before he was so suddenly taken away from us. Matthew was so great with Marc. Every time he'd see Marc he'd come over and do his Jump, Jump dance. He'd tickle Marc and laugh with him."

Morgan went over and wrapped both her arms around Hope. "It is such a tragedy."

Hope noticed Morgan's injury. "What happened to your hand?"

Morgan blushed once again. "I tripped over Mini." Morgan looked over at Elliot who gave an adoring supportive smile.

Hope couldn't help but notice. *I remember when Jay used to look at me in such a doting way.* "Is it broken?"

"It's just a sprain, I'll live." As the words came out, Morgan wished she could take them back. "I'm sorry, poor choice of words."

"Speaking of living, Nathan here says that you and he suspect foul play in Matthew's death. How have you come to that conclusion?" asked Elliot.

"I'm not jumping to any conclusions, but I believe that

there are some loose ends that need to be cleared up. We have a good place to start, don't we, Nathan?"

"Yes, we do. Today while we were inside Matthew's house, we listened to the last message on his answering machine. Let's just say it was not so friendly."

"Really? What did it say?"

"Basically, it was football player Russell Weathers threatening Matthew." Hope provided, "Detective Callahan is planning on tracking down Russell Weathers and confirming his whereabouts yesterday."

"A detective is investigating Matthew's drowning?" Elliot's brow creased. "They said on the news this morning that it was just a drowning. There was no mention that it could be a possible homicide."

"That's because the police department wants this high-profile case closed. They believe it is a drowning, an open and shut case." Hope cleared her throat. "However, Nathan here feels otherwise. Detective Callahan is currently willing to look a little deeper. He surprised us a short while ago at Matthew's house. He told us that based on his past experiences with trusting authority..." Hope gave Nathan a slight wink, letting him know that he still owed her answers to what happened between him and Jake years ago, "...he's come to the decision that it couldn't hurt to give this case a second look."

"A possible murder right here in our own Gold Coast Estates." Morgan pointed out, "I feel like I'm in an Agatha Christie novel!"

"I think that is as close to murder as this goes. Matthew drowned. Whether or not it was an accident may remain a mystery." Elliot grabbed hold of Morgan's right hand. "I hate to think that anyone could do such an unthinkable act, especially here in our lovely community."

"You might be right," Hope acknowledged. "However, it doesn't hurt to tie up any loose ends, especially one where Matthew's life was threatened just hours before his death."

Nathan's cell phone began to ring. "Hello?" He put his hand over the receiver and whispered, "It's Detective Callahan. He's located Russell Weathers." Nathan proceeded to walk away from the group.

Click, click, click

The photographer leaned against the fence alongside Matthew's house. *Just as I thought.*

Click, click, click

Hope and Nathan will never leave well enough alone.

CHAPTER 56

BACK AT THE MANSION

Folding his phone closed, Nathan caught up with Hope and Marc, who were walking along their usual walking path. Elliot and Morgan had left a few minutes ago; the cold was causing pain in Morgan's wrist.

"Jake tracked down Russell Weathers. He's in New York. You'll never believe where." Nathan took hold of the stroller steering it away from Hope and in the direction of the golf course leading to Maltz. "He is at the mansion. I say we head over there."

"Did Detective Callahan talk to him yet?"

"No, he was just getting there now. He stopped to talk with the security guard who manned the gate last night. He had him check the list of guests who signed in yesterday. There was no one listed visiting Matthew."

"So, does that point us away from any possibility that Matthew could have been murdered?"

"Not necessarily. There is a possibility that someone could enter the community unnoticed if they got their hands on a gate remote."

"Would Russell have access to such a remote?"

"I don't know. It's possible."

CHAPTER 57

SIX DEGREES OF SEPARATION

Entering the Green Light Bar, Nathan's eagle eyes spotted Detective Callahan and immediately walked over to the table he was seated at. The maître d' chased after Nathan calling out for him to wait to be escorted to his table.

Detective Callahan shook his head. "Why am I not surprised?" Jake let out a slight giggle and directed his attention to the two gentlemen sitting at the table. "This is Nathan Freidman and Hope Klein. They were with me at Matthew's house when I heard your message."

Russell Weathers extended his hand toward Nathan. "Nice to meet you. This is Tim Drady." Russell waved and smiled at the maître d alerting him that he was okay with Nathan and company being at his table.

Nathan shook Russell's hand and then moved his hand over to shake Tim's. "I know who Tim Drady is. You have some arm."

"Thanks." Tim stood up. "I was just getting ready to go. I have a sick young man waiting at the hospital for my visit. I promised his mom at last night's fundraiser I would stop by."

Russell stood up and hugged Tim. "I'm glad you made it to the fundraiser this year. It feels good to know that there will be other kids like us who will get to attend such a wonderful football camp in the summer. I'll be gone when you get back here. I fly back to Philly in the next few hours. Have a safe flight back to Pittsburgh tonight."

"Thanks, I'll probably be half asleep. My flight isn't until ten thirty."

"Nathan and Hope were Matthew's neighbors," Detective Callahan informed Russell after Tim walked away from the table. "Mr. Weathers, I know you have cleared everything up with me, but would you mind if they ask you a few questions?"

"Please take a seat. I can't believe Matthew is dead. Such a loss of a great player and friend."

Nathan seized the opportunity and began his inquisition. "You two were friends? It sounded more like frenemies on the voicemail you left on his machine just hours before he was found dead."

Russell gave out a hard laugh. "You're a cool old dude. Frenemies! Ha! As I told the detective here, that message was left to make an impression on Aliza."

"Do you always leave threatening messages on people's machines to impress women?" Hope interjected.

Russell's upper lip rose. "No. This was a special circumstance." Russell's eyes widened; his lips tightened. "Let me start from the beginning. When I got to Maltz yesterday Aliza was waiting for me. She knew I would be here for the event. I have been participating in the annual Mighty Athletic Stars Foundation fundraiser for the past five years. It has always been held here. They raise money for inner city athletes nationwide to provide athletic opportunities they wouldn't normally receive in their own neighborhood due to limited funds. But I digress. So, there she was, standing at the top of the bridal staircase when I entered. I could see she was upset, so we went here, to the Green Light Bar, got a few drinks and talked. She told me how Matthew filed a complaint against her with the Cold Spring Harbor police department for a restraining order."

Hope interrupted, "Why did he do that?"

"Aliza was showing up unannounced anywhere Matthew would be. It was getting out of hand. Matthew got a restraining order stating that Aliza was not permitted to be within five hundred feet of him. Aliza had thought Matthew would have lifted it by now, but he hasn't. She was devastated. She and Matthew were high school sweethearts; they broke up years ago but remained friends. The only thing is she still loves him. And I believe he loves her..." Russell sighed, "Or should I say, loved her? He just wasn't in love with her. I could see how hurt she was, so I told her I'd speak to Matthew and convince him to drop the restraining order. I called right then and there, but he didn't pick up. I didn't want to simply say, 'It's me, Russell, call me back.' I knew that wouldn't make Aliza feel any better, hence...the message you heard. I didn't know that Matthew was going to drown that very night! I would never harm Matthew. I was planning on calling him in the morning to clear everything up. You can ask anyone who was at the bar last night. They can vouch for me. I was there all night. In fact, Tim was at the bar, too."

Nathan and Hope looked at each other. "That's some story." Nathan asked, "Do you mind if we ask you a few more questions?"

Russell shook his head approvingly.

"How did you come to be friends with Matthew's ex-girlfriend?"

"We met at the summer football training camp I attended way back when I was a high school junior."

"So, you knew Matthew since high school, too?"

"Yes. He was an instructor at the camp. He was playing college football at the time. He and Aliza were still dating. She would come to watch him train us at the workouts. She would talk with all the players while they sat out. One day we got to talking and we found out we had a great deal in common growing up. Both of us lost our parents when we were very young to drugs; we were both tossed from foster home to foster home. We instantly became fr-amily, a family we didn't have. The three of us hung out that whole summer and remained friends ever since. We made it a tradition to meet back up at the camp every summer."

Nathan nodded. "It makes sense that she would come to you then. You said that you were at the Green Light Bar all night yesterday. Was Aliza with you?"

Russell hesitated, then snorted in annoyance. "No, she left shortly after I left the message. I know Aliza...she would never harm Matthew."

"You said you two had drinks. Was Aliza drunk when she left you?"

Russell's face brightened. "Aliza isn't a big drinker; she's more of a binge eater. She eats pretty much anything you put in front of her when she is upset. I remember the last time we were together, a few weeks ago, I thought she'd eaten everything in her kitchen that wasn't nailed down. She was eating away her breakup with Shaun Smith."

Hope and Nathan locked eyes as if a bell went off in both their minds triggering a connection. Shaun Smith's name was on Matthew's list as was Russell Weathers. This was not a coincidence.

"Another football player broke her heart," said Hope.

"You misunderstand. Aliza broke Shaun's heart. There were many reasons she broke it off. The age difference started to become a problem. Shawn acted very immature at times, landing him in the news. Aliza was growing tired of his antics. She realized she still had strong feelings for her high school sweetheart."

"Maybe that's what caused that scuffle on the field a few weeks ago."

"Probably. Shaun hasn't taken it well. I think he's displacing all his aggravation and disappointment out there on the field."

"Maybe Shaun continued their battle last night?"

"That's not possible. He's in L.A." Looking at his Rolex, Russell added, "If there's nothing else, I really need to head to the airport."

Nathan asked, "Can you give me Aliza's address?"

Russell went into his carry-on bag, took out a paper pamphlet and started writing. "I put all the information on the program from last night's fundraiser. Maybe you'll find it's an incredible organization worth donating to! Let Aliza know to return my calls. I've been trying to get in touch with her all day to see how she's handling Matthew's death."

"You haven't spoken to Aliza yet?"

"No, I figured she wants to be alone to mourn."

"Oh, by the way," Hope said as she pulled out the chart. "We found this at Matthew's house. What do you make of it?"

"Looks like Matthew was keeping an eye on some of the players." He smirked. "Including me!" Russell stared at the chart. "Looks like there are more green footballs than red ones. More wins than losses."

Hope looked at the chart. "More wins than losses? Perhaps you're right. I didn't think of that. Russell, would you mind giving me your cell number? In case something comes up?" Hope handed him the chart to write the number on.

Detective Callahan looked at his watch. "Russell, we better get you to the airport or you'll miss your flight." The two men got up from the table, leaving Nathan and Hope.

CHAPTER 58

MIGHTY ATHLETICS STARS SUMMER FOOTBALL CAMP

Nathan and Hope remained seated at the table digesting everything Russell shared with them.

Hope spoke first.

"Don't you think it is highly suspect that Russell Weathers, Shaun Smith and Tim Drady went to the same camp and they all happen to be on Matthew's list of players from the chart?" she questioned.

Hope opened the program Russell gave them from the fundraiser. Her eyes read through a description of The Mighty Athletic Stars Foundation. "Mighty Athletic Stars Foundation is a not-for-profit charitable organization set up to raise money to provide athletic services and opportunity to inner city children who have a strong aptitude for sports." Hope moved her eyes farther down the description to where there was a header titled "Mighty Athletic Stars Summer Football Camp; MASS Football Camp." It read, "We are extremely proud of the accomplishments of our Mighty Athletic Stars Summer Football Camp. It has become one of the premiere summer camps on the Island, reaching athletes from the Tri State area. Located on Hofstra's Campus, the home field for the NY Titans summer practice, MASS Football Camp has earned its reputation for helping develop the excellent athletic skills of those who attend." When she got to the last sentence, she raised her eyebrows: "We are pleased to state that many athletes who have attended MASS Football Camp have gone on to play in the NFL. Dylan Jackson is our latest addition to the NFL!"

"Dylan Jackson went to this camp, too! That makes four players on Matthew's list who went to this camp. That can't be a coincidence." Hope flipped through the program pages.

Nathan pointed out, "Didn't Russell say that Matthew coached at the camp?"

"That's right." She lifted the opened program and pointed it in Nathan's direction. "And I just found the last player from Matthew's chart, Andy Rees."

Nathan took the program and read the small print under a photo. "Andy Rees at last year's MASS Football Camp. The student has become the teacher!"

"They all attended the MASS Football Camp. This has me wondering about what Russell said about the chart, how the green footballs are wins and the red footballs are losses. Maybe he was onto something. Maybe a person at the camp blackmailed each of these players to throw the game? You know, so that they can win a lot of money. Maybe Matthew figured that out? I bet those videos on his desk were only the games represented by the red footballs. He was watching to see how the players threw the game."

"Let's not jump to conclusions. I think we need to speak to Aliza. She may very well know what this chart actually means."

"I really think I am on to something here. I want to go back to Matthew's house and look at those tapes. I bet anything they are the games represented with red footballs."

"Fine, you go to Matthew's and I'll go to Aliza's. We will regroup later."

They got up from the table and gathered their belongings when Hope heard her name being called.

CHAPTER 59

A SENSELESS LOSS

"Hope, Hope Klein is that you?" bellowed a voice from across the room. Hope knew only one person so self-absorbed as to not care if all eyes were turned on him, never mind on the person he was calling out to.

"Joey De Angelo, what a nice surprise."

"I didn't know you were joining Jay and me."

This took Hope back a few notches. She had no idea that Jay was meeting Joey. "No, I'm here with my neighbor."

Turning his attention toward Nathan, Joey extended out his right hand. "Mr. Friedman, it's a pleasure to finally meet you."

Nathan's eyes raised up in surprise. *He knows who I am?* "Finally? Were you looking to meet me?"

Joey gave one of his whimsy smirks. "Your name has been spoken many times to me."

Hope deduced, "Jay has mentioned Nathan to you?"

"That's one way his name has been presented to me," he said coyly.

"Really? I didn't think Jay concerned himself much with me." Nathan's interest peaked. "And how else has my name come up?"

"You underestimate yourself, Mr. Friedman. Your relationship with Matthew over the years has been very entertaining."

Hope gently smacked her hand to her forehead. "Data for your algorithm. Of course, you would know about Matthew having a relationship with Nathan."

Joey lowered his eyes forlornly. "And I know how special that relationship was. You were like the father Matthew never had. Please accept my most sincere and solemn sympathies. Such a tragic loss."

"Thank you. This has come as a terrible shock to me. He wasn't suicidal or reckless. It doesn't make any sense. You obviously have collected a great deal of information on Matthew. Do you think there is a possibility that Matthew was murdered?"

Joey didn't skip a beat. "I could see how you would think that way. He was like a son to you, and no parent wants to believe that something like this could happen. A simple act of relaxing in a hot tub could end up so tragically. I do agree with you that Matthew was not in a suicidal mindset; however, there is nothing that I have learned through my data collection on Matthew that would lead me to believe that he was murdered. I think it was nerves and alcohol."

"What about this Aliza Allan? You must have come across her name?"

"Aliza is a sweetheart; hers is a sad story. She lost her parents when she was young, and she has gone from foster home to foster home. She finally felt she had her own family when she met Matthew in high school. They dated all throughout Matthew's college years. Then when he got into the NFL, he told her they needed a break. Aliza dated other players in hopes of getting over Matthew or at the least making Matthew jealous. It appeared she finally found someone that she loved, Shaun Smith. However, I heard she recently broke it off because she still had feelings for Matthew. I don't believe Aliza would hurt Matthew, if that is what you are suggesting."

"You sound more like a TMZ host than a gambler," Hope blurted.

"It's all part of the equation. I've won big bets with this knowledge. There were games that Matthew played so poorly because his mind was on Aliza drama." Motioning over to Nathan, Joey placed his hand on his arm. "I know it's difficult to accept such a senseless loss."

He should only know how much practice I have had with senseless loss, thought Nathan.

"Dada!" Marc cried out.

Hope turned to see Jay walk into the room. He was not alone—Dr. Conrad was with him. Jay made eye contact and walked over to her.

Hope greeted Jay coldly. "I didn't know you were meeting with Joey and Harry today. I'm surprised you were able to get away from the clinic."

Dr. Conrad smiled at Hope as he walked passed her toward the table Joey was seated at.

Jay bent down, gently kissing Marc on the head. "I thought I told you last night I was going to lunch with Joey."

"No, no, you did not mention it last night! All you said to me was goodnight, Gracie."

Jay laughed. "Yesterday was an extremely rough day. Finding Matthew really had me shaken."

Hope stood there in shock. She couldn't believe her husband's flippant, blasé attitude. Once again Jay was not acting like himself.

"Yes, we all were taken aback by last night. Matthew's tragic and sudden death has us all concerned. Nathan and

I have been looking into Matthew's drowning. Something about it just doesn't feel right."

"He drowned Hope! It shouldn't feel right." Jay looked at his watch. "Hope, can we talk about this when I get home? I only have an hour before I have to go back to the clinic and Joey, Harry and I have a lot to go over."

Hope stepped out of the way. In a sarcastic tone, she said, "Sure thing. You go have your lunch. Nathan and I have more investigating to do."

Hope motioned back to Nathan. "I think it's time to go."

CHAPTER 60

THE RED FOOTBALLS

Hope and Marc strolled up Matthew's walkway. Hope smiled as she lifted up the Doc statue and picked up a key. "Right where I left it."

Entering the quiet home, Hope felt uneasy. She wasn't comfortable being in anyone's house by herself uninvited, let alone a dead person's. Yet this would be the second time she's doing so in one day! Looking down at a sleeping Marc, she pushed the stroller alongside the couch in the sunroom. She looked at her watch. *It will be at least a half an hour before he gets up from his nap, she thought.*

As she walked to Matthew's desk, Hope stopped by the television and turned it on. *Better to have the background noise then deafening deadly silence,* she thought. Sitting down at the desk she pulled the stack of DVDs over to her as she took out the chart from the diaper bag. Picking up the top DVD, Hope read out loud, "New York Titans versus New York Colonists Week One." She looked down at the chart and nodded. "A red football with three slashes in Shaun Smith's box for that week." She lifted up the next DVD: "Pittsburgh Coalminers versus Miami Manatees Week Three." Looking down once again, she said, "Another red football! This one had two slashes and is in Russell Weather's box." Hope continued to go through the rest of the pile.

"Just as I suspected, Matthew was only watching games where he marked the player's box with a red football," she whispered. "Could it be that these players are responsible for losing these games? I need to confirm that this is the case. I can't remember which team won each of these games." She glanced over at the pile of DVDs. "That's a lot of hours of video to watch," she said to herself. "There's got to be a better way."

Hope's concentration was interrupted by the reporter on the TV.

"Coming up at the bottom of the hour, our very own Lauren Kelly will share her latest interview with Joey De Angelo. You asked for it and we got him."

"That's worth watching!" Hope looked at her watch; she had time to go back and watch the interview in her own house.

She pushed Marc across the street and up the walkway to their house when a thought presented itself. She recalled Joey telling her about a website he used to gather information about a team's score and player's performance. "What was the name of that site? Sports Score? No, that's not it. Pick Score? No, that doesn't sound right. Boxscore!" she exclaimed. "That's it."

Hope diapered Marc and put him in the pack and play. She then went over to her computer and typed "Boxscore" into the search bar. She clicked the link for the website, and the Boxscore header appeared. She typed in the Titans Colonists game into the website's search bar: "The Titans won." She looked at the chart and there was a red football in Shaun Smith's box. Hope then typed in Pittsburgh vs. Miami. "Wait a minute! Pittsburgh won. Yet Pittsburgh's Russell Weather's box has a red football." She entered another game, the Dallas Atlanta game. "Atlanta won, yet Atlanta's Dylan Jackson has a red football in his box."

Hope was more confused than when she started. *This throws a wrench in my theory. I thought all the games Matthew watched would prove to have the team the player played for lose. That doesn't seem to be the case.* It was a good thing the interview was about to air; it would make for a good distraction for Hope's frustration.

"We are here with Joey De Angelo in his stunning hotel room at Maltz Mansion. Perhaps the cameraman can move the camera over to the window so our viewers can see the beautiful view of the grounds. Thank you for taking the time to speak with me. Shortly after I first interviewed you, we've been inundated with tons of emails and calls from viewers requesting we do a spotlight on the handsome Joey De Angelo. We were so pleased you agreed to sit down for this interview with us today."

"It's my pleasure. Thanks for having me on. First off, I'd like to send my condolences to the Russo family. My heart goes out to his dear mother. I only wish Dr. Klein and I could have done something, but it was too late." Joey lowered his head and sighed. "That's all I wish to say on this tragedy."

"We share those thoughtful sentiments as well. Our prayers go out to his family and friends, especially his poor mother who has gone through a great deal these past couple of months with Matthew tearing his ACL and not knowing if he would ever return to playing football. Speaking of that fateful game, how did you make out betting-wise on that game? I expect you must have had a great deal of money riding on the Titans, as they were favored to win. As many of our viewers know, you have won a lot of money during your illustrious gambling career. It is rumored that your total winnings are in upwards of two hundred seventy million dollars. So tell us, the viewers want to know, did the great Joey De Angelo suffer a loss?"

Joey's lips spread to the sky. "Actually, I won big. Your assumption that I bet on the Titans is misguided. I wouldn't be the gambler I am today if I always bet on the favored team."

"Isn't it better to take the safe bet?"

"What's the fun in that? Besides, who's to say it's not the safe bet? As most of your viewers know, I have developed an elaborate algorithm that guides me in my decision process for the bets I place."

"So, I'd imagine for this past week's game, Dallas versus Atlanta, you bet on the underdogs, Dallas?"

"In this case you are correct, and I did win."

"Yes, Dallas lost and you won only because Atlanta didn't cover the point spread," Lauren pointed out. "Actually, they almost did if Dylan Jackson had made that catch in the final minute of the game. I remember thinking he should have had that catch. I guess you can say his loss was your gain."

Hope got up and walked back to her computer. She repeated Lauren Kelly's observation, "His loss was your gain." Hope went back onto the Boxscore site. *It's not about who wins or loses the actual game, it's all about the spread.* For the next half hour Hope researched each player's performance for the game that had a red football in their box. She checked to see if they made any errors in that game and tracked how many there were.

Wait until Nathan hears what I've discovered, Hope thought as she picked up her phone and dialed.

CHAPTER 61

YOU NEVER REALLY
LEAVE AUSCHWITZ

Nathan hadn't been in this part of town since he coached high school wrestling. It was considered dangerous by many folks. It was zoned section eight housing, which provided housing to low-income individuals with rental assistance. There were four different apartment building complexes; each were only two stories high, following town code guidelines, housing 45 units. The area had a nice residential feel with oak and maple trees lining the street, and a playground with children running around and park benches occupied by the elderly. One would not expect the transformation that happened upon nightfall. Unfortunately, many of the tenants had fallen on hard times, which is part of the reason that they were provided the housing in the first place; however, this had not solved all their problems. Most nights the police and fire department got called there for domestic violence, burglary or drunken outbursts, to name a few. Today was no different—the sun hadn't even been down for an hour, and there was a police car and an ambulance parked outside the building Nathan pulled up in front of.

Nathan looked down at the program where Russell wrote down Aliza's address. Apartment 207. He got out of the car and began walking up the steps. When he got to the second floor, there was a sign—Units 201-210 and an arrow pointing to the right. Nathan turned right and proceeded to walk past units 201...203. As he moved farther ahead, he noticed a police officer was leaving an apartment. He appeared to be holding the door ajar; it read 207...Aliza's apartment. Nathan stared at the door as an EMS worker appeared pulling a gurney.

Nathan was in shock. Two gurneys in two days. What are the odds? he thought. He froze for a minute. His mind was taken back to Auschwitz...

It is a battle of the senses: a horrific stench permeates through your nose into your stomach. You gag as your startled eyes bear witness to staggering ghost-like figures in tattered striped pajamas, shaven heads and bulging terrified saddened eyes. Blood curling sounds capture your attention: barking dogs, shouting SS guards, cries from children and their parents. The ground is a sea of bile, muddy brown. Gray smoky fog floats as black smoke fills the powder blue sky gray. A shiver of cold blows through you as you survey the area: barbed wire fences along the perimeter, funereal longhouses in rows and a towering watch tower filled with armed SS guards prepared to take action. You wish you could go back on that crammed filled train, but there's no turning back. You are at Auschwitz, where there is a thin line between life and death.

Crying in his bunk, calling out for his mama, a young scared Nathan attempted to fall asleep. Unable to find a comfortable position, his entire body ached. He ached with pain. There wasn't any part of him that the SS hadn't hit, whipped, burned or punched. He ached with hunger. What little food he did receive he gave most of to the elderly who were ill from malnutrition. He ached with loneliness.

At the camp, he worked as a slave laborer producing munitions, synthetic rubber, and other products that were essential to Germany winning the war. Whenever he saw the opportunity, Nathan would sneak out. He'd investigate. His innocent eyes witnessed atrocities the devil himself couldn't even imagine. Barbaric inhumane medical experiments conducted on innocent prisoners inside the torturous vile labs within the walls of Auschwitz. What Nathan saw would forever haunt his nightmares. So many bodies—mutilated ones, dead ones and living dead ones. All these cruel inhumane acts were designed to achieve the Nazis ultimate goal—to break the Jews' spirit, their stomachs, their hearts, and their humanity. But fortunately for Nathan, all the Nazi torment was countered by the acts of kindness from fellow prisoners. It sparked a light inside him that the Nazis couldn't extinguish. No matter how they tried. And they tried.

"Hey, buddy, get out of the way!"

"Officer, what is going on?"

"Girl OD'ed," the officer said as he proceeded to walk. "Another life taken by drugs. Unfortunately, an all too common occurrence in this neighborhood."

Nathan walked on toward Aliza's apartment. The door was still open. Something inside Nathan took over, and before he knew it, he was inside Aliza's apartment.

He looked around at the claustrophobic studio apartment. There was a small weathered-looking dark brown futon which must have served a dual purpose of bed and sitting area; there was a rickety old wooden chair and a battered wooden coffee table. There was a blanket sprawled out across the floor. It must have been wrapped around Aliza and EMS tossed it off of her in an attempt to revive her. There was also a newspaper on the coffee table. The headline read "Football Star Matthew Russo Found Dead." Off to the side was the kitchen area, cluttered with dirty dishes, pots and pans. On the kitchen counter there was a single coffee mug with a lipstick stain and a hot pink scrapbook. The title cover read "Aliza and Matthew" with a huge heart around the names. Nathan headed over to the counter to view what was inside but got distracted by what he saw on the wall alongside the kitchen. The entire wall was covered in photos. They were lots of photos of Matthew. Some were of him alone, while some pictured him with others. Most of the photos were taken outside on the football field and at Gold Coast Estates.

Aliza was Matthew's stalker!

He walked over to the wall to get a better look and discovered he was in many of the photos. Aliza arranged the photos into sections—each section was dedicated to a specific person that was with Matthew. Nathan gasped. *She was watching us too!* There was a dedicated section of Nathan photos, Hope photos, Jay photos, and some of Matthew's teammate photos. Some had Matthew in them, but not all. *Aliza must have taken them while she waited for Matthew.* Nathan stared at the wall of photos. Aliza must have dedicated uncountable hours shooting them. Nathan leaned closer to one photo in particular. It was of Jay and Matthew talking outside Matthew's front door. Nathan focused on Matthew's face. He knew that face. It was one of concern and fear.

Why would Matthew be making that face when talking to Jay? Nathan wondered.

CHAPTER 62

SOMEONE'S BEEN
WATCHING YOU

Nathan's concentration was broken by the ringing of his phone. He quickly answered it hoping the noise did not alert anyone's attention that he was in the dead girl's apartment.

"Nathan, I was right about the DVDs!" shouted Hope into the receiver. "Matthew was watching the games that he had given red footballs to. However..."

Nathan interrupted her mid-sentence. "That's really interesting, Hope, but I have some bad news," Nathan whispered, and walked back over to the counter where the scrapbook was. "Aliza is dead."

There was silence on the other end, then Hope uttered, "What! What happened to her?"

"Apparently she overdosed. The police officer believes that this is a common occurrence in this neighborhood. He is called down here at least once a week on an overdose."

"That is so tragic. She must have heard the news about Matthew and she just..." Hope couldn't complete the rest of the sentence. "Russell! He has no idea. We must let him know. I'll call him. No wonder he never got in touch with her."

"Hope, there's more, Matthew was right. He was being watched. Aliza was stalking Matthew."

"Aliza was stalking Matthew?! What? Why would you think that?"

"Because of what I am currently looking at in Aliza's apartment." Nathan rested his hands on the scrapbook staring at the wall. "A wall plastered with photos of Matthew! Well, mostly Matthew, she also took photos of us!"

"What? There are photos of us on her wall?"

"You bet there are. Aliza must have hidden to circumvent the restraining order and watched Matthew without being seen. She must have spent hours clicking pictures as she waited and watched Matthew. I guess she decided to pass the time by watching us too. There are photos of you, Marc, Jay, and me. Most are of us with Matthew, but there are some of us without him."

Hope couldn't believe her ears. "I can't believe she was spying on us? I feel so violated," Hope's mind was in overdrive, "Nathan, did you say that there were photos of Jay with Matthew? That's surprising to me, I never thought Jay had the time to socialize."

"Funny you should say that. There's a photo of the two talking and it doesn't look like he is socializing. Matthew looks concerned, almost fearful."

"I wonder what they were talking about? This is crazy. How did no one ever spot Aliza in the community?" Suddenly Hope quickly suspected, "Do you think that's what Matthew meant when you heard him say *I know I'm not the only one?* He figured out that she was not only stalking him but watching us!"

"That could be, however, I wonder..."

"Wonder what?"

"What if Aliza had left Russell that night and went to go stalk Matthew. Maybe she saw more than she bargained for?" Nathan sighed, "I think her overdose is a little too convenient."

"You think she captured something incriminating through her camera lens?"

"Sir, sir, what are you doing in this apartment? Who are you?" called out a man wearing a blue Yankees baseball cap, a white t-shirt and a pair of green work pants with a bunch of keys hanging from his belted waist.

"Hope, someone's here, I got to go." Nathan hung up abruptly. Realizing that his time in the apartment was limited, Nathan quickly performed his best magic trick—with a sleight of hand he slid the pink scrapbook under his coat unnoticed.

Moments later the super of the building was escorting him out.

CHAPTER 63

CLOAK AND DAGGER

Hope hated that her phone call with Nathan got cut short. She didn't like the way the conversation ended. She had more she wanted to discuss. So many thoughts swirled around inside her head. *Aliza might have seen something the night Matthew drowned? Her overdose was a little too convenient. Matthew looked concerned, almost fearful? What could Jay have said to him?*

Looking at the phone, Hope refocused; she had a call to make. Lifting up the chart she found, Hope wasn't quite sure what she should do. Should she leave a message? If she did, what should she say? Hearing the beep, she blurted out, "Russell, it's Hope Klein. Please call me back when you get this message." She paused a second then added, "We met earlier today at Maltz."

Hope's adrenaline was pumping; she needed to do something. She started dinner. There is nothing like following a recipe to distract you, although Hope didn't really *follow* a recipe. She had a way of putting her own spin on recipes. A pinch of this and a dab of that; she let her taste buds determine the measurements. Surprisingly, it always turned out great. Hope had attempted to do the same with baking, but that didn't work so well. Baking is a precise science, one needs to have exact measurements, no fooling around. It was hard cookies and flat cakes! So it would be cake mix and store bought cookie dough for Hope.

Hope enjoyed listening to classical music when she cooked. Today she banged her spoon to the rhythmic beats and catchy melody of Mozart's "Turkish March," the third and final movement of Mozart's "Sonata No. 11." The rondo form with its quick and simple repetition made it one of Mozart's most popular. Hope was so entranced keeping up with the hypnotic pattern, she didn't even sense Jay as he came up behind her. Feeling a wet tongue circle her ear, Hope jumped and turned to see Jay laughing.

Hope placed her hand on Jay's arm. "You startled me! You haven't been home at this time for dinner in weeks."

Jay swayed from side to side as he hummed Marvin Gaye's "Let's Get It On." He raised his eyebrows suggestively. "Maybe we should take advantage of this situation?" He moved in back to Hope's ear.

Hope's face reddened; she was caught off guard. She let the moment take her away. Taking hold of Jay's hand, she guided him to the bedroom.

Lying in bed, Hope stared at a resting Jay, who it should be noted had a huge smile on his face! *It's like old times*, thought Hope. She felt ashamed to think that Jay was hiding something from her. She gently rubbed his face, and Jay opened his eyes and casually asked a question that not only raised the tiny hairs on the back of her neck but her suspicions. "So how did your cloak and dagger investigating with Nathan go?"

A chill waved through Hope's body. It was uncharacteristic for Jay to ask about what she and Nathan were doing, much less refer to their activities as cloak and dagger.

"Why would you say cloak and dagger?"

"When we spoke at Green Light, didn't you say you were going to investigate? For some reason, when I envision you and Nathan investigating, I think cloak and dagger."

Hope shook her head. "You may think Nathan is a crazy old man, but the more we investigate the more suspicious Matthew's death becomes."

"How so?"

"How about another tragic death, this time a *convenient* overdose."

"Convenient overdose? That's Nathan talk." Jay rolled his eyes. "I've heard enough. I want you to stay away from Nathan until he comes to terms with Matthew's death."

Hope couldn't believe her ears. This was not what she expected from Jay...well, at least not from old Jay. Old Jay would have joined her and Nathan in their investigation. "There's more. I think Matthew figured out that some of the players were throwing games. I think Joey is involved."

Jay's face turned bright red. "Just because I don't want you hanging around Nathan right now doesn't give you the right to make stuff up about Joey."

Before Hope could tell him about the chart and the suspicious games, Marc's cries erupted over the monitor beckoning her.

Hope finished diapering Marc and brought him into her bedroom to see Jay. To her surprise, Jay was fully dressed and on his way out.

"Sorry, Hope, I got called into the hospital." He kissed both Hope and Marc before walking out of the room.

Well, wasn't that convenient! thought Hope.

CHAPTER 64

A REVEALING PHOTO

Nathan pulled into his driveway, turned the car off and sighed as he looked down at his son's watch positioned on his left wrist. If he was a superstitious man, he'd think that this watch brought the worst of bad luck to whomever he gave it to. From this point on he would be its sole owner.

Nathan was a man who continually challenged the world around him, a quest filled with lots of questions and a journey seeking the answers. It was this ability to find meaning and significance in life that had enabled him to survive the darkness that had seeped into it. No matter how many times the light had been turned off, Nathan was able to put it back on.

Matthew's death brought back many of those dark times Nathan faced in his long life.

Maybe it is me who attracts the darkness, bringing harm to those I love most? Nathan shook his head, and he picked up the pink scrapbook and began to browse through the pages.

It was a touching book Aliza created of a young girl's first love. The album was filled with photos of the two—a picture of the two standing on the high school football field, Matthew in his practice jersey and Aliza wearing short shorts and a tank top. Another picture was of the two holding school books, another on the couch and still another of the two of them all dressed up in their evening best: tuxedo and gown, likely prom or junior prom. There were also photos of Aliza with Matthew with his knee casted, another with him lying in a hospital bed. Nathan was impressed by Aliza's dedication to Matthew while in the hospital as he read the caption under the photo—"Visited Matthew every day until he got better."

Turning to the next page in the scrapbook, Nathan stopped and stared at the photo. It was a photo similar to the one on the previous page; however, there were other people in this photo. Nathan gently pulled and untucked the picture from the scrapbook page. It was hardly secured to the page by pieces of old dried up scotch tape. Bringing the photo closer to his face, he focused his attention on one person in particular. He turned the photo over; there was writing on the back. "Matthew's life was saved by these great men." Nathan wondered if this referred to the crash Matthew was in back in high school. He recalled how Matthew joked that he came out better than when he went in. He turned the photo back around. Nathan felt his whole body tingle as he started processing what he was seeing. His eyes zeroed in on one of the young men. There was an icy sparkle in the man's eyes that reminded him of someone he knew. *But who?* He thought. Nathan sensed the sparkle had a darkness to it, ones like those he looked into and away from in Auschwitz. There was something soulless behind the sparkle. Nathan continued to stare at the photo. He got the feeling that this photo somehow was key to this whole tragic situation. What was it? He couldn't figure it out just yet.

Nathan put the photo into his coat pocket, then picked up the scrapbook and proceeded to look through the pages when he heard a knocking against his car window. Turning toward the clanking sound, Nathan's eyes met a pair of jet brown eyes that appeared to be piercing daggers at him.

It was Jay Klein.

Nathan rolled the window down. "Jay, you startled me. What is it I can do for you?"

Jay said firmly, "You can drop this wild goose chase you and Hope are on. I don't like the idea of Hope and Marc playing amateur detectives. Hope should be focused on Marc, not entertaining a foolish old man's wild suspicions."

Nathan found Jay's behavior concerning but wasn't looking to escalate the situation. He nodded. "I understand."

Jay's stiffened body loosened. "Thank you for understanding. It's for Hope and Marc's sake."

Was it really for their sake? wondered Nathan. His thoughts were interrupted by barking. Mini came running up the driveway pulling along Morgan and Harriet with her.

Nathan opened the car door, and Mini jumped right up onto his lap. She licked his face as he giggled. "This is such a wonderful greeting." Nathan pet Mini. "I am happy to see you, too."

"She smelled you a few houses ago and had us on the run ever since!" Morgan exclaimed catching her breath. "Good thing Elliot wasn't here to see how fast we were going. You know him—he would be so concerned I would fall and have both wrists in braces."

"You did just fine. Elliot needs to realize your symptoms are not worsening as fast as he is imagining. He worries too much." Harriet gave a reassuring smile then directed her attention to Jay. "Are you coming home from the clinic just now?"

Jay sighed. "No, I'm going to the hospital, Harriet." Jay made eye contact with Nathan. "Nathan, this is Harriet. She works at the clinic with me. Harriet, this is Nathan."

Nathan's eyes sparkled. "Nice to meet you." He put his hands under Mini's belly who was now chewing at his necklace.

"It's nice to meet you as well," Harriet said and raised her brow quizzically up as she turned her attention back to Jay. "Who's the patient?"

"It's Mr. Stuart. I saw him earlier at the clinic. I didn't like the way he looked; his blood pressure was extremely high, but he wouldn't hear of me admitting him to the hospital. I guess he had no choice tonight."

"That Mr. Stuart is so stubborn. I warn him all the time to keep his diet in check because of the diabetes but he just won't listen—thinks he knows better than the medical professionals. He's a regular at the clinic, going on eight years. I'd like to go with you."

"Don't be silly. How often do you get a day where you can visit with a friend? I can handle things."

Morgan noted, "Harriet is very dedicated to her patients!"

Jay laughed. "I will admit, many of our patients look for Harriet for treatment over any of us doctors."

Harriet shook her head. "I wouldn't say that. Many of the patients have been coming to the clinic for years and have grown comfortable with me. They trust me."

Jay motioned down the driveway. "I best be going or I'll be late and that won't do any good in developing trust in my patients."

Harriet waved, then thought, *I didn't think Mr. Stuart was back from visiting his family in Delaware.*

Nathan pushed Mini away from his neck and placed her in the seat next to him. "I need to get her a leather necklace of her own to chew!"

Morgan rushed around to the passenger side of the car, opened the door and grabbed Mini who was eyeing the pink book on the dashboard. "It looks like she'd be willing to accept that leather scrapbook as a consolation prize."

"Anything that is made of leather, she thinks is a chew toy," laughed Harriet.

Morgan laughed. "You should see Elliot's wingtips!"

"So, Nathan, are you taking a trip down memory lane?" Morgan pointed at the pink scrapbook.

Nathan pursed his lips. "I guess you can say I'm taking a trip down someone else's memory lane. It belonged to a friend."

"Well, I'm sure you would love to get out from the cold car and into your warm house and continue your trip."

And with that the girls left. Nathan found himself alone with his thoughts. He pulled out the photo from his pocket and stared at those familiar eyes again. *He is older now,* thought Nathan. Then it came to him. He knew who those eyes belonged to. With this realization Nathan's mind went back to what Matthew had said when he spoke about the car accident, he was in years ago: *I came out better than when I came in.* Nathan hadn't thought much of it at the time but now it sat on his stomach like a bad tuna sandwich.

He picked up his phone and dialed Hope.

"You have reached Hope Klein. I'm sorry I missed your call. Please leave me a message and I'll get back to you as soon as I can. Have a great day!"

"Hi, Hope, it's Nathan. The scrapbook confirmed it. There was foul play here…" he paused. "In more ways than one."

"When will there cease to be evil in the world," he whispered to himself. "It runs in their blood." He then went back to staring at the photo before putting it back in his pocket.

CHAPTER 65

IT DOESN'T ADD UP

Hope carried Marc over to the front window to see Jay off. "There goes Daddy off to work. Bye, Daddy!" Hope lifted Marc's arm, making a waving motion.

Hope stood up a bit taller as she watched Jay walk past the car and over to Nathan's car. Her instinct was to rush out, but she quickly rejected it knowing that it was far too cold out to take Marc outside. She decided to wait for Jay to leave and then call Nathan—they had so much to discuss.

In the meantime, she knew Marc must be hungry. "How about some dinner? Mommy made you your favorite—chicken fingers and candied carrots."

After placing Marc into his highchair, Hope walked over to the counter and prepared his plate. Now that she had discovered how much Marc enjoyed dumping his food into things, she started giving him dipping sauces! Chicken nuggets, frankfurters, cut up hamburgers, French toast sticks, to name a few. Marc joyfully dipped, dumped and splattered. He might have been a messy eater but he was also becoming an excellent one.

Hope was just finishing cleaning up and was about to dial up Nathan when the phone rang.

"Hello!"

"Hi, it's Russell. I got your message. Everything okay?"

"Ahhhh, it's Aliza."

"What about her?"

Hope could not get her lips to open until her mind had chosen the right words, which felt like an eternity. "She is no longer with us."

"What do you mean, she's no longer with us?!"

What was I thinking…She's no longer with us?

"Earlier today she was found in her apartment. She died of a drug overdose. I'm so sorry."

"That can't be. Aliza didn't do drugs."

"Maybe she couldn't handle Matthew's death?"

"Not a chance. Aliza might have been hopelessly in love with Matthew, but she knew the importance of life. She was making a new start. She was going back to nursing school, becoming independent."

"I didn't know she was interested in becoming a nurse."

Russell laughed as he recalled, "Aliza has always behaved like a nurse. From the first day we met, she took care of me. Actually, many of us when we were at the football camp. We all used to tell her that nursing was her calling. It wasn't just the players who took notice. Even Joey De Angelo would tell her…"

Hope interrupted, "Joey De Angelo? Why would he be at the camp?"

"Oh, Joey would come every year to the camp. He would show up and sit on the top bleacher with his fingers typing away on his laptop."

"Really. Isn't that very interesting." Hope paused for a moment and reflected to herself. *Joey was at the same camp as all of the players on the chart. He won huge bets on games these players made errors in. Should I ask Russell about this?* Hope quickly thought better of it. *If Russell is involved, that's the last thing I should do.* "He must have been collecting data on high school players. Isn't he thorough?"

"I guess. Anyway, the point is Aliza had more to live for than just Matthew. Overdosing is not something Aliza would do."

"Nathan felt the same way. Maybe you should contact the police and tell them your concerns."

"That's my next call. I will insist on an autopsy."

"Let me know what you find out."

As Hope disconnected her call, she noticed a little blinking picture of a phone in the right top hand corner of the phone. She had a message.

CHAPTER 66

EVERY TIME I THINK I'M OUT, THEY PULL ME BACK IN

Jay yawned with exhaustion. He was glad to be wrapping things up at the hospital. "I'm going to head out. Contact me if anything changes with Mr. Stuart," Jay informed the night nurse.

"Sure thing, Dr. Klein."

As Jay left the emergency wing, EMS workers came rushing in pushing a gurney. A tall, dark-haired medic called out for guidance, "We have Tim Drady here. He's in cardiac arrest, a possible blockage."

Every time I think I'm out, they pull me back in, he thought, as he rushed over to treat the patient.

CHAPTER 67

FOUL PLAY

Hope entered her voicemail password.

"Hope, it's Nathan. The scrapbook confirmed it. There was foul play here." There was a pause, then, "In more ways than one." Hope thought the message was over and was about to disconnect when she heard faintly, "When will there cease to be evil in the world." Silence, then, "It runs in their blood."

Hope leaned closer to the phone. She wasn't quite sure what Nathan was saying. *What scrapbook?* She could only assume it was Aliza's. Her instinct was to disconnect from the messages section of her phone and dial Nathan. It rang six times before she got an automated voice saying, "You reached Nathan Friedman. Leave a message at the beep."

"Nathan, it's Hope. It's eight o'clock. I'll be up late. Call me when you get this message. I don't know what to make of your cryptic message. Foul play? In more ways than one? It runs in their blood? I can't wait to tell you everything I learned today. I think Joey has been blackmailing the players into making errors so he can win huge bets. Russell told me that Joey was at the camp every year. I think he got dirt on the players there and has been using it to blackmail them.

I wonder what he has on them?" Hope took a breath. "Lots to talk about, call me back."

Hope walked over to the front window and looked out at Nathan's house. His car was no longer in the driveway and all the lights were off. *Could you really be asleep this early?* she thought. *Perhaps you went out?*

Either way she would have to wait until Nathan returned her call.

—

Nathan rushed out of the bathroom toward the family room in search of his phone. *I knew I should have taken it with me into the bathroom.* It was just his luck that he'd been waiting to hear back from Hope all night and when he heard his phone ringing it was not with him. Lifting his coat off the couch, Nathan reached into the coat pocket. He flipped the phone open only to discover he was a little too late. There was no one on the other end. There was, however, a voice message.

"Nathan, it's Hope. It's eight o'clock. I'll be up late. Call me when you get this message. I don't know what to make of your cryptic message. Foul play? In more ways than one? It runs in their blood? I can't wait to tell you everything I learned today. I think Joey has been blackmailing the players into making errors so he can win huge bets. Russell told me that Joey was at the camp every year. I think he got dirt on the players there and has been using it to blackmail them. I wonder what he has on them? Lots to talk about, call me back."

Nathan looked at his watch considering if it wasn't too late to call when he noticed that the scrapbook he left on the coffee table was no longer there. He walked closer to the table. Maybe it had fallen onto the floor. While searching the area around the table, Nathan felt something hard hitting the back of his head. Placing his right hand over the area that was hit, his eyes spun until the room went black.

Part Three

GOOD INTENTIONS,
DEADLY CONSEQUENCES

CHAPTER 68

WHERE'S NATHAN?

The next morning, Hope awoke with a headache. She tossed and turned most of the night. She kept thinking about Jay and how he had changed since moving to Gold Coast Estates. How he had become so consumed with work and Joey DeAngelo, and less focused on her and Marc. She wondered about the photos Nathan saw at Aliza's apartment of Jay and Matthew together. Jay never mentioned even seeing Matthew in the community, let alone, being close enough to him that they would be captured in photos together. Then there was Nathan's message.

Hope replayed it in her mind: *There was foul play? In more ways than one? When will there cease to be evil in the world?* She especially wondered what he meant when he said "it's in their blood."

Hope looked over at the time: 8:30 a.m. "Why hasn't Nathan returned my call? He knows Marc gets me up early." Hope picked up her phone and stopped mid-dial when she heard the doorbell ring. She smiled in relief. "That must be Nathan!" she said to Marc as she raced to the front door.

Hope's smile turned upside down when she opened the door. "Detective Callahan? Is something wrong?"

"I'm sorry to bother you this early. I was hoping to find Nathan here. I knocked on his door, but no one answered. I promised him I'd stop by today to take him to Matthew's funeral. It's a small intimate gathering, but Nathan was concerned with the reporters and paparazzi. He wanted me to escort him so no one bothered him."

"I forgot today is the funeral. Nathan isn't here and he hasn't returned my call from last night. I should have heard from him by now." Hope looked down at her phone and double checked that there were no messages from him. "You rang his bell and he didn't answer? I'm worried. Maybe he is hurt. We need to get inside his house." Hope pulled open a kitchen drawer and took out a key ring with a singular key hanging from it, then picked up Marc and placed him in his stroller. "Let's go."

Rounding the corner of Nathan's walkway, Hope immediately noticed something curious. She bent down and lifted up today's newspaper. Looking over at Jake, she asked, "Don't you think it is odd that today's newspaper is still outside?"

Jake raised a brow. "I'm sure there is a reasonable explanation. Let's not jump to any unnecessary conclusions." From the tone in Jake's voice, Hope wondered if he was not only trying to convince her, but himself.

As Hope entered Nathan's home, her heart raced as she called out, "Nathan, it's Hope. Are you okay?" There was silence. She prayed that he was alright. Hope and Jake went from room to room, but Nathan wasn't in any of them. Jake looked in the garage. "His car is gone. He probably forgot I was picking him up and left for the funeral himself."

"I don't think so. He would have called me before he left. We had lots to talk about."

"Was he still looking into Matthew's drowning?"

"We both are. I believe Nathan was onto something. He told me so in a voice message he left me."

"That sounds like Nathan. He could never just leave things alone."

Hope took this moment to ask Jake something that she has been wondering about since the first day they met. "What happened between you two?"

"In high school I was manipulated by the wrestling coach into fudging my weight so I could get into a lighter weight group while truly belonging in a heavier one. I respected the coach and followed whatever he asked of me. It was Nathan that figured out what was happening and turned the coach in. As a result, I got kicked off the team and lost all scholarships."

"Wow. I can see why Nathan felt you would never forgive him."

"Believe me, I hated him for a long time. But I came to realize that I was doing something wrong by blindly following someone in authority. In the end, it was this incident that led me to pursue a career in law enforcement."

"Oh, now I understand why you felt the need to investigate Matthew's death even when the higher ups wanted the case closed. I remember you saying to Nathan that sometimes you need to challenge authority."

"That's true. Nathan stood up for what he believed in. He sought out the truth."

"I am starting to wonder if he sought out the truth here, and now has found himself in trouble."

"Let's not jump to any conclusions. Nathan may be at Matthew's funeral. I'll check it out and follow up with you."

Just as Jake was leaving, he heard a faint buzzing sound. Searching for the sound, Jake walked over to the coffee table.

Bending down, he reached under the table and pulled out a small black flip phone. Nathan's cell phone. Jake held it up for Hope to see. "Now we know why Nathan hasn't called us back." Flipping the phone open, he said, "Four missed calls."

CHAPTER 69

A CURIOUS PHOTO

Hope decided to hang out at Nathan's a little bit longer. *Oh, Nathan where can you be? Was looking into Matthew's drowning a mistake? How did your phone end up under the table?* Looking over at his emergency to go bag, she was certain he would be returning soon. At least, she prayed that was the case.

Thank goodness for PBS, thought Hope as she watched Marc stare and sway to the opening song of Sesame Street on Nathan's television. She enjoyed hearing the song as much as she had as a child herself. She was so glad that she could share one of her favorite childhood shows with Marc. It was incredible how much of the show had remained the same, with its loving characters, catchy melodies and fun learning. Hope could now understand why her mom let her watch it so often.

Hope picked up the newspaper and pulled it out of the clear plastic bag. *Newsday* was the leading news source for Long Island and New York City. Most Long Islanders read *Newsday*, allowing them to keep up with national, as well as more localized, news. Hope appreciated the color printing incorporated into the paper.

Flipping through the headlines, she sighed. *The news can be so depressing.* Moving deeper into the paper, she got to the local news. Her eyes widened. A headline caught her eye. "Football Player Tumbles—Rushed to Hospital."

"Early last night, Tim Drady passed out after tumbling off his barstool at Maltz Mansion. Drady was at Maltz participating in a fundraiser for Mighty Athletic Stars Foundation the night before. A witness at the Green Light Bar said Tim appeared flushed; beads of sweat were easily visible. Additionally, he was breathing heavily. It was no surprise that he collapsed. Probably dehydrated or exhausted. Mr. Drady was taken to Huntington Hospital where he is said to be in stable condition but will remain in the hospital for further tests. No further information has been provided regarding why he collapsed or what tests are being run."

In stable condition but will remain in hospital for further tests? That doesn't sound like an innocent case of dehydration or exhaustion, thought Hope. *What are the odds that a name from Matthew's list ends up in the hospital? He might have ended up like Matthew. That's some coincidence.* Hope was starting to think there was more than a coincidence here.

Marc cried out looking for his mom.

Hope squatted down from the couch and sat next to Marc. She pulled over her diaper bag and dug her hand in, searching for the bag of Cheerios she knew was in there. A smile ran across her face as she pulled out the Ziploc bag.

"The Sesame number of the day is seventeen!"

"Today's number is seventeen," she announced in her best Count voice. "Let's count seventeen Cheerios. Yah yah yah!" Hope pulled out a Cheerio from the bag. "One Cheerio, two Cheerios...yah, yah, yah. She placed each Cheerio into Marc's cupped hand. He imitated Hope the best he could as he put the Cheerios into his mouth. "Sixteen Cheerios, and seventeen Cheerios... yah, yah, yah!" Marc giggled as he took the last Cheerio and tossed it over toward Hope's mouth. Unfortunately, he missed and it rolled under the couch. "You silly boy. I'm not hungry." Hope bent down to find the lone Cheerio. "Nathan wouldn't be happy if we left food under his couch."

Feeling her way under the couch, Hope felt a bunch of papers and dust bunnies. She pulled everything out, figuring the Cheerio was stuck somewhere in between. Looking through the papers, she found what looked like an old photo. She smiled thinking it was an old photo of Nathan, but her smile disappeared when she brought the photo into focus. Nathan wasn't even in the photo. It was a young Matthew Russo lying in what appeared to be a hospital bed. Next to him was a young girl Hope assumed was Aliza.

What was Nathan doing with a photo of a young Matthew in the hospital? thought Hope. Then she realized it was probably from the scrapbook Nathan told her about.

She brought the photo closer. Matthew and Aliza weren't the only ones in the photo. Three men adorning white coats stood on the opposite side of the bed. *They must be Matthew's doctors,* thought Hope. She intently stared at the younger doctor. She couldn't believe her eyes…she recognized him.

A chill ran up her spine at the same time the doorbell rang.

"Nathan!" Hope called out as she rushed to the front door.

CHAPTER 70

SURPRISE!

Hope opened the door and did a double take upon hearing the word "Surprise" shouted out at her.

"Mom! Dad! I forgot you were coming today." Hope couldn't believe her eyes. "How did you know I was here?"

"When we stopped by your house, you weren't there so we figured you were either on a walk or at Nathan's." Her mom looked around. "Where is Nathan?"

"That's the million-dollar question. No one knows. He's disappeared. I haven't heard from him since yesterday. He should have been here this morning preparing for Matthew's funeral."

"That is odd. Have you tried his cell phone?"

"Of course." Hope rolled her eyes. Leave it to her mother to state the obvious. "It's not with him; he left it here. Detective Callahan thinks Nathan forgot he was picking him up to take him to Matthew's funeral and went himself."

"That sounds reasonable. Who is Detective Callahan?"

"He's a friend of Nathan's. A former athlete Nathan trained years ago. He was supposed to drive Nathan to the funeral but Nathan wasn't here."

Hope's mother went to sit down in Nathan's favorite chair when she spotted the photograph on the coffee table. Lifting it up to get a good look at it, she said, "Jay looks so young here. Still very handsome. When was this taken?"

Hope's mouth dropped. It wasn't her creative imagination running wild—it really was Jay in the picture. A picture with Matthew in a hospital bed. Once again, Jay had not been forthcoming with her about his relationship with Matthew. *Why?* she wondered.

"Yes, he does look so handsome in that white coat. I'm not sure when it was taken. If I had to guess, it must have been when Jay was an intern or completing his residency." Hope motioned over to her mom and took the photo. "You know, mom…" placing the photo in her pocket, "I think it is time for me to have a talk with my husband. Would you mind if I left you for a bit and went to the hospital to talk to Jay?"

Hope's mother looked concerned. She knew her daughter and could tell something was truly upsetting her. "Of course, you can. I'm sure Marc will keep your father and me plenty occupied while you're gone."

With that, they all returned back to Hope's house where she gave her mother last-minute Marc instructions. She grabbed her cellphone wallet and keys out of Marc's diaper bag and off she went.

What are you up to, Dr. Klein?

CHAPTER 71

EMERGENCY ROOM SEVEN

Hope took a deep breath as she entered the hospital. There was so much she hated about hospitals—the smell, the blood, the worried families, the gowned patients. Walking through the lobby she followed the signs to the ICU. Jay would be just about finishing up with the patients he needed to follow up with.

Pressing the buzzer to gain admittance into the ICU, Hope watched as the doors magically opened. She approached the desk and informed them who she was. The nurse smiled and pointed to room number seven. The curtain to the room was pulled closed, which meant that the doctor must be doing something with the patient. Suddenly the curtain was pulled away, and two men sporting white medical coats came out. One was Jay. Hope couldn't believe who the other person was with him. *That doesn't even make sense,* thought Hope. *Or does it?* she countered to herself as she grasped into her pocket, taking out the photo she found at Nathan's. The man that was walking out of the room with Jay was also in the photo.

Just as the two men exited room seven, a heart-wrenching sound burst from room six. A flushed nurse ran out from that room calling a code red. The two men rushed into the room. The buzzing sounds jolted Hope, another aspect she hated about hospitals—the chaos.

"Should I leave?" Hope asked the nurse, who had the phone to her ear.

The nurse put her hand over the receiver. "No, don't be silly. The ICU is never dull." She smiled and instructed Hope to wait by the chair just beside the room.

Hope thanked her and proceeded over to the room. She kept her eyes forward, doing her best not to look into any of the other rooms.

As she went to take a seat next to room seven, another curious bit of information surfaced on Hope's radar. The name of the patient posted on the dry board outside the door. *Could it possibly be? What are the odds?*

Tim Drady. The football player she just read about in the paper at Nathan's house, the player whose name appeared on Matthew's list.

Hope's instinct overtook her, and she went into room seven.

CHAPTER 72

THOSE ARE SERIOUS NEEDLES

Fortunately for Hope, there was no one else in the room besides a sleeping patient lying in a prone position. It appeared that Tim Drady was sedated for some sort of procedure that could be done right here in the ER room. Hope looked at the medical table beside the bed; there were two huge syringe needles.

Those are serious needles, thought Hope just as she heard the nurse approaching the room. Quickly she hid behind the bathroom door.

"Okay, Mr. Drady, it is time to get you cleaned up so the doctors can do their thing."

Tim's eyes opened; he was half awake and groggy. He gave the nurse a slight smile and a nod, letting her know he understood.

The nurse removed the sheet off Tim's lower back area and began to apply disinfectant.

Hope peeked out and watched. She was having difficulty seeing exactly what the nurse was doing, so she stood on top of the covered toilet seat, which provided a perfect aerial view.

Hope realized that the nurse was preparing Tim for a

procedure; however, when she focused in on the area she was prepping, Hope noticed there were already markings. Scars actually. They were in some sort of pattern. *Almost like a football play pattern,* she thought. *Not unlike the scar markings Matthew turned into the Statue of Liberty play tattoo on his back...in the same location.* There were fewer markings, but what are the odds to have any such markings on one's back and in the same location? This was another connection the two players shared. Too much of a coincidence to ignore.

Hope's concentration was interrupted when Jay entered along with Dr. Conrad. Hope could not make heads or tails as to why he would be at the hospital. He didn't practice medicine anymore. This was highly suspect, especially since he was also in the photo she found at Nathan's.

Hope observed as Jay put on the latex gloves that were lying beside the needles. "Tim, I'm going to begin with the aspiration now. I will insert a needle and remove a small liquid amount of bone marrow. You will feel some pressure and a tugging sensation going down your leg. I will then insert a second needle into the same place to expunge a small core of your marrow."

Tim nodded.

Meanwhile, Dr. Conrad appeared to be focusing on the markings as he whispered something into Jay's ear. Hope couldn't make out what he whispered, but she did know exactly what procedure Jay was conducting on Tim.

He's testing for leukemia. This is precisely the procedure they conducted on my dad.

Jay removed his gloves and set the syringes on the table. "Get these down to the lab ASAP."

Hope was impressed by Jay's skill. He got it on the first attempt. Her father's doctor needed to make three insertions before he got it right. Just as that thought entered her mind, a light bulb went off.

The markings on Tim's back are insertion scars! Was he tested earlier in his life for leukemia? Hope shook her head; that seemed unlikely. What other reason could there be for such markings? And why did Matthew have similar markings? Why were Jay and Dr. Conrad involved with Tim Drady's medical concerns? Were Tim and Matthew somehow connected, and if so, were Jay and Dr. Conrad a part of that connection?

So many unanswered questions!

CHAPTER 73

SIMILAR MARKINGS
ON THEIR BACK

Hope took a deep sigh as she entered her car, relieved that she got out of room seven unnoticed. Her mind was in overdrive— so much information to digest. *Tim was being treated by Jay. Jay treated Matthew. Both have similar markings on their back. This has Dr. Conrad all over it. I bet he is involved in this, and somehow, he got Matthew involved! That man is a reckless rule breaker. He thinks he's God.*

Hope jumped out of her seat upon hearing the ringing of her phone. "Hello?"

"Hey, Hope, it's Jake."

Hope didn't give him a chance to continue. "Did you find Nathan? Is he okay?"

Jake let out a sigh. "No, there's no trace of him at the funeral or anywhere else. I put out an alert for him and his car, but nothing's turned up."

"Did you check the area hospitals?"

"Yes, thankfully he isn't there." Jake paused. "Give me a minute, Hope. I'm receiving a text, maybe it's about Nathan, let me check...Hope, are you still there?"

"Yes!"

"The text wasn't about Nathan. It was the medical examiner getting back to me with a more detailed autopsy. It appears that Matthew's spleen was enlarged indicating leukemia."

Hope couldn't believe her ears. "Matthew had leukemia?"

"From the way the report reads, he would need to undergo chemotherapy. He had a long, difficult trying road ahead of him. Perhaps his drowning was a suicide?"

Another coincidence! she thought. Hope's mind raced. *Matthew had leukemia and Tim is currently being tested for leukemia. Jay treated Matthew when he was younger. Now he is somehow treating Tim. Why was Jay even involved with Tim Drady's medical issues? He has nothing to do with the Colonist players.*

Hearing no response, Jake raised his voice. "Hope, Hope… did I lose you?"

"No, no I'm here. Just concerned that we haven't heard from Nathan yet. I'm worried something's happened to him."

There was a pause. "I'm starting to think the same. I believe we would have found his car by now whether it was involved in an accident or went over any toll bridges. All that's left is someone has him and has hidden his car. But why would someone take him?"

Hope wondered that, too. Her thoughts brought her back to Nathan's voice message—*There was foul play here. In more ways than one.* Then Nathan's voice grew lower—*When will there cease to be evil in the world? It runs in their blood.*

"I believe Nathan discovered something that put him in danger. The last voicemail he left me said there was foul play, in more ways than one. He then whispered to himself thinking he was done with the voice message."

"What did he whisper?"

"When will there cease to be evil in the world? It runs in their blood."

"What did he mean?"

"I'm not quite sure. However," Hope paused and picked up the photo. "I think I'm on to something."

"What's that?"

"I need to speak with someone first. Make sure what I'm proposing is possible. Perhaps I have read one too many mystery thrillers and what I'm thinking is ridiculous. I'd rather save myself the embarrassment."

After a few failed attempts, Jake finally gave in. "Well, keep me posted. I'll be at the precinct working on my next move."

Hope went into her contacts, selected the name she was looking for and dialed, "I need to pick your medical brain again. Can you spare a few minutes? Great! You're where? I'm not far from there. I can be there in ten."

CHAPTER 74

MORE THAN A COINCIDENCE

Once again, Hope found herself at Maltz Mansion. On her way to the library, she peeked into the bar, and the television screen headline caught her attention—"Shaun Smith Donates To Suicide Awareness Charity in Honor Of Matthew Russo." Hope moved closer to the television and asked the bartender to turn up the volume, but he didn't hear her. Thankfully the gentleman drinking at the bar who was obviously a regular noticed and called out, "Hey, Michelini! Turn it up."

"As many fans recall, Matthew and Shaun had a scuffle the last time they played. Today, Shaun Smith announced he will auction off that very shirt that was torn. All the proceeds of the sale will be donated to a suicide awareness charity," informed the commentator.

Hope recalled that game very well; she was there after all! She remembered the expression on Matthew's face as he watched Shaun walk off the field. Hope's eyebrow raised. *Did Shaun Smith have a scar too? Is that what Matthew spotted that day? Is that why he added Shaun's name to the list. Maybe that's what started the chart?* Hope gasped, *I know I'm not the only one! Matthew discovered he wasn't the only athlete to have something done to him!*

Hope attempted to piece it together. *When Matthew saw the scar, it triggered him. He recognized that whatever was done to him was also done to Shaun. Matthew said he got that scar when he was in high school, a young aspiring football player. When Shaun was younger, he went to Mighty Stars Athletic camp...a camp Joey regularly went to watch young aspiring football players. Somehow the scar and the camp were connected.*

Hope thought back on Nathan's voice message. *It runs in their blood.* Hope pondered. *Dr. Conrad! Somehow Harry figured a way to do something to their blood to create a super athlete.* She would not put it past him to cross the line from experiments on animals to humans. *Joey found the perfect subjects from the camp, promising them an NFL career in exchange for throwing a few games. He didn't have to blackmail them, they owed him. They felt beholden to him.*

How or what was exactly done, she didn't know. She hoped Elliot would be able to figure that out. Leaving the Green Light Bar, Hope followed the hallway toward the library. Entering the regal room, she found Elliot on the phone.

"I'll be fine. She's here now, I have to go." Elliot disclosed into his cell phone, "I'll meet up with you right after."

Elliot walked over to the bar and poured some twenty-three-year-old Kentucky straight bourbon whiskey. "From the way your voice sounded over the phone earlier, I expect you can use this."

CHAPTER 75

THIS SOUNDS LIKE
SCIENCE FICTION

Hope accepted the drink. "Maybe this will help put my nerves in check. It's been quite a day."

"When you called you said you wanted to pick my medical brain. Is everything okay with your dad?"

"It's funny you should mention my dad. I think what has happened to him has led me down a path that I would not have known existed."

"I'm not quite sure what you're talking about."

"I think Jay has gotten caught up in something unethical and illegal." She hesitated. "I believe that it all stems from Harry Conrad, that sanctimonious man, along with your friend Joey."

Elliot's eyes squinted "How could you believe Jay would be involved in anything sordid? I know you've been unhappy with his friendship with Joey, but I highly doubt they are involved in anything close to being illegal or unethical. Let me make you another drink, then I'll set you up in a room here at Maltz and you can get some rest and clear your mind."

"No, I don't need a drink or some rest, what I need is information. Maybe my mind has gone over the top with imagination? That's why I came to you. I believe that Harry Conrad discovered a way to do something medically inside an athlete's body to create a super athlete. He neglected all ethical guidelines and restrictions and implemented this discovery on actual human subjects. Joey found the perfect young willing athletes, ones who would jump at the chance to become incredible enough to become an NFL player. All they had to do in exchange was to throw a game from time to time. Joey gets to place bets he is certain to win and reaps a financial windfall. Dr. Conrad gets to use his medical scientific abilities to play God."

Elliot took a deep breath. "Do you hear yourself? What you are saying sounds like something out of Shelley's *Frankenstein* novel. Do you have any proof?"

"Nathan and I found a chart in Matthew's house the day after he drowned. Matthew must have discovered something was going on. The chart contained a list of players including Matthew's going down one side of the chart and a list of numbered game weeks running across the top side. The chart was filled with football symbols that were colored green or red. The red ones had slashes running through them. This chart left us with lots of questions. Why was Matthew tracking these specific players? What did the green and red football symbols mean? And why were there slashes through only the red footballs? It took me a while, but I think I figured it out. There had to be a connection linking all players together. That connection was the Mighty Athletic Stars Summer Football Training Camp. All the players attended this summer camp during their high school years. I believe it was at this very camp that Joey found the perfect subjects for Dr. Conrad's procedure to create his *super athlete*. Most athletes who participated in the camp came from low socioeconomic backgrounds with the father out of the picture. They were willing to do anything to provide for themselves and their families. I remember Matthew's mom telling me at the ball how lucky she was that Matthew rescued them."

Elliot concentrated on what she was saying.

"Next I needed to figure out the football symbols. That wasn't as easy to solve. I believe the red colored footballs represented games in which the player made minor errors in a game that would not necessarily alter who won the game but *would* affect the outcome for the spread. Matthew was watching these particular players and discovered that the fix was in!"

Elliot appeared frustrated. "What are you talking about?"

"Let me be more specific. The chart had the players' names running down vertically and the game week numbered from one to seventeen running horizontally. Boxes corresponded to a specific week and the player. These boxes had either a green or red football in it. Matthew's focus was on the red colored footballs, which he had put different numbers of slashes through. At first, I thought the red footballs meant losses, figuring the player Matthew was watching threw the game. But that wasn't the case; some of these games the teams won. Then I heard Joey being interviewed by Lauren Kelly. They were talking about players' errors. She suggested that a player's loss was Joey's gain. That got me thinking, what if the players Matthew was tracking made errors that didn't lose the game for their team but helped them not obtain the points that would allow them to cover the spread. Making an error that lost the game was too obvious, but having some minor errors here and there like a ball fumbled, a running back not blocked, or an incomplete pass didn't necessarily lose the game but affected the spread. Matthew made a notation of this error by placing a slash across the red football symbol in the box that coordinated with the game played and the player's name. The number of slashes equaled the number of errors. Your friend Joey knows about spreads. I remember finding out at the Titans–Colonists game how he still won the bet he placed because his team covered the spread even though they lost the game. He and Dr. Conrad came up with the perfect play. No one's suspicions would ever arise by an error here or there when it didn't necessarily keep the team from winning. It's a master plan."

"That is some elaborate theory." Elliot joined his opposing fingers together forming a pyramid shape. "And how does Jay fit into all of this?"

Hope grasped the picture out of her pocket. "I found this photo." She handed it over to Elliot.

Elliot looked at the photo. "What am I looking at?"

Hope leaned in closer and pointed her finger out at the photo. "This is a young high school age Matthew Russo in a hospital bed surrounded by what I assume are his doctors and girlfriend. Do you recognize this man?"

"Is that Dr. Conrad?"

"Yes, and standing next to him is Jay." Hope shook her head. "Why is Dr. Conrad, a researcher, in a hospital room with Matthew Russo and my husband?"

"There could be many reasons. One that comes to mind is that back then Dr. Conrad was also an advisor for the medical school. Perhaps he followed up on patients his students treated."

"Perhaps. However, I don't think it is a coincidence that these three are in the room because of advising. It has come to my attention that Matthew Russo and Tim Drady, and likely Shaun Smith, all have the exact same scar on their backs in the exact same location. That is more than a coincidence, it means something. It reminded me of my father's disease, Polycythemia Vera. Remember, they thought he had leukemia and needed to do a bone marrow biopsy? He was left with a similar scar. I think Dr. Conrad did something involving their bone marrow enabling them to enhance their athletic abilities. I'm not exactly sure how he did it. I'm not a doctor, but you are! Am I insane? Have I read one too many thriller paperbacks? Can what I am proposing be done?"

Elliot placed two fingers up to his lips. "I think anything is possible." He paused. "Scientific technology used in the human body has grown in leaps and bounds ever since scientists have mapped out the human genome. Scientific advancements arise from the basic premise of helping to cure human diseases. Altering DNA is one way researchers are working to find cures. Researchers have come up with the ability to cut and edit a gene. This ability to modify genes has opened up the floodgates of possibilities." Elliot paused and lifted a drink to his lips. "Except, of course, in Morgan's case."

"What do you mean?"

"I mean, imagine my pleasure when I found out about technology's latest amazing accomplishment, the ability to cut and edit a mutated gene with what they call molecular scissors, only to find out that the Huntington gene is far too long to use such scissors. We held many tests in the lab attempting to edit the mutated Huntington gene to no avail. The technology to cut and alter genes was there for shorter genes like the ones that control the production of red blood cells, for example, but we could never reach the target area involved in the Huntington gene. You could understand how that realization brought me to my lowest point. To be so close yet so far." He lifted up the photograph and laughed. "I took to eating my frustrations away." Elliot threw the photo back onto the coffee table.

A chill ran up the back of Hope's neck as she lifted up the photo from the coffee table. She stared intently at the unidentified man. *I took to eating my frustrations away.*

CHAPTER 76

I RARELY TOOK PICTURES
BACK THEN

I very rarely took pictures back then. I hated the way I looked.

"It was you!? You're the third doctor in the photo. You created the super athlete?"

"It's not what it seems. I'm not some doctor with a God complex. I was in a dark place back then. I remember Joey and I were in a bar and we were both drinking. I was drinking away my disappointment with being unable to use the molecular scissors, and Joey had just lost everything on Wall Street. Hopelessness ran through our veins. The lab was low on funding. We were drunk; we hit rock bottom. We came up with the idea of obtaining large amounts of money to continue the research by altering a gene that could enhance an athlete's abilities and then placing bets on games we knew we'd win. We laughed it off when we sobered up, and then it sort of fell into our laps. There was the car accident involving a promising young athlete."

"Matthew?"

"Yes, it was a sign. It all happened so quickly. We never

meant for anyone to get hurt. We figured it was a win-win. Matthew was given the incredible endurance to enhance his already athletic skills. And I would have the funds to continue my research."

"A win-win? I don't think Matthew feels that way."

There was a knock on the library door. Elliot walked over and slightly opened the door. Mini squeezed through the small opening before Elliot had a chance to completely open it.

"Morgan, is everything okay? Why are you so dressed up?"

Mini ran over to the couch and jumped up beside Hope. To her pleasure, Mini dropped the toy she was carrying in her mouth onto the couch and gave her lots and lots of kisses. "You're such a good girl. I love you, too."

"Why aren't you dressed? We're going to be late for the New York University gala." Morgan shook her head. "I tried calling but you didn't pick up." As she entered the library, she said, "Oh Hope, I didn't see you over there."

Hope stood up and gave Morgan a hug. "I just needed to tap into that medical brain of your husband's. I think I got my answers." Hope proceeded over to the door where she was held up by Elliot.

"I believe I have more to add. Please stay." Elliot guided Hope back to the couch. Without Hope seeing, Elliot picked up her cellphone wallet off the end table and slid it into his pants pocket. As Hope went to sit down, she sat on a toy that Mini left behind. Retrieving a leather chain from under her, Hope gasped "Wait a minute, I've seen this chain before... this isn't a doggie toy." Hope hid the leather chain with three charms dangling from it in her left hand. "Sorry, Mini, this doesn't belong to you."

Elliot redirected his attention back to Morgan. "Honey, the gala is next week."

Morgan's face turned ashen. "I mixed up the dates again?! My memory isn't what it used to be."

Elliot could see the concern on Morgan's face. Her symptoms were worsening. "I guess you'll have to start using an organizer like the rest of us. You do look so beautiful. Let's go out. Let me escort you to the Green Light Bar and you can wait there until I finish up with Hope." He grabbed hold of her hand and guided her and Mini through the library doors as he closed them shut behind them, locking Hope inside.

CHAPTER 77

OPEN SESAME

Hope felt an awful pang inside her stomach upon hearing the door lock. Walking over to the library doors, she hoped they unlocked from the inside. No such luck. Hope quickly went over to the sitting area searching for her cellphone wallet. *Where is it?* Hope looked all around. No phone. *Why didn't I keep it in my pocket with my keys? He must have taken it!* Pacing back and forth, Hope surveyed the room. All of the windows were picture windows that couldn't be opened. Hope's options were running out. Then it came to her—she remembered the secret door Elliot used the day of the ball. Hope felt a rush of nerves shutter across her face causing her to feel faint.

Think, Hope, think how he accessed it.

Hope rushed over to the bookshelf. A book, the book is the key. But which book? Hope's mind went blank. Her hands were very moist and clammy as she aimlessly pulled on every book she could get her hands on.

Think, Hope! There are too many books to pull, and Elliot will be back soon.

Soon was an understatement. In the distance, Hope heard footsteps approaching. She continued to pull the books but nothing happened. Finally, it came to her—*The Great Gatsby*! Hope's eyes searched the stacks. There it was. Of course, it was on the top shelf. Pushing over a chair, Hope pulled the spine—open sesame! The panel next to the fireplace slid open. Hope rushed in. Just in the nick of time.

Hope entered the darkened wine cellar. The last time she was inside the lights were on. Hope stumbled along the wall searching for the light switch. Feeling a singular switch, Hope flipped it up. A row of lights flickered on over in the red wine section of the cellar.

That's it? There has to be another switch that lights up the rest of the cellar!

Hope glanced around.

Hope frantically searched her mind trying to remember the cellar layout.

Were there any doors?

She didn't recall seeing any doors, except the one she just entered from. A door she knew Elliot would be entering through any minute. She needed to do something fast.

Hide, she thought. *I have to hide.*

Hope went over to the reds section seeking a place to hide. That is when she remembered the window!

There's a window over by the nook area, just past the reds!

Motioning out of the light into the darkness, Hope stumbled deeper into the cellar. Thanks to the partial light shining in from the window, she found the nook.

Jumping up onto the cushioned bench, Hope made her way over to the window. She pushed up on the single hung window, but it wouldn't budge. To make matters worse, Hope heard a noise.

The creaking sound of the cellar door opening.

It's Elliot!

Using all her strength, she pushed up on the window. Happily, she felt some movement. But to her dismay she couldn't get the window to fully open. Looking at the opening, Hope wasn't so sure she would be able squeeze through.

Upon hearing footsteps enter the cellar, Hope decided not to try.

I have to hide!

Looking down at the bench she smiled.

She found the perfect hiding space.

CHAPTER 78

HOPE, YOU CLEVER GIRL

Elliot unlocked the library door and entered.

"You see how this disease has attacked my poor wife's cognitive abilities," Elliot announced as he re-entered the library before noticing Hope had disappeared. His eyes combed the entire library until they stopped at the chair in front of the bookshelf.

His lips widened. "Hope, you clever girl. I forgot that you knew about the secret door." Elliot pushed the chair out of his way. He pulled the spine that read *The Great Gatsby* and moved through the opening.

As Elliot moved deeper into the wine cellar, he called out, "There's no reason to run from me. I just want to talk." Elliot's eyes canvased the area with the Cabernets. No sign of Hope.

Hope remained still, motionless as her eyes were fixated on the photo she held in her right hand. *You think you know a person*, thought Hope, struggling to make sense of everything that just unfolded. She shook her head. *How did I not see it?*

I trusted you. Quietly, she put the photo in her back pocket. *How did it get this far?*

Elliot continued onto the Merlot aisle, then the Pinots. Still no sign of Hope—however, there was an open window.

The hairs on the back of Hope's neck raised; her body tingled when she heard footsteps approaching. *He found me!*

Elliot jumped onto the bench, then climbed on top of the cushions over to the open window.

Hearing a thump on top of the bench, Hope feared she'd been caught.

She heard him shout out the open window, "You can run Hope, but you won't get far."

"Did you find her?" asked an annoyed voice entering the wine cellar from the other side of the cellar. "I knew I should have stayed with you when you talked with her."

Slamming the window shut, Elliot said, "Looks like she snuck out the window."

"How much does she know?" asked the angry voice taking a seat at the table.

"She knows everything."

"Then shouldn't we be going after her? We can't let her go to the police."

"She won't get far."

"How can you be so sure?"

Elliot's upper lip rose with pride. "I spiked her drink with ketamine. It should be kicking in about now."

Hope's brow-line creased and her eyes bulged out. *I've been drugged?* Hope did her best to control her movements. The slightest bang of a bottle would reveal her location.

"This is a big mess. We better go find her. I'll start at the back end of the mansion. We can put her in with our other unwelcomed guest."

An enraged Elliot shook his head. "That makes two unwelcomed guests I have to contend with thanks to you."

The pair got up and separately exited the way they entered.

Hope gasped, then forced herself to settle down. She glanced over at her left hand, which was still holding the black leather necklace with three charms dangling. *They took you. I knew you would never have left without telling me.*

CHAPTER 79

GIVE ME A CHANCE

Elliot returned back to the library, and headed right to the bar. He grabbed the whiskey bottle and did something he hadn't done since he was in college—put his lips to the bottle and drank. *I can't believe how out of control this has gotten.* Elliot put the bottle down and headed out to look for Hope when Joey entered.

"Elliot, what's going on?" Joey got up in Elliot's face. "I just left the bar, and Morgan's really upset. She's worried that Hope's father took a turn for the worse."

Elliot sighed, "Isn't that just like Morgan? Always concerned about others, regardless of what is going on with her."

Joey's brow raised as he stared at Elliot's body language. *Was he shaking?* "What's really going on here? You seem shook. I don't think you'd react this way to news that Hope's dad has taken a turn for the worse."

"Hope Klein has figured out what we've been doing," Elliot blankly stated.

"She what?! How?"

"She's smarter than you think. She saw that interview you did! She just paid me a visit thinking *you* got her husband involved in something illegal and immoral. She portrayed you as a monster. I couldn't allow her to continue. What you and I have been doing couldn't have been further from that. We were searching for a cure to a *monstrous* disease. We needed the funds to do so. We had no choice."

Joey poured himself a shot of whiskey and swallowed it down. "Where is she now?"

"She's somewhere on the mansion grounds. I was just going to search for her. If I could just speak with her, I know I can convince her not to turn us in. She couldn't have gotten far."

Joey paced the library floor. "It's time we face the facts. What we did *was* against the law. I don't think there's any convincing her. I knew this would happen one day. No one ever gets away with it. At the very least we need to tell Morgan before she finds out when the cops come to arrest us."

Elliot barked, "I'm not willing to concede yet. Everything we worked so hard for will be for nothing. If I can't convince her, then we are sealing Morgan's tragic fate."

Elliot's phone rang. "Hello? I'll be right down." He began walking toward the exit doors. "Hope is downstairs. I've got to go. Please give me a chance to fix things before you go running to Morgan."

Joey closed his eyes for a moment. "Fine, you have one shot." He followed Elliot to the library doors and called out as Elliot rushed out into the hallway, "You have one hour, then I go to Morgan."

Elliot raced out of the library at record speed, not noticing the gentleman walking toward the library doors.

Joey, on the other hand, did. He whispered under his breath, "What's he doing here? I don't have time for him today." He put on his best happy-to-see-you voice. "Jay, what brings you here?"

CHAPTER 80

EVERYTHING WENT BLACK

Hearing the door shut, Hope waited a few moments before leaving the security of the bench. She felt a bit woozy. Was the ketamine kicking in? How much time did she have before she blacked out?

Hope wasn't sure how many people would be out looking for her. She had to figure a way of getting out of the mansion undetected and before she succumbed to the drugs. Her mind was already starting to become dazed and confused. Realizing that the second pursuer's voice entered from the other side of the wine cellar, Hope deduced there must be another way out. She remembered that the mansion has hidden passageways the servants used to get around unnoticed. There must be a door that the servants used to gain access to the cellar. This pathway would be the perfect way out of the mansion. If only she knew where it was.

Hope went deeper into the wine cellar seeking any sign of a door. Passing the Pinot Noirs, she saw nothing. Moving on, she rushed up and down the Zinfandel aisles, still no door. Finally, Hope smiled as she got to the Chardonnays. At the very end of the aisle was a narrow wooden door.

Once through, she descended down a stairway. Arriving at the bottom, she adjusted her eyes to the darkness. Her vision was starting to blur. Time was running out. She proceeded through the long narrow hallway that stretched roughly twenty yards, then turning out of sight toward the left.

Hope raced as fast as she could, trying her best to keep her balance, which was becoming more difficult with each step. Hope's stomach turned; she heard something. Was there someone trailing behind her? She wasn't going to wait to find out.

Hope kept moving forward. She was certain that this pathway led to a way out. *I must be close.* A few feet away she saw a beam of light. A light at the end of the tunnel! Unfortunately, she could not go any further. A woozy Hope collapsed mid-step.

Then everything went black.

CHAPTER 81

HOW'S THAT POSSIBLE?

Jay stormed in neglecting all social protocols and niceties and got up in Joey's face. "Tell me where Hope is."

Joey's face showed surprise. "Why would I know where she is?"

Without waiting to be invited in, Jay moved farther into the library and looked around. "Where is she? You can drop the charade. I know more than you think."

"What do you think you know?"

"I know Elliot played mad scientist with Matthew Russo's DNA."

"I think you're the one who is mad."

"Numbers don't lie," Jay declared. "Both Matthew Russo and Tim Drady had red blood cell counts through the roof! Two NFL players close in age having such incredibly high numbers is not a coincidence. That doesn't just happen."

First Hope figured out what we were doing and now Jay. "We never meant to hurt anyone." Joey fell back onto the couch in defeat. "Do you know how much money goes into the kind of research needed to find a cure for a disease? And this isn't cancer we're talking about. Only a small amount of people have Huntington's disease. No one is donating to us huge amounts of money. We had no choice. It seemed harmless at the time, even a win-win." Joey poured himself a double. "Elliot engineered super athletes in exchange for them fixing a game from time to time. We took athletes from underprivileged communities and gave them the boost they needed to make it to the pros. All they had to do was fix a game once in a while for me to bet on. Everyone benefited."

"So, this was just a way for you to make money for yourself?"

"Aren't you listening to what I am telling you?! It wasn't for me; it was for Morgan."

"How exactly did Elliot decide that altering an innocent person's DNA would help?"

"When Elliot heard about the discovery of molecular scissors, he was certain that it was the exact tool he needed to alter the Huntington gene; however, he quickly discovered that the Huntington gene was too long to properly cut and alter. He just couldn't wrap his mind around the idea that he could alter a short gene like the one that controls athletic endurance ability but not the Huntington gene."

"So he mutated the gene responsible for the production of red blood cells enabling skilled athletes to have super endurance? He must have suspected that there would be side effects to such a procedure. I guess you both overlooked that pesky problem."

"There haven't been any side effects," Joey stated naively.

"Matthew Russo would disagree. He had leukemia. Elliot had to know that when he altered a player's body's production of red blood cells, he put them at a high risk."

"How did you find out Matthew had leukemia? You weren't his doctor."

"Matthew approached me at one of the games. He remembered me from my resident days. I had no idea I ever met him before. He said I saved his life when he was in high school. At first, I thought he was pulling my leg. Then he informed me that he was the patient I saved when I was a resident. His last name was different back then. He changed it to his mother's maiden name after he turned pro. He said he hadn't been feeling right and wanted my help. I thought it unusual but was happy to help. I ran tests and found an extremely high red blood cell count." Jay rubbed his chin, then paused for a moment. "That led me to do a bone marrow biopsy. When I told him he had leukemia, he said something strange. He said he knew karma would come back to bite him one day and that he must tell the others. At the time I figured he meant telling his family and friends, but from what I heard today I wonder if what I told him led to him being killed."

"You're wrong—we had nothing to do with his death. He drowned."

"I thought so, too, but I'm beginning to think Nathan and my wife were right. Something about Matthew's drowning isn't kosher. And if that's the case I think she's in danger. I think Matthew was silenced before he could tell the other players about what was going on. Please Joey, if you think Elliot has lost control, who knows what he could do to Hope. If he does have her, where would he take her?"

Joey put his right hand over his forehead. "I think I might have an idea. Follow me."

CHAPTER 82

TRAPPED!

Hope could feel the panic kick in as she awoke in unfamiliar surroundings. She felt her way in sheer darkness, pressing against the walls until she stumbled upon what felt like a steel door. She began banging on the door. Her face was drenched, flushed beet red. "Help, help! Can anyone hear me? Is anyone out t -h -e -r -e?" All of a sudden, a hand covered Hope's mouth.

"Shush, shush. They must be out there, that's why they turned the power off. They want us to panic and reveal ourselves. They are searching. They will hear you. We must be quiet," uttered a man's voice in a childish tone.

Hope's eyes froze, fixated upon a frightened old man. "Nathan, it's me Hope. Thank God you're alright! I knew they were holding you somewhere here inside the mansion; I never imagined it would be in such a confined dark place. We need to find a way out of here. We're running out of oxygen." Hope continued to yell out for help, until she felt Nathan's hand cover her mouth again.

"There is hope if you stop yelling. We must be quiet. Nazi soldiers are listening for us."

Hope struggled both physically and mentally when a revelation overcame her. *He thinks he is back in hiding. He fears the Nazis will hear us. I need to get Nathan to come back to his present situation.*

Hope stopped her screaming. Nathan settled down.

Hope reached out desperately. "Nathan, we are not in hiding. We are locked in a vault with the vents closed off. We are losing oxygen. I need you to help us get out of here."

Nathan shook his head. "I know you are scared, but we must be quiet. We can't leave just yet. We must wait for Lara or Lucas to give us the signal when it's clear to get out."

Hope's breathing was becoming labored. She was feeling faint. Despair was consuming her. She was losing all hope. The vault grew darker than it already was. Her inner light was burning out. Hope collapsed onto the cold floor making a loud thump.

A half-conscious Hope wasn't quite sure if what happened next was real or in her upset mind. Shortly after landing, she could swear she heard a thumping sound right outside the vault door.

CHAPTER 83

KNOCKED OUT

Jay followed Joey through a door that led to the hidden passageways the servants took back in the day. These days they were used by a select group to get to the man cave to play poker.

Jay cautiously followed Joey down a staircase. The stairway was eerily dark and silent. Upon stepping down the final step, Joey switched on the light to discover a body lying on the cement floor.

"Elliot!" He rushed over to an unconscious body. "Wake up, Elliot."

Jay looked around expecting that Hope would be somewhere close by. "Where's Hope?"

"I don't know. Help me lift Elliot up and maybe we will find out!"

Groggy and rubbing the back of his head, Elliot said, "My head. Oh no. Am I too late? I...I need to open the vault immediately. My head!" Elliot's eyes rolled back as he fell back to unconsciousness.

"Vault! There's a vault? Maybe Hope's in that vault. Open it."

"I would if I could. I don't know where it is. I know it's somewhere hidden in this room. Elliot had told me how when

Morgan created this man cave, she found a hidden vault. She didn't tell anyone and used it to be a private space for Elliot. She knew Elliot would love a hidden space for his research."

Jay walked along the walls and pressed, pushed and pulled his fingers along the walls hoping it would magically open.

Joey went over to the wet bar and grabbed a dish towel, put it under running water and brought it back applying it onto the huge bump on Elliot's head. "Who did this to you?"

Elliot stirred his head back and forth, but his eyes remained closed. However, his lips moved and with great difficulty; he uttered three words: "It was H -a -r -r -y."

"Harry? Harry's somehow involved in this?" Jay continued to walk along the perimeter of the room attempting to open a wall. "Wait a minute." Jay walked over to the framed painting of Cassius Marcellus Coolidge's Dogs Playing Poker, known for its anthropomorphized dogs smoking and drinking around a card table. "This frame is hanging too low." He ran his fingers along the frame…nothing. Disappointed, Jay stared at the kitsch artwork. "This has to be it. I can just feel it." Then he saw it. "This dog's eye is not the same as the others. It's dull." Jay placed his finger onto the dog's eye and pushed down, hearing a sound that made him smile—the creaking of a door moving open.

CHAPTER 84

I'M COMING FOR YOU

Not waiting for the door to fully open, Jay thrusted himself inside. It was pitch black. His eyebrow raised, making out what appeared to be two shadowy bodies in a seated position clinging to one another. "Hope, Hope! It's me Jay!" he called out. Deafening silence. Jay grew flush as his worst fears came rushing over him. As he got closer, he placed his hand on one of the body's arms. It was warm. He let out a deep sigh; the two bodies were unconscious, holding each other up. "Hope, please wake up. Please wake up." Looking over at the second body, Jay exhaled. "I see you found Nathan. He needs you." There was a pause. "I need you. Please wake up." Jay put his lips on Hope's forehead and kissed it warmly. Then he moved to her cheek, then her lips.

"My Prince Charming!" Hope coughed and wrapped her arm tightly around Jay's. Then she went in for a full bear hug. "How did you find me?"

Jay reached into Hope's pocket, pulled out her keys and jingled them. "I put a GPS locator on them a few days ago. I wanted to surprise you the next time Marc misplaced them!" Jay and Hope laughed. Hope's laughter turned to coughing.

"Joey, get her some water!"

Hope coughed again. "Check on Nathan." Then she stared back at Jay. *How did I ever think you were involved?*

Jay moved over to Nathan and checked his neck for a pulse. It was weak but there. "We need to get him to the hospital." He flipped open his phone and dialed 911.

Hope's eyes turned to ice as she stared down Joey and called out, "Tell them to have the police come, too." She added, "Tell them to ask for Detective Callahan."

Joey quickly brought Hope water. "You've got me all wrong."

Hope placed the glass up to her lips and gulped down the water. Her eyes widened. "I know what you did. Gambling on games you had fixed. Did Matthew finally decide to rat you out? Is that why you killed him?"

A shaky voice interrupted, "It was Harry." There stood a wobbly Elliot with a river-like blood stain running from his forehead down the side of his face. "Gone mad I tell you. Harry killed Matthew, kidnapped Nathan and locked you inside the vault. I tried to get you out, but Harry knocked me out. Drowning Matthew started a chain reaction that Harry didn't bargain for."

Hope digested this revelation. *So, Dr. Conrad was involved.* Rubbing two fingers over her forehead, she asked, "Where is Harry now?"

"We are not sure. If I were to guess, as far away from here as possible and on the next plane to a non-extradition country out of here." Elliot was fading in and out. He directed his attention to Joey. "Please go to Morgan and explain everything to her before police get here."

Hope pondered and stood up. "The safest and fastest way at this hour would be by train. Didn't I read that there is a way to get to the Cold Spring Harbor train station from here by foot?"

"That's right! That's how the servants got to the mansion. It's not far. You just follow the path across the backyard greens."

A second wind overcame Hope as she quickly moved toward the staircase, passing Joey who was on his way upstairs to talk to Morgan, disregarding Jay's calls for her to wait for the police to arrive.

Hope climbed up two steps at a time until she reached the narrow passageways that would lead her to the cocktail room where she would use the French doors to exit into the backyard lawn.

Looking out the arched Palladian floor to ceiling window, Hope was surprised by what she saw. The picturesque sprawling green lawn had remarkably been transformed into a huge white blanket since she entered the mansion earlier. Hope recalled hearing this morning's weather report predicting snow later in the day. Hope braced herself as she opened the door.

Moving closer to the freshly first laid snow, Hope noticed something that confirmed she was on the right trail. Fresh footprints. These footprints continued in the same direction she was taking to get to the train station.

A chill ran through her body. Looking down at her snow-covered sneakers, not the best foot attire to be wearing, she wondered if it was the weather or the fact that she was heading to confront a killer that brought on the chill. She assumed a bit of both.

Hope's breathing intensified as the train station came into view. Would Harry still be there?

The station consisted of a small area with wooden benches next to the tracks. There was no indoor seating area. Hope looked over at the lined-up benches. They were all empty. She shook her head; she didn't make it in time.

She sat down at the closest bench and slouched in defeat, when she noticed a person leaning against the ticket machine. She quickly got up and approached her captor.

"Never thought you'd see me again?" Hope whispered into her abductor's ear. A chill ran down Hope's back when the figure leaning against the ticket machine turned around. "YOU! You're not Dr. Conrad. Why?"

"Why? Why do you think? I would do anything to protect Elliot and Morgan. He was going to ruin everything."

"Who?" Then it came to her. "Matthew Russo?"

"Yes, I overheard Joey talking with him on the phone. Matthew was clearly upset. I went over to his house that night to talk to him. He was already a bit buzzed. He was irate. I suggested he relax in the hot tub. I tried reasoning with him, but he wouldn't listen. He said that there were other athletes that could be affected and it was his responsibility to notify them. I told him that there was nothing they could do about it. No matter what I said, he wouldn't listen. There was no changing his mind. He was going to ruin everything. His actions were going to hurt the people closest to me. Elliot would be forced to stop his research; Huntington's disease would consume Morgan. I was getting ready to leave when Matthew slipped into a slumber. In that split second something came over me—it was a sign. I took my hand, placed it on top of his head and pushed it completely under the water. I silenced him for good." There was a pause. "And now I realize it's time for you to be silenced." Harry pulled out a knife, grabbed Hope by surprise, and pressed the knife against her neck.

"Harry, please listen to me, you don't have to do this."

"Don't call me Harry. You haven't earned that right."

"You're right, Harriet, but you don't need to do this. We

can speak to the police and explain that what happened wasn't your fault. You weren't in the right state of mind."

She laughed madly. "Do you think the police will accept a temporary insanity plea for Aliza's overdose, too? She stuck her nose where it didn't belong, taking pictures of Matthew all the time. Of course, she would be hiding out in the bushes that night."

Hope recalled Nathan's phone call from Aliza's apartment. *She took lots of pictures...maybe she saw more than she bargained for?* "Nathan thought her death was suspicious. But how did you know she knew what you did? Maybe she wasn't there that night?"

"Oh, she was there. She called me the next day demanding that we meet. She was cryptic. She actually said she had something I needed. I knew exactly what she meant. She never identified herself, but I knew it was her. I went to her apartment to see if I could find the memory card. However, Aliza got back earlier than I expected. One thing led to another, and I pushed her. She hit her head on the coffee table. It all happened so fast. I rushed into the bathroom, and found sleeping pills. I made it look like an overdose. And that's precisely what the police believed it was." Harriet took a deep breath. "Just as they were ruling Matthew's drowning accidental. It would be very difficult to prove otherwise. I would have gotten away with it, too, but you and Nathan had to stick your noses where they didn't belong. You see, there's no way out for me. I have no choice but to silence you."

"I think you do have another option. Turn yourself in. It seems to me that you never intended to kill anyone. You're a victim of circumstance. You are a good person, Harriet, a nurse not a killer. You took an oath to heal people, not hurt them. You have helped so many patients. They love you."

"You're right." A light bulb went off in Harriet's mind. "I *was* a good nurse. What have I become? I can't bear to witness my patients finding out what I've done. No more talking! I'm sorry, Hope, I liked you." Harriet tightened her grip around Hope.

A loud tooting echoed through the station, announcing the imminent arrival of the train.

Harriet moved them closer to the track. The intense roar of the oncoming train drowned out their voices.

Hope screamed, "Don't do this!"

Harriet yelled back, "It's what I have to do."

In the distance, Hope heard police sirens.

Harriet's grip loosened, and Hope seized the opportunity. The thunder of the train erupted as the beaming headlight spotlighted the two women battling.

The train screeching to an unexpected stop was deafening, far worse than nails on a chalkboard. Bewildered passengers got off, curious what caused their train to come to such an abrupt, bumpy halt. Human screams blasted out as the train's passengers witnessed a lifeless female body lying crushed on the train tracks.

Making his way past the horrified passengers over to the train tracks, Jake frantically looked onto the tracks. To his relief he did not recognize the woman hit by the train. He did, however, recognize the woman collapsed on the platform just above the fallen woman.

"Hope, are you okay? I got here as fast as I could."

A hysterical Hope grabbed onto Jake. "I tried to save her. I really tried."

"What happened? I thought you were the one in danger."

"That poor woman was lost. Blinded by her love for Elliot."

"Hope, Hope, Hope! Thank god." Jay called out, as he rushed over to Hope and Jake. "I was so worried. I got here as soon as I knew Nathan was taken care of. His condition has stabilized. They took him to Huntington Hospital."

Jake smiled. "I'll head off there now." Before walking off, Jake gave Hope a final hug. "I'm sure you two have some catching up to do."

Hope embraced Jay. "Thank you for taking care of him. He certainly is a survivor!"

"That he is." Jay pulled back. "What were you thinking going after Harry? He's a killer!"

"It wasn't Harry. It was Harriet!"

"Harriet? What? No way."

"I couldn't believe it myself. She killed Matthew to stop him from revealing what Elliot and Joey were doing. I think her love and need to protect Elliot overtook all commonsense." Hope shook her head. "She hadn't planned on killing Matthew."

"I knew it. My telling Matthew he had leukemia set off a chain reaction that ultimately killed him."

"You can't think that way. You were treating your patient. How were you to know that it was a part of an elaborate money scheme that would lead to two murders."

"Two murders?"

"Aliza didn't overdose. Harriet killed her."

"How do you figure that?"

"Oh, that's right, you don't know. Aliza was stalking Matthew. She hid in the shadows around the community, watching and taking photos of him. She captured Harriet running from Matthew's yard the night he drowned. She was blackmailing Harriet."

"Blackmailing? That's what got her killed. She should have gone to the police with what she knew."

"Yes, she should have. But I guess since Matthew had a restraining order on her, she thought the police would think she had something to do with his death." Hope raised her left eyebrow. "You know she also took photos of us. There was one photo of you and Matthew that Nathan described Matthew as having a concerned, almost fearful look. It was that photo that raised my suspicions that you might be involved in Matthew's death in some way."

"Why would you be suspicious of me?"

"You were becoming distant; you were hardly around. It felt like you were avoiding me."

Jay nodded. "I guess in a way I had been avoiding you. After we attended the Titans game, Matthew reached out to me. He remembered me from my resident days. He asked if I could run some tests on him. I suspected something was up. Why would Matthew need me to run tests on him? There were other doctors in the group I'm sure he used. I knew if you got wind of it, your curiosity would get the better of you."

Hope shook her head. "Now you know why I suspected you. I can always sense when you are hiding something from me."

Jay grabbed hold of Hope's hips, bringing her in toward him. "I promise I won't keep anything from you again." They tightly hugged.

CHAPTER 85

THERE'S SOMETHING
YOU NEED TO KNOW

A sweaty, disheveled Joey entered the Green Light Bar, found Morgan and took a seat beside her.

Morgan's eyes widened. "Joey! What's going on? Are you alright?"

"Do you know how much you mean to me? Since the first day we met at NYU, I knew you would always be a part of my life. There is nothing I wouldn't do for you. You know that, right?"

Morgan sensed Joey's urgent need for an answer, a confirmation. "Yes. I would be lost without you. I know that you are always there for me." Joey's odd behavior made the hairs on the back of Morgan's neck tingle. "What's going on? You're scaring me."

"Elliot and I did something that was risky and idiotic. I'm amazed we've gotten away with it this long; however, the time has come. The police are on their way."

"Police? Where is Elliot? What exactly did you two do?"

Sirens were blaring outside the mansion.

Joey ignored Morgan's questions. "I always knew we would get caught. That is why I implemented a plan B." He hesitated. "I must confess, I opened up the sealed envelope you gave me."

Morgan frowned and closed her eyes. "Why did you do that?"

"I'm glad I did. It guided me toward making preparations for you in the event I'm not around, which seems very likely now."

The police entered the bar.

"What preparations?"

"I wrote you a note. It explains everything. Please read it," Joey called out as he was escorted out by two broad uniformed officers.

CHAPTER 86

HAPPY ENDINGS

Nine months later.

Hope's phone rang and she picked up on the first ring. "I expected your call a half hour ago. What time is it there?"

Morgan glanced over at her watch. "It's almost five o'clock at night. It's six hours ahead here in Amsterdam. I wanted to catch you before the party started, but I'm still at the house. Did your special guest arrive?"

"No, not yet." She looked at the wall clock. "She should be arriving soon. So, you spent all day at the house?"

"Yes." Morgan paused. "I know you had your reservations with Joey, but he set up a magnificent home in the warm picturesque countryside where people like me can go to live out their final stage with dignity—the way they choose."

"That is terrific."

"I met with the doctor who will be running the home. He is very supportive and understanding of the heartbreaking impact this disease inflicts. Joey really did his research. I'm glad Jay was there to help him. Joey made certain that I would be taken care of while helping so many others. I'm not quite ready for this place yet, but knowing it's here makes all the difference."

"Yes, it was smart of Joey to ask Jay for his advice on selecting the right doctor. I can't believe I thought they were doing something nefarious. I misjudged them." Hope hesitated. "I really barked up the wrong tree. Have you decided it's time to speak with Elliot?"

"No. I just can't get around the idea that he would risk the lives of young innocent athletes in the name of finding a cure for me." Morgan sighed. "Kiss Marc, and tell him happy birthday from me. Oh, and tell Mini I miss her and will be home soon. I hope it all goes well at the party."

Morgan hung up the phone and looked around. She smiled as she exited the home, reading the sign: "De Angelo's House of Angels."

Hope placed her phone down and thought, *Faith and trust. I will never lose that in Jay again.* Her thoughts were interrupted by the doorbell ringing.

An elderly woman holding a glass jar with a bow waited at the front door.

Hope answered the door, and a huge smile appeared across her face. "I am so glad you were able to make it."

The elderly woman shook her head up and down. "Zhere'z novhere else I'd rather be. It'z been far too long."

Hope guided her guest into the backyard that was transformed into Neverland, with tents set up, a huge inflatable pirate ship that the little ones were running around and climbing up, and green and silver pixie dust glitter spread out all over the ground. Marc had some all over his hair as Jay held him up in the air singing, "All it takes is faith and trust and a little pixie dust! He can fly, he can fly, he can fly!"

Marc yelled out, sticking out his pointer finger up to the sky, "Secon star 'til mornin!"

Seeing another guest had arrived, Jay flew Marc over to

say hello. He landed Marc gently down onto a wooden bench where Nathan was seated. Nathan smiled. "It's Peter Pan! Protecting us from the evil Captain Hook." Marc giggled, swinging his dagger in the air.

Hope joined them with their latest guest. "Three cheers for Peter Pan!" she joyfully proclaimed. "Hip, hip, hooray! Hip, hip, hooray! Hip, hip, hooray!"

Marc giggled as he eyed the glass jar filled with delicious treats. Nathan noticed the jar too.

"Are those Goo Goo Clusters in that jar?" asked Nathan. "I haven't had them since I was a child myself."

The elderly woman giggled. "It'z a zhame, zhey were your favorite."

Nathan did a double take. "How would you know that?" He stared into the woman's eyes. "It can't be! It is not possible. Sadie?" Nathan's face went white, drained of all color. "In Auschwitz I was told by a neighbor that you and Mama were shot fleeing the Nazis."

"I played dead just how Mama taught me." Tears were streaming down Sadie's face. "I zearched for you but zhere vas never any documentation on you. Until thiz past year."

Hope gave a half smile, lifting her shoulders up. "Your story needed to be recorded."

Nathan wobbled. Jay held him up. "I got you, old man!" Jay and Nathan had grown closer the past few months. Jay had become like a son to Nathan and vice versa.

Jay gently walked Nathan closer to Sadie. The siblings tightly embraced, bawling tears of joy and sorrow.

Life is full of surprises.

The End

PLEASE SHARE YOUR THOUGHTS

Thank you for reading my debut novel. If you enjoyed my story, please make your feelings known by writing a review on Amazon, Goodreads, Instagram and/or Barnes and Noble. Your support would be greatly appreciated. Thank you!

If you would like to connect with me,
checkout my Instagram page

@followmywritingjourney

After reading *The Perfect Move*, I think there's a lot to ponder. Whether you're in a book club or read the book independently, the book kit I've created is *perfect* for you! It is filled with thought provoking discussion questions, recipes, interesting facts about Huntington's disease, the Holocaust, Long Island's Gold Coast, sports gambling, and more. *The Perfect Move Book Kit* is available for free by going to my website:

www.alisahklinger.wixsite.com/alisaklinger

or email at

alisahklinger@gmail.com

AFTERWORD

Between 1890 and 1940, more than 1,000 magnificent private estates were erected in a measly 70-square-mile radius bordering the Long Island Sound which would come to be known as the "Gold Coast." Both locally and around the world, one hears stories of the fabled Gold Coast with its grand mansions and lavish roaring 20s parties—parties so famous they inspired F. Scott Fitzgerald's *The Great Gatsby*.

Personally, there was one estate in particular that always stood out—OHEKA CASTLE. It is the beautiful Gold Coast mansion, designed in the style of French chateaux, that inspired Maltz Mansion in this novel. Egg hunts with $1000 bills inside the eggs, secret doors, and hidden passageways are just a few of the fanciful things that feature in stories told about Oheka.

OHEKA is an acronym for its owner Otto HErmann KAhn, said to be the inspiration for the iconic Mr. Monopoly, who built OHEKA CASTLE in 1919. Kahn was frustrated with the social scene in many upper-class communities where Jewish people were prohibited from joining social clubs, or using "exclusive" amenities such as golf courses. In response, he purchased a 443-acre plot of land on Long Island where he could build his own estate, and make his own rules. Workers spent two years constructing a hill so the castle would have views of Cold Spring Harbor and other estates, including that of the Vanderbilt family.

OHEKA CASTLE is the second-largest private residence ever built in America.

Of the more than 1,000 grand estates that once existed on the Gold Coast, today less than a third remain. After World War II, many Gold Coast mansions were demolished, and their parcels of land subdivided into suburban developments. Additionaly, as private fortunes disappeared, some of the most prominent Gold Coast homes were turned into museums, conference centers, resorts, and others non-residential uses.

Fortunately for OHEKA CASTLE, Gary Melius, a Long Island developer, purchased the devastated estate. At the time he acquired the property, it had no electricity or plumbing, or even windows and doors, left on its 23 remaining acres. Melius took on the painstaking challenge of successfully restoring the estate back to its original grandeur.

Today, OHEKA is listed on the National Register of Historic Places and is a member of Historic Hotels of America®. OHEKA hosts hundreds of wedding receptions, celebrations, and corporate events each year. The estate serves as a destination for photo shoots and movie scenes, as well as weekend getaways on which guests can enjoy packages with the Cold Spring Country Club for tennis and golf.

I'm thankful to the Melius Family for indulging me, and providing me with many interesting historical facts to share about Long Island's Gold Coast and OHEKA CASTLE.

For more information go to their website: www.oheka.com

ACKNOWLEDGMENTS

Setting out to write a novel is an overwhelming task. I could not have completed my novel if it were not for my supportive family.

Thank you, Mom and Dad, for all your continued encouragement and emotional support. When the seed for the story sprouted, it was Mom who I first springboarded ideas with, and continued to do so throughout writing the book. I've enjoyed our many conversations and collaborating together. I was happy to share this experience with you. You're my biggest fan.

Thank you to my two wonderful sons, Matthew and Marc, who make me so proud of all their accomplishments, and how encouraging you both are towards me obtaining mine. I love you both so much, you are my proudest accomplishment. You both fueled my desire to write this novel. Your faith in me is inspiring. I am indebted to you, Marc, an incredible writer in your own right, for brainstorming, fleshing out ideas, and helping me to create a more cohesive story. You were always there to help me find my way through the writing process, turning what I envisioned in my mind into words on the page. Thank you to Matthew, my tech support, for helping me with all my computer questions. I'd be lost without you.

A thank you shout-out to my sisters, Cheryl and Lauren, who provided support and willingness to beta read the book. Cheryl, I'm thankful for all the holes you found!

A special thank you to Nancy Melius, In-House Interior Designer & Marketing Director at OHEKA CASTLE, who from the moment we met has been very supportive.

Thank you to my graphic designer, Domini Dragoone, for creating an incredible book cover and formatting the book. You are extremely thorough, very creative, and patient. Thank you to my editor, Ashley Brown, for editing my manuscript.

Thank you to all of my beta readers! Your support, feedback, and encouragement are greatly appreciated.

Lastly, thank you to my devoted husband who has never stopped me from ever pursuing anything I've dreamt of doing. Your unwavering faith in me is greatly appreciated. I love you always.

To find out more about Huntington's disease, or if you'd like to make a donation, please visit the Huntington's Disease Society of America website:

www.hdsa.org

ABOUT THE AUTHOR

Alisa H. Klinger, author of *The Perfect Move*, has worn many hats before putting on her author's cap. They include New York City teacher—Talented and Gifted Specialist—and New York State Licensed Real Estate Associate Broker. This is her debut novel.

Everyone starts somewhere, and for Alisa it began with making up bedtime stories for her two wonderful sons. Alisa has always enjoyed creating stories where she puts herself in other people's shoes. This passion has helped her create colorful, well-developed characters that readers truly become invested in and care about. Alisa admits she's become very attached to the characters in *The Perfect Move*.

When Alisa is not writing, she spends time with her family, plays Pickleball, takes long walks on the beach, and explores grand estates.

Alisa currently lives on Longboat Key, Florida, with her supportive husband. They have two amazing sons who they are extremely proud of. Alisa grew up in Queens, New York, and raised her family in a quiet Long Island suburb. Even though it's been a few years since she's lived in New York, she hasn't lost her accent—which puts a smile on many Floridian's faces whenever they hear her ask for a cup of *cawfee*! You can take the girl out of New York…but you can't take NY out of the girl!